Dov Hoenig

Triumph Street, Bucharest

A novel

*Translated
from the French by*

GAVIN BOWD

First published in 2022
by Istros Books
London, United Kingdom
www.istrosbooks.com

Originally published as
Rue du Triomphe
© Editions Laffont, Paris, 2018
Translation © Gavid Bowd

The right of Dov Hoenig to be identified as the author
of this work has been asserted in accordance with the
Copyright, Designs and Patents Act, 1988.

Typesetting: pikavejica.com

ISBN: 978-1-912545-87-2

The publishers would like
to express their thanks
to the Arts Council England
for the financial support that made
the publication of this book possible.

Supported using public funding by
**ARTS COUNCIL
ENGLAND**

For Zoe,

*without whom I would be
'o frunză pierdută',
a lost leaf*

Contents

'That eternal human wish: to leave!'

ANNA DE NOAILLES

I

The Courtyard, the House, the Hall

Today, my childhood home no longer exists. In the 1980s, mass demolition work took place in Bucharest and my courtyard, my street and my whole neighbourhood were reduced to dust. In the name of Marxism-Leninism and the holy class struggle, the tyrant Nicolae Ceaușescu had decided to give the capital wider avenues with monumental prospects and immense constructions. Thus, the magnificence of marble and the fury of reinforced concrete were to intimidate a people starved and condemned to despair. On the dictator's orders, thousands of inhabitants were expelled from their homes and dispersed to the city's periphery. They had to pack their things and agree, at barely a day's notice, to relocate to housing blocks still under construction, without water or electricity, often without even doors and windows. The bulldozer's blades and caterpillar tracks razed their homes, turning them into a pile of bricks, stones and scrap metal. More than forty thousand houses, along with many priceless churches, monasteries, synagogues, hospitals, theatres and monuments, were demolished or moved. Among the many neighbourhoods annihilated was the old Jewish quarter stretching across the suburbs of Vacaresti, Dudesti and Vitan, where thousands of poor emigrants, mostly from Russia and Ukraine, had settled since the nineteenth century. This is how several streets of my childhood, with their houses, whose bright, joyful colours guided me in winter like morning stars on my way to school, were wiped out with the occasional exception of a few mutilated, pitiful segments.

At the very heart of Ceaușescu's urban ambitions was his megalomaniacal plan to build in the city centre a gigantic House of the People, conceived, in his imagination, as the Eighth Wonder of the World. He wanted this project to mark the apotheosis of his reign, ensuring him an eternal place in history. The construction works for the House of the People were launched in 1984 and a fifth of the old city of Bucharest (a surface equivalent to three Parisian arrondissements) was converted into a vast cemetery of rubble.

Ceaușescu and Elena, his wife, did not have the chance to attend the completion of this project in all its grotesque majesty. On 21 December 1989, a series of riots in Bucharest and other cities in the country led the population and the army to rebel and provoked the fall of the communist regime. The brutal and degrading execution of the Ceaușescu couple, on 25 December 1989, was worthy of their ignominy and the suffering they had inflicted on their people.

I had left Romania well before Ceaușescu came to power. For me, on a personal level, he was just the thief of a few precious traces of my childhood. I cast him into oblivion now in order to devote myself to the period preceding the Second World War, when my neighbourhood of Vacaresti-Dudesti enjoyed a quiet life, just like Triumph Street and the big combined courtyards of numbers 47 and 49, at the centre of which nestled the little house where we lived, behind the branches of an old plum tree.

Most importantly, there was our courtyard. It was entered through one of the two gates that opened onto two parallel alleyways where the two properties joined one another. On the left was number 47 with the house inhabited by the landlord, Nae Theodorescu. Although he was short of stature, and a little overweight, his elegance, intimidating look and powerful voice commanded respect and submission: 'A man of great class', said those in the know. I have kept quite a clear image of Theodorescu: greying hair under a wide-brimmed felt hat; bulging eyes; bushy black eyebrows; a long nose poised above a perfectly trimmed pencil-thin moustache. He liked striped suits of fine wool and double-soled English shoes that made him a little taller. A white silk handkerchief often spilled out of his breast pocket, like cream overflowing from a cup of coffee.

Proud of his social position and his success in life (he was the son of a rich landowner), Theodorescu had never been too familiar with his tenants. But, since his marriage to Lutetia Filotti, his distant and unapproachable manner had only become worse. In the courtyard, this attitude had, to quote Balzac, 'aroused unfavourable suspicions about his character', and malicious tongues began to wag: 'If he wasn't chasing after money, even though he already had plenty, why would he, at the age of fifty, have married a woman like Lutetia Filotti?' Apart from the fact that she was skin and bone, morose and haughty, Lutetia brought, by way of dowry, her old mother, Valeria, while poor Nae already had a mother of his own to look after. His mother's mind had gone since the death of her husband, Tudor Theodorescu, and she lived in her son's house in a small isolated room, just behind the kitchen, under the care of a nurse. We often heard the old woman's wails, like heartrending appeals for help, but with time the neighbours learned to ignore them. She was eighty-two years old, to believe Theodorescu's young servant, Maria – a petite brunette, young and full of life, who liked gossip as much as Sunday dances in the Municipal gardens.

In contrast, Valeria Filotti, Theodorescu's mother-in-law, maintained, despite her seventy-six years, robust health and a sound mind. Small and thin and always dressed in black, she would spend hours behind the curtain of her window, spying on the goings-on in the alley. She desperately sought someone to speak to and, as soon as the opportunity arose, she flung open the curtains, darting her head out like a snake flicking its forked tongue to taste the scents. 'Ah, what a beautiful day!' or 'Oh, what awful weather!' she would exclaim, her face cleft from ear to ear in a syrupy, toothless smile revealing three or four yellowing and decaying stumps clinging to her rotten gums. She knew how she looked and to hide her embarrassment, her smile vanished just as fast as it had come, her face returning to its severe and assertive expression. She would then launch into endless litanies that went from the national crisis to the rampant corruption in King Carol's palace, not forgetting the punishment of sinners and rewards for the righteous. That would set off a series of imperious sighs, sometimes followed by a few tears, and ending with the interjection *vai de loume!* ('world of misfortune!'). Motan, her big black cat, with long whiskers like those of an old Hungarian hussar, did

14

not seem to worry about the misfortune of this world as much as she did. Seated like a sphinx on the windowsill, he ran his bushy tail across his mistress's face with the regularity of a windscreen wiper. Motan had little time for the old woman's conversations with passers-by, but his misanthropy did not bother Valeria. No cat was going to dictate to her how much of her time to spend on humans, for this depended solely on the interest she had in the passer-by. Those considered 'poor of mind' were summarily dismissed, whereas she latched on to the 'elevated souls' and I, *vai de loume*, was at the top of her list of elevated souls. 'Bébé is one of us, he's one of us', she would tell Motan in the unlikely hope of persuading him to endure my presence, but despite her coaxing, Motan continued to observe me with the disdainful green-grey eyes of a spoilt and spiteful creature. I have never liked cats, black ones in particular, and Bébé is not my real name: my name is Bernard, but family and the neighbours had saddled me with the nickname 'Bébé', or even worse, to cajole me, 'Bébéloush'. Naturally, I hated the one as much as the other.

In the same alley, facing the Theodorescus', was the house of the Cassimatis couple, Radu and Cornelia. They too were of Greek origin like Theodorescu. Radu, dark-skinned and well-built, who smelled of perfume a mile off, was the director of a small import-export company trading with Greece. Cornelia, his beautiful wife, was a teacher at the primary school on Labyrinth Street, not very far from us, and she was the one who aroused in me the precocious desires of a barely pubescent boy.

The two conjoining alleyways of 47 and 49 Triumph Street, led from the entrance gates to a communal roundabout bordered with flowers that served as the meeting place of our little community. From this roundabout, three more alleyways ran in parallel to the back of the courtyard, where sturdy walnut trees and a fence separated us from a large empty lot. On either side of the alleyways, little houses succeeded one another like train carriages pulled up at a railway siding. About twenty families lived in our courtyard and with the exception of the Theodorescus, their servant Maria and the Cassimatis couple, all were of the Mosaic religion, in other words: Jews.

The entrance hall and the living room at the front of our house were situated opposite the Cassimatis' kitchen, near the roundabout. But, other than on days when we received guests, we came in and out of our home, that is, of the Davidescus' home which we rented, through the kitchen. The tall narrow door, with a rectangular transom, faced west, which was a pity, as the sun did not light up the room when my mother Jenny, started her day's work, long before my father George, my brother Leo, and I, Bernard (and not Bébé!) began to stir.

On entering the kitchen, a table with four chairs was placed near a large cupboard in which the crockery and glassware were kept, along with a number of cooking utensils. An imposing old blackened cooker with a large oven held court from the opposite wall, beyond which a door led into a spacious square room, the *dormitor*,[1] where my parents slept, where we took our meals and where Leo and I did our homework. A large Turkish rug with geometrical motifs, but without crosses (we did not like crosses!) covered the floor. In addition to our parents' bed, a dining table, some chairs, a chiffonier and a wardrobe with three drawers, the room also contained a tall, brown, glazed-ceramic stove that looked like an old pagan tomb. It was this fine wood stove that kept us warm in winter when the ill winds from distant Siberia blew across the plains of the old kingdom

1   Bedroom.

16

of Wallachia, from whose womb the city of Bucharest was born. The room was a bit dark. Its two windows opened onto a small yard, on the other side of which lived an old widow, mother of the strange neighbourhood doctor, Samuel Lebensart. She had cancer and her son often came to look after her while trying to keep his visits discreet, which wasn't hard, given that his mother's windows and curtains were permanently closed. But what the house withheld from the eye, it offered to the ear. The mysterious doctor had one leg shorter than the other and used a cane, the noise of which was amplified by the resonance in the inner yard, betraying his presence. As my mother only very rarely left the house, she knew the days and times of his visits by heart as he attended his appointments with exemplary punctuality.

The doctor was a handsome man. His raven hair was combed back in a wave like that of Tyrone Power, the famous American actor in *The Mark of Zorro*. He had a long, thin face, a powerful nose and his pale, cold eyes resembled those of an inquisitive wolf. I dreamed of having a Prince of Wales suit like Doctor Lebensart's, but I was too young to wear one... The doctor lived in a two-storey house with his wife and daughter, further up our street, where he also had his medical practice. When his old mother passed away, rumours circulated in the neighbourhood that it was he who had killed her to save her from unnecessary suffering. Rumours, as we know, have a logic of their own. He was disliked because his precise and honest diagnosis was often delivered with brutal frankness, and because he was accused of being too fond of money. He was believed to be heartless, when in fact he was not.

Next to our bathroom, which was situated at the back of my parents' room, a door opened to the living room. It was a

17

beautiful and spacious room reserved for family festive dinners and *musafiri*,[2] but in which my brother and I shared a bed, for want of another solution. The main piece of furniture was a large oak table that could seat twelve. My father had bought it from an antique dealer for a price well above our means. Finely decorated baroque style chairs accompanied the precious table, five on each side and one at each end reserved for my mother and father. From the middle of the ceiling, centred above the table, hung an imposing bronze chandelier with twelve branches ending in lions' paws, each holding a light bulb in its claws. It came from an old retired general whose wife was a client of the luxury fur shop where my father worked as a salesman. A big oval mirror, in front of which I often enjoyed conducting an imaginary orchestra, and a dresser of Viennese origin where my mother kept the silverware, crystal glasses and plates of the finest porcelain, completed the living room's furniture. All this symbolised, for my father, the fulfilment of his ambition to succeed in the illustrious metropolis of Bucharest.

To the right of the big living room window, opposite the Cassimatis' kitchen, a door led to the entrance hall of our house, a small bare room. On one of the walls, in front of the only window, hung an old painting of a Moldavian landscape, in front of which a small round table and a coat-stand were condemned to reclusive co-existence. A Persian carpet with floral motifs dominated by faded reds and blues, covered the parquet floor. That was all the room contained, but it was precisely its nakedness, its silence, that I liked. In winter, I went there very rarely, as we did not have the means to heat it, but during summer and autumn, I spent long hours there reading

2   Guests.

or playing chess alone; I felt protected, free and happy in my solitude.

One winter (was it in 1938?) I was gravely ill with scarlet fever and double pneumonia. At that time, before the discovery of penicillin, the law required that any child with scarlet fever had to be quarantined in a government hospital for infectious diseases and that the Ministry of Health take charge of the decontamination of their home. On a previous occassion, I had witnessed this procedure in Nerva Traian Street. Dressed in outfits resembling deep-sea divers, men surrounded by a crowd of curious bystanders stormed a hastily evacuated house. Each man was equipped with a canister with a long pipe connected to a white tanker-truck bearing the emblem of the Red Cross. They made me think of gangsters carrying out a hold-up in a silent action movie.

As anti-Semitism was already rampant in Romania at the time, my parents hesitated to send me to a government hospital where they feared I would be treated by hostile and surly nurses. Doctor Lebensart agreed to look after me at home, but for a short time only. He advised my parents to consult the head of the paediatric service at Caritas hospital, a Jewish hospital that only treated non-contagious diseases. The doctor was called Rafael Fruchter, and when he came to see me, my temperature was over forty degrees. He promised my parents he would take care of me, and he kept his word. The following day, I was admitted to Caritas and transferred to an isolated room where, with the exception of the head nurse and her two assistants, nobody knew that my pneumonia was combined with scarlet fever. We never found out why Doctor Fruchter had consented to such a risk, although we knew it was not for money, as my parents did not have any. Even Doctor Lebensart, little known for his philanthropy, had stopped making us pay for his visits. Had they discovered something unique in us, or was it rather the uniqueness of the doctors of those times?

After a week, my health had not improved, but the pains I suffered, especially in the ears and throat, were nothing compared to the terror caused by the punctures made to extract pus from my lungs with the use of terrifying long-needled syringes. I refused to undergo them, unless it was Doctor Fruchter himself who carried out the procedure. A week later, despite the punctures and the medication, my situation worsened. Exhausted and dehydrated, between two bouts of feverish delirium, I could read the fear on the faces of my parents and the nurses. They were afraid I would die. Only doctor Fruchter remained calm and confident. If he had his doubts, his face showed none. His serene voice and the reassuring look in his eyes revived hope and the will to live in me. Nevertheless, late at night, knowing he was no longer in the hospital, I feared that death was lurking by my bedside. I thought I could see his awful skull leaning over me and could sense his icy breath on my face. I was terrified that death would seize me all of a sudden and drag me into the land of shadows; that night would swallow me up forever. The past and the future would no longer exist, the present would come to a full stop. Everything would stop. The very instant when death took me would be my last breath of life. After, I would remember nothing. There would be no after, there would be no more me, ever... To protect me from these horrific thoughts, my mother brought me an old Hebrew-Romanian prayer book, which I kept under my pillow. Holding it close, I prayed silently early in the morning and late at night. Two weeks later, Doctor Fruchter's treatments and the prayers proved that they were stronger than the illness. I was cured!

I spent the desquamation period in the house, happy to find my bed again, to be at home. I rejoiced in being well again, in knowing that soon I would be back at school and that I would walk, exhilarated, in the streets of the capital, as tirelessly as before! But I kept the habit of praying and the hall was the only place where I could pray unseen. In my own words, I thanked Heaven for having kept me from death and I prayed to the Almighty to guide me along my life's path. I often mentioned the name of Doctor Fruchter in my prayers, who I was certain had been sent to my rescue by Providence.

Many times I've thought about the time spent at Caritas hospital with strange nostalgia, as though I wanted to feel again an old pain. How could I forget the strong odour of disinfectants and medications, the rattle of trolleys wheeled along icy corridors, the impenetrable mystery of voices and footsteps, coming and going with no rhyme or reason, the whisperings of the nurses, their white, starched bonnets crisscrossing against the blue background of the walls? And how could I avoid reliving the feverish agitation that took hold of me as I waited for the bleak stillness of night to relinquish its hold at the dawn of a new day? Through a gap in the curtains, a charitable ray of sunlight would come to settle on my bed as the hospital roused itself from sleep, filling each ward with morning clatter at the same time as it spread everywhere the aroma of the first coffee.

If scarlet fever had rewarded me with a new skin, the effort demanded to overcome the double pneumonia had armed me with a newfound vitality. In my mind, I had sketched out a precise plan: fortify my body, regain the position of top of the class and enjoy again the youthful pleasures that the long illness had denied me. I wanted to be like the other boys of my age, knowing full well that it was not possible, if only because I was Jewish. At my primary school, which was Christian, as well as in the street, the tram, and in the cinema theatres, I encountered this reality on a daily basis. Despite being Romanian by birth, like my parents and grandparents, I remained in the eyes of Christians a *jidan*, a dirty Jew, a Yid. How many times had anti-Semitic hooligans spat at me as I went to and from school? And in how many streets did my heart break to see, on billboards, deplorable posters caricaturing my race as spiders and rats?

It is in no way surprising that I began to hate the country of my birth. I hoped that soon fate would take me to the Jewish state that Theodor Hertzl had dreamt of, where my real life would begin. This hope was going to become reality sooner than I thought.

2

Pouica, History and Memory

I had learned to read before I started school, as I could not stand my brother being ahead of me, and always wanted to be his equal. Since he could read, I had to read too. One day, I asked him to help me and step by step, faintly amused, but hardly enthusiastic, he gave in to my pressures. After some effort, thanks to him, I realised my ambition. Later, when I started my fourth year at primary school, my brother entered his fourth year at high school. I was trailing behind him, without the slightest hope of ever catching up, which was hard to swallow except that with time, this disadvantage, which was due to the order in which our parents had conceived us, brought me an obvious benefit: I had access to his school books, which were much more advanced than my own. Therefore, in certain subjects, I was ahead of the others, helping me to reinforce my status as top of the class despite my mediocre marks in mathematics.

From my first year in school, I had shown a particular interest in history. I was fascinated by the lives and works of the great heroes of the past and by the ups and downs of peoples and nations. Unlike arithmetic and geometry, which I felt belonged to a lifeless and sterile planetary space, history offered me all that was most exciting in the adventure of humanity on earth. My passion for this subject ran alongside my interest in politics. This interest, which was unusual for a boy of my age, was greatly down to the fact that during my childhood, from 1938 to 1945, I had been the involuntary witness to a series of historic events of great importance, as much for the world as for Romania.

I was seven when, on 13 March 1938, Germany annexed Austria. In the month of September, Hitler, Ribbentrop, Mussolini, Ciano, Chamberlain and Daladier signed the infamous 'Munich Agreement' that forced the Czechs to cede the Sudetenland to the Third Reich. In Romania, King Carol II established a monarchist dictatorship. He outlawed the traditional political parties and created his own 'mass' party, the Front for National Rebirth, Jewish membership of which was forbidden. I was eight when in 1939, Czechoslovakia was annexed by the Reich and Albania fell to the Italians. In the same year, Ribbentrop and Molotov announced the Germano-Soviet non-aggression pact and Germany and the USSR carved up Poland. On 4 September 1939, France and Great Britain declared war on Germany and two months later the USSR invaded Finland. Between the months of April and June 1940, Denmark, Norway, the Netherlands, Belgium and France were defeated by the Wehrmacht. Thanks to the heroic effort of a flotilla of thousands of boats, most of the British Army in France could be evacuated from the port of Dunkirk as well as the French units that had fought ferociously to slow the Wehrmacht's advance. In the month of June, Italy joined Germany. We were thrown into the Second World War.

In our courtyard, the subject that preoccupied us, as Jews, was knowing what Romania's position would be in this bloody conflict. Our future, our very existence, depended on it. Now that the guarantees by France and Great Britain, its traditional allies, were no longer worth even the paper they were written on, preservation of its territorial integrity demanded that Romania ally itself to Germany. But King Carol II's persistence in remaining neutral far from satisfied Hitler. When in June 1940, the USSR issued Romania an ultimatum demanding that it cede the territories of Bukovina and Bessarabia, Hitler did not oppose it. On the contrary, he demanded that the King submit unconditionally to the Soviet demands. More than to punish the King, the Führer wanted to subdue Stalin, while in secret he prepared to attack the USSR.

On 14 June 1940, petrified in front of the radio, we heard that the German Army was parading in the streets of Paris. A few days later, France chose a new head of State, Marshal Petain, who signed an armistice with Hitler on 22 June and installed his government in Vichy. Great Britain, where Winston Churchill had replaced Chamberlain at the head of the government, remained isolated, alone in Europe to have taken up the challenge against Hitler's Germany and Mussolini's Italy.

Such was the face of the world in which I grew up. And yet despite all of this, during the summer Sundays, with their blue skies and scent of acacia, the spectre of war did not prevent us from getting up late and enjoying the day of rest. Once

25

Theodorescu's servant Maria had hosed down the gravel and the boiling asphalt of the alleyways, doors began to open slowly, inviting into each home the scents of the refreshed earth. It was the awaited signal. Like theatre actors at the sound of the three strikes, who rush onto the stage to take up their places before the curtain rises, people came out in front of their doorways, sitting down on straw chairs and deckchairs, and the courtyard sprang alive like a fair. The women exposed their arms and shoulders to the burning sun – their legs, out of decency, only to the knees – and the men gathered in the shade around small tables covered with multicoloured cloths to discuss politics or to tease each other during animated games of poker and backgammon.

The lively political debates took place in front of the house of the Bercovici family, situated at the beginning of the alley opposite our kitchen. I was the main attraction of these animated discussions: Having passionately devoured the daily newspapers my father brought home, I had memorised the names of all the political parties and their leaders, as well as those of former and current ministers, and I knew about the dramas and intrigues of Romanian political life, thereby dazzling the adults. Every Sunday, weather permitting, a faithful audience of a dozen men gathered to listen to my analyses of the week's events. I was proud of myself as much as my father was proud of his offspring, but the responsibility often weighed too heavily on my shoulders. Keeping up with the news was not everything in my remit. My audience included Radu Cassimatis, an Orthodox Christian and fervent supporter of a host of ferociously anti-Semitic politicians. This obliged me to filter my analyses and deliver them in such a way as not to upset the 'goy'. For example, Kleinfeld, the father of

Sergiu, my brother's best friend in the courtyard, once dared to criticise King Carol II for having given, in his new government, three ministerial posts to the anti-Semitic Iron Guard, one of them going to its leader, Horia Sima. Radu Cassimatis responded drily that Horia Sima was above all else a very great Romanian patriot. That was a dreamed-of opportunity for me to show my objectivity by giving him my unconditional support: 'On the contrary,' I said, 'the King was right to give a voice to Horia Sima. That's democracy!' While shooting Kleinfeld a triumphant look, Cassimatis rewarded me with a broad smile and complimented me with: 'Bravo, Bébélush, you're a good democrat!' Another time, I expressed my sympathy for General Antonescu, then under house arrest on the King's orders. I had read that, from 1923 to 1924, the general had served as military attaché in France and in England, and that, ever since, he had hugely admired these two western democracies. However, I had omitted the fact that after the humiliating defeat of France, Antonescu, persuaded like his supporters that the Germans were going to win the war, turned coat, becoming a great admirer of the Führer and the Wehrmacht. I had again wanted to please Cassimatis, who, being Greek, hated King Carol for having chased Queen Hélène, his Greek wife, out of the country in order to further his affair with the flame-haired Magda Lupescu, a converted Jewess with captivating green eyes. After all, Queen Hélène was none other than the daughter of the King of Greece, Constantin I, and of Princess Sophia of Prussia, as well as the great-granddaughter of Queen Victoria of England!

When I was facing difficulties during these political séances our neighbour opposite, Nicu Bercovici – a tall, paunchy man with owl-like eyes – came to my rescue. Well-versed in politics, he had the advantage of age and experience. He was director of the bedding department of the Bucharest branch of Galeries Lafayette, a position the importance of which was manifested by his imposing moustache. Unfortunately, his wife Sofia, who was tiny and frail, suffered from a serious heart condition. That those two had been able to bring into the world a creature as bubbly as Rozica, their thirteen-year-old daughter, with breasts as firm and round as cantaloupes, remained an impenetrable mystery for the courtyard. Rozica's best friend was a girl of the same age called Chichi Herescu. We teased Chichi saying that, because of her height, she must surely bash her head on every ceiling. I was mean with Rozica, but kind to Chichi, under the spell of her sad eyes, which looked ready to fill with tears at any moment. 'Chichi the weeping willow' would have suited her perfectly. As the only adolescent girls in the courtyard, Rozica and Chichi were as inseparable as Siamese twins. They were always whispering something in each other's ears and made no effort to hide their contempt for the courtyard's three male adolescents: Nellu, Sergiu and my brother Leo. 'Their loss!' sniggered the three in retaliation; they were attracted neither by Rozica nor Chichi and did not lack success with other girls in the neighbourhood.

The political debates were exclusively the business of the 'men's club', but there was nevertheless one exception: a nineteen-year-old girl, Pouica Marcovici, who I called Pouia. She had just finished her first year at the Faculty of Letters and sometimes joined the men, although she was too shy to express an opinion. Her parents, Mishu and Neta, lived in a house adjacent to the Bercovicis and I fell in love with Pouia. It was a boy's first love for a shy, dreamy-eyed girl with freckles and a thick fringe of black hair cut straight across her forehead.

Whether shy or not, the unfortunate fact was that, just when I fell in love with her, Pouia developed a crush on Marcel Fein, a young hairdresser from a salon on Vacaresti Street, which she sometimes frequented. Who could have imagined a university student taking a shine to a hairdresser?

At least once a week, in the afternoon, when she was alone in the house, Pouia received Marcel in her room. Though the big window was shut, the transom above it, kept open by a hook, let the noises from inside filter out as far as the alley in which I roamed nervously, pretending to be hunting butterflies.

Many times, as I approached the window to listen better, consumed by what was simply plain jealousy, I heard giggles, taunts, clicks of the tongue, and little stifled cries followed by long silences. One day, I heard Pouia whisper: 'I don't want to,' and then Marcel's voice insisting 'Just a little, I promise'. Rapid and unintelligible words followed and when Pouia suddenly shouted, 'If you continue, I'll scream!' I heard Marcel mumble hoarsely 'Trust me' and at that moment, in a state of agitation, I turned on my heels and fled home.

Not long afterwards, Pouia and I became good friends. It is possible that this friendship helped her to contain the attraction she felt towards Marcel – an inclination unworthy of the image she had of herself. To have an affectionate and innocent relationship with a boy like me (affectionate maybe, but innocent?) provided her with the serenity to better understand her torment. I made a habit of going to her place once I had finished my homework, on the days when she was not expecting Marcel.

Once, she received me in her little room, the window was wide open and the net curtain undulated at the whim of a light breeze. It was hot, and an iridescent light flooded the room. In the distance could be heard the cries of children playing at tzourka, the cricket of the poor, of gypsies and of ruffians. Intermittently, nightingales exchanged short staccato-like and repetitive musical phrases. Apart from the birdsong, it was as though all of nature had fallen asleep. I was sitting with Pouia on the couch. She had a very beautiful mouth and pink, finely drawn lips. Her teeth were gleaming white, like those of the black women I had seen for the first time in American films. A breath of air lifted the collar of her half-unbuttoned blouse (was it through negligence or to keep cool?). My eyes strayed briefly to the hollow where her breasts separated to hide in her brassiere, pinching the fine white cotton of her blouse. Her warm brown eyes smiled at me candidly: a smile that I could read as clearly in her eyes as I could have on her lips. A floral skirt covered her thighs up to her round and silky knees. Seized by emotion, I suddenly blurted out: 'I think you're very beautiful, Pouia.'

'I think you're a bit of a crazy boy!' she replied in astonishment.

I felt my face turn crimson. She was right next to me and when our bodies happened to touch, I felt the heat of hers like a sudden blaze. She lifted my chin to raise my head, which I had lowered through shyness, her thumb brushing my lips.

'Tell me the truth: how many beautiful women have you known?'

I placed my hand on hers, as it held my head up: 'Only you. You're the only one.'

Surprised, she blushed in turn and said, 'So you see...'

'I don't see anything!' I protested as she placed her finger across my lips to silence me.

'You... can... see... that... you... are... lying,' she said, detaching each word, her lips taking the shape of a kiss. 'Like all men, in fact,' she added, her body moving away from mine. I felt the separation like a sudden cold wind blowing in from Russia. As she took her finger away from my lips, her expression changed strangely and I exclaimed in a manner more childish than I would have liked: 'But I am not yet a man!'

She scratched her head, looking for some way of getting out of this impasse. 'Give me an example of another woman you find beautiful,' she challenged. I hesitated. 'Come on!' she insisted.

As I was still hesitating, she pointed her finger at me and scolded in an amused tone, 'Big or small, men are all the same. I'll bet that she is blonde!'

'No!' I denied categorically. 'I was thinking of Merle Oberon! She's not blonde, she's brunette and beautiful like you!'

Pouia jumped as though stung by a bee.

'Where did you get that name from? The New Testament?'

'From a film, not the New Testament!' I proudly asserted.

And it was perfectly true. One day, I had taken my mother to the Tomis, my favourite neighbourhood cinema, to see *Wuthering Heights*. The film had touched me so deeply that I spent nights thinking about it. I was haunted by the sad love story between Catherine Earnshaw, from a rich aristocratic family, and Heathcliff, the poor boy with no family. Merle Oberon played Catherine and Lawrence Olivier, Heathcliff. Catherine was dying of remorse, having broken Heathcliff's heart by marrying, under family pressure, the wealthy Edgar Linton. Just like Heathcliff who, late at night, heard the ghost of Catherine knocking at his window, I, during my sleepless nights, could not escape from the evanescent face of Merle Oberon and the tragic expression of her haunting dark eyes. Pouia had not seen the film, but she had read the book and she knew the works of the Brontë sisters well. She particularly liked Charlotte's novel, *Jane Eyre*, which she considered better than Emily's.

Coming suddenly back from work, Neta, Pouia's mother, put an end to my tête-a-tête with her daughter. But, as I was 'her Bébéloush' as well, she would not let me leave before tasting her pastries, which, I have to confess, were not as delicious as my mother's.

At the end of the courtyard, just opposite Theodorescu's kitchen, was an alley less frequented than the others. An old oak tree with heavy, gnarled branches watched over the entrance with a Cyclops eye under a frowning brow. To the left of the alley lived the Halpern family, and to the right lived Nora Freiberg and her daughter, Anca. It was rumoured in the courtyard that Nora Freiberg, petite, slender and with slightly reddish hair, was a woman of questionable morals. Since the death of her husband, she had become, according to the same gossip, the mistress of a rich businessman, a married man, who kept her in exchange for the gifts in kind that she offered him. She was not seen often, as she came and went at unusual hours, leaving a trail of heady perfume behind her. She wore jersey-knit Chanel cardigans with a certain insolence over slightly short skirts, two-toned boots and, depending on the circumstances, either a cloche hat or big black straw one with a veil. For reasons that were hard for me to understand, her slightly bowed legs caused great excitement among the men of the courtyard. I had often even heard my brother and his friends talk about them. Sergiu, who was fifteen or sixteen, repeated the words 'eroticism' and 'erotic', which I did not understand. The dictionaries were hardly any help: according to them, the word referred to love, not legs.

When I had asked Pouia to explain, she blushed and laughed nervously, before launching into a long and convoluted speech, typical of grown-ups when a child asks them an embarrassing question. Subjects linked to the sexuality of men and women were too complex for my age, she said to me. It was better for me to be interested in less adult subjects. Childhood, she concluded, is the most precious period of our lives; it should be spent as much as possible in joy and happiness, far from the passions, worries and responsibilities inherent in the lives of grown-ups.

Anca, Nora's daughter, was a little blonde girl with blue eyes. Everyone adored her cute nose and her cherry-shaped mouth. Her mother dressed her up like a doll: plaid skirt with cloth braces across a white blouse, and pink socks that covered her skinny legs right up her calves, along with patent leather shoes.

As Nora was rarely at home during the day, a governess, Sarina, took care of Anca, collecting her from kindergarten at midday and preparing her meals. But on Saturdays, if the weather was nice, Anca spent her time playing outside. One Saturday, taking advantage of the fact that the Halpern family next door had left on holiday and that Sarina was doing the shopping at the Vitan market, my brother and his two friends, Nellu and Sergiu, had the idea of playing 'mummies and daddies' with Anca. The game was conceived as a one-act play: Anca to play the mummy and Nellu, the daddy, whilst my brother and Sergiu took on the responsibilities of co-directors. I must have been about six, Anca five and my brother, Nellu and Sergiu ten or eleven, about the same age as Rozica and Chichi who were assigned the role of passive aunties (at that time, they hadn't yet given themselves the airs and graces of

33

the unapproachable princesses that they later adopted). I was permitted to remain as long as I kept quiet. The old oak, with its knobbly roots and a carpet of leaves spread around the foot of its trunk, served as a natural décor. When the imaginary curtain lifted, signalling the start of the play, Nellu, who already saw himself in a white medical coat, kneeled before Anca, grave and solemn like a priest reading from his breviary. We sat by in a semi-circle. Anca, propped up on her elbows, was lying on the ground, her legs wide apart, and her panties down to her ankles. Transfixed, we looked at her impudent little sex that resembled a fine cut vertically between the undulated triangle of her thighs. All we could hear around us was the drone of bees as Nellu succeeded to insert a straw into little Anca's sex, after having carefully separated the lips with his other hand. Perfectly at ease in the role of mummy, Anca followed attentively, and without the least embarrassment, the activity of 'Daddy' Nellu. I was never to know the outcome of the scene that the directors have envisaged, as Sarina came back from the market earlier than expected and the curtain dropped prematurely before the end of the play.

A few years later, when I asked Anca if she remembered the game of 'mummy and daddy', she turned red and stalked off. Poor beautiful Anca, she still had the same angelic face and cherry-shaped mouth, but her legs were beginning to be bowed like her mother's.

This children's mischief, which fortunately never reached my mother's ears, brings back the memory of two significant moments that we did share together. The first is linked to the image of a poor bear, reared up on its chained hind paws, its russet fur matted and filthy. At some forgotten intersection, a couple of dozen gawkers jeer and whistle over the frenetic, rhythmical sound of a tambourine as the gipsy's whip goads the wretched animal into a shuffling dance. In the crowd, the gipsy woman, with one hand clutching an infant to her breast, picks up the coins that rain down on the pavement like manna from heaven. Clinging to my mother, I witnessed this scene in a street in Galatz, the lively and cosmopolitan port on the Danube, where I was born. The image of this bear, robbed of its freedom and all dignity, took root in my mind as another striking example of the acts of barbarism, ignominy and injustice that man is capable of. From the mistreated animal to man treated as an animal, the road is very short.

The second memory is linked to my induction into primary school. One day, just before the end of the last class, I felt terrible pains in my stomach and the urgent need to go to the toilet. As soon as I heard the liberating bell, I rushed for the door. Though I was quick, a dozen other boys were right behind me, no doubt headed for the same place as me. They were shouting, swearing, swinging their satchels at each other and giving each other kicks in the backside, like a bunch of hooligans. I didn't like the look of them, nor their rough voices and coarse language and was afraid of finding myself alone with them in the toilets. Locking myself in one of the narrow, foul-smelling stalls wouldn't have made me safer. How would I have defended myself if they prevented me from getting out and pushed lit papers or firecrackers under the door, just as they had done recently to another boy? I decided that I had to change my plan. I turned away suddenly and, taking the shortest path, made for the school gate. Once in the street, I bolted, making my way blindly, rushing between pedestrians, cars, trams, cyclists and carts, like someone possessed. The road ahead was still quite long and, afraid of not being able to contain myself, I clenched my muscles with all my strength and ran on, gritting my teeth and biting my lips until I tasted blood. I ran and ran. Cold sticky sweat, mingled with tears of shame and anger, streaked down my face. Everything was blurred, but I just kept running: haggard faces of men and women, street dogs, beggars, vagrants, prams, telegraph poles, walls – some blank, others covered in posters – windows and unfamiliar doors flashed by on all sides. This maelstrom of images whirled by like a dream, or as though seen through the grimy carriage window of a tram travelling at great speed. Suddenly, at the corner of Triumph Street and Nerva Traian, scarcely a few hundred metres from home, what I had feared happened: my muscles gave way. I froze, horrified: what had I done? Why hadn't I been able to keep it in? After a few seconds, I calmed down somewhat, as the worst had already passed. I now had to prepare myself for what I was going to face at home. I had little chance to dodge between my brother and my mother without their realising the situation, but whatever happened, I had to get home as quickly as possible. However, the weight of the calamity in my pants prevented me from running. Dragging my feet like an old cripple and squeezing my thighs tight together, I made my way home at a snail's pace, avoiding everyone on my path.

Reaching the house, I hammered on the kitchen door, which was opened by my brother. Seeing that my eyes were red, he asked why I was crying: 'For nothing,' I answered, pushing him aside roughly with my satchel. I saw my mother and Fanny, a distant cousin, with cups of coffee and a spoonful of cherry conserve set before them. Fanny, 'the shame of the family', was a prostitute by trade and had recently spent a month in a hospital specialising in nervous disorders, at the edge of the city. The conversation I interrupted touched on a certain 'trafficker of living flesh' who had ruined her life – a reference to her pimp, as my brother explained to me later. When things were going very badly for her, Fanny always turned to my mother, who out of all the family was the only one to treat her with kindness and compassion. Seeing me, Fanny rushed to kiss me. Turning my face away, I tended a cheek while protecting my mouth. She smelled of eau de Cologne and beer, quite a disgusting mixture, but, given the circumstances, the smell of eau de Cologne suited me perfectly. 'How you've grown, little Bébélush! I almost didn't recognise you!' she exclaimed, pinching my ear with nails that looked like the claws of a predator. She had very black hair, large prominent blood-shot eyes and an enormous mouth with fleshy mauve lips. I freed myself from her thick arms to approach my mother as though to kiss her, but quickly whispered in her ear: 'Mother, I've done it in my trousers!' Taken aback, my mother rose quickly from her chair and, making her excuses to Fanny, rushed me out of the kitchen.

From then on, at family gatherings, the story of my misadventure made everyone laugh except my mother and I. She understood me. I had inherited her aversion for stupid and vulgar crowds; she who fled social life and disapproved of the indecency of the outside world to the point of avoiding restaurants, cafés, parks and street traders. As for my difficulties in adapting myself to the primary school in a Christian milieu, my mother could do nothing more than comfort me. I did not know why our parents had sent us to a State, and therefore Christian, primary school, rather than to the Moriah primary school, a Jewish school near our home: was it because the State school was free while Moriah would have cost them money?

The fact is that, just like my brother before me, I had to spend my 'primary' years in a Christian school. And just like him, during those four years, I had to bite my tongue every morning, refusing to make the sign of the cross when 'Our Father who art in Heaven' was recited.

After a few months, Pouia broke up with Marcel. Well before admitting it to her parents, she told herself that the handsome hairdresser was not for her. Was it by pure coincidence that at the very same time, Aurel, son of Marta and Aron Halpern, became the young man that Pouia's parents got it into their heads to have as their son-in-law? He was the complete opposite of Marcel Fein. Marcel was the same height as her, dark, virile, sporty, a cunning charmer and a smooth talker. Aurel was blonde, pale, skinny, shy, and shorter than her. There may have been doubts about how Pouia would react to her parents' choice, but amazingly she seemed interested! When the meeting was craftily 'arranged' by Pouia's family, with Aurel's parents' complicity, it wasn't love at first sight for her, but a pleasant surprise: how could she have crossed paths so often with this young man always in a hurry, with his unruly blonde locks covering his forehead, without the desire to know him better? Then, during subsequent encounters, she discovered that she felt good in his company; comfortable, assured and, for the first time, in harmony with a man.

In our courtyard, the time a secret stayed secret is equal to the time it took for a whisper to travel from lip to ear. The word engagement spread at vertiginous pace, but, for once, even malicious tongues held back. The new couple inspired only good feelings in us! We were delighted to see them, arm in arm, confident and happy. I was not less happy for Pouia than the others, although since she had got involved with Aurel, she no longer had any free time for me. That my visits to her ceased, goes without saying. One day, meeting by chance in the street, she apologised for not having been able to see me due to her end of year exams. She had had to shut herself up in her bedroom, day and night, condemned to swot up on Latin, French and German, not to mention the writings of the great bearded and bald philosophers. I assured her that I understood completely, having my own ration of studies to digest.

In the meantime, the gravity of the situation in Romania made my role as political commentator more and more complicated. On 30 August 1940, Hitler, in agreement with Mussolini, imposed the Vienna Diktat on Romania, according to which it had to cede to Hungary the north-west of Transylvania, populated by more than two million inhabitants, the great majority of them Romanian. Weakened in the eyes of the masses and the political parties for already handing over Bessarabia and Bukovina to the USSR, King Carol II was forced to abdicate in favour of his son Michael. On 14 September, a fascist coup d'état brought General Ion Antonescu to power. By royal decree, Romania was proclaimed a national legionary state. Horia Sima, head of the Legionary Movement, became vice-president of the Council of Ministers. He had taken the leadership after Corneliu Codreanu ('the Captain', as his disciples called him), founder of the Legion of the Archangel Michael and of the infamous Iron Guard, its paramilitary wing, had been arrested and later assassinated in prison, on the King's orders. On 6 October, in Bucharest, during the Festival of the Legionnaires, General Antonescu appeared at the rostrum wearing the green shirt with a Sam Browne, the uniform of the Iron Guard. He officiated at the Legionnaires' march-past, with his arm raised in the arrogant salute of the fascist phallocrats, except that the gesture was not accompanied by 'Heil Hitler' as in Germany, but by its Romanian equivalent: 'Long live the Legion and the Captain'.

With the rise to power of the Iron Guard, the Jewish community found itself under serious threat. What was I going to say about this subject to my adult audience in the presence of the 'goy' Cassimatis? My father and Nicu Bercovici had advised me that I would need to be careful, but the warning turned out to be unnecessary, as Radu Cassimatis deserted our Sunday political discussions. His decision shocked us. Although he had never hidden his sympathy for anti-Semitic politicians, because he wasn't any less anti-Semitic than they were, we had adopted him as our 'goy', a 'good goy' who relished our Jewish jokes and seemed to feel good in our company. His presence at our tables, in our inner circle, was for us a constant, but enriching, challenge. He embodied difference, but also our acceptance. His rejection sentenced us to isolation. Why would he have wanted to break with us if he had not heard something terrible about our imminent fate? In all truth, although I was as concerned as the adults, the idea of being able to deliver my political dissertations to an exclusively Jewish audience freed me from a great responsibility. Granted, without Cassimatis, the excitement was not the same, but I felt freer and more relaxed.

Curiously, Antonescu's accession did not immediately impact the situation of the Jewish community in Bucharest. Despite the seriousness of political events, in particular the increasing influence of the Iron Guard and the German Army's resounding successes, both indications of the storm brewing, we could still live our daily lives more or less as usual in the hope that we would survive.

3

Barbu

The academic year was coming to an end and the summer holidays were rapidly approaching. Aurel was preparing his university exams in the company of a classmate and close friend, Barbu Stanescu. You might think that Stanescu is not a common surname for a Jew, and with good reason, as Barbu Stanescu was not Jewish, but came from a family of peasant farmers in south-west Romania. I was fascinated the first time I laid eyes on him: Barbu's features were even less Jewish than his name. The first thing that struck me was his powerful, almost triangular neck and his square head that looked as though it had been hewn from a block of stone; my attention was then drawn to his fiery black eyes with wild brows, and by his deep and melodious voice that in exuberance or in anger, rose to a volcanic roar. The friendship between him and Aurel intrigued me. They had prepared their final-year exams at the Polytechnic together and I often saw them sitting at a table covered with an oilcloth in the shade of the old oak tree. While they were absorbed in their textbooks, I passed silently behind them, stopping in a distant part of the alley from where I could watch them without being seen. Occasionally, they got into heated arguments about an equation or a trigonometry problem, which taught me some spicy insults and a multitude of very colourful epithets. At other times, they lounged about on deckchairs in the sun, exchanging dirty jokes in hushed voices. I did not have any friends of my own age in the court-yard or elsewhere, and I was envious of their friendship. When the time came for Barbu to leave, they embraced as if they were never going to see each other again and Aurel frequently accompanied him as far as the street. I found it strange that I had never seen Pouia join them. I started to believe that the two young men shared a secret and that this secret was what their friendship was built on.

Both of them passed their exams brilliantly and as soon as she heard it, Marta, Aurel's mother, spread the good news throughout the courtyard, but soon after, for some mysterious reason, the meetings between Barbu and Aurel stopped. One day, my mother heard Nora Freiberg say to Marta: 'So much the better. The voice of that loud young man in front of my win-dows woke me up every morning. You know, I come back from my work quite late at night, and without my ten hours sleep, I can't function like a human being.' After Nora left, Marta remarked to my mother: 'She comes back "late at night"? She calls that work?'

On 13 October 1940, a German military mission arrived in Romania, made up of several thousand soldiers and about a hundred officers. Two generals headed the mission and, if

I am not mistaken, Speidel commanded the air force. About fifty Messerschmitt fighter planes and a dozen Heinkel bombers flew over Bucharest, sowing terror in the hearts of all the Jews, along with admiration mixed with anguish in those of most of the Romanians. Among them, the less blind wondered if, as a matter of fact, the mission was not an army of occupation. Officially, the German military had been invited by the Romanian government with the aim of training and modernising the Romanian Army, but the true reason for their presence was to ensure the defence of the strategic oil fields of Ploesti, near the capital. Romania then having the richest oil deposits in Europe on which the advance of the Wehrmacht panzers depended.

With all the bad news at the end of that month of October, autumn appeared to be particularly bleak. One Saturday afternoon, I went outside to cool off after a heated dispute with my brother: I felt that he had betrayed me and I was furious; the reason being that, at the start of the school year, I was to enter, at long last, high school – hip, hip, hip, hooray! I was going to Cultura, a secondary school founded in 1898 by the Jewish community that had two branches, one combining science and arts and the other purely commercial. I would finally be a secondary school student, in a Jewish secondary school, amongst Jewish pupils, with Jewish teachers! But, contrary to my desires, my parents wanted to put me in the commercial branch of Cultura, as they had done with my brother before me. And my older brother, who said that he was, with lofty authority, my protector and guide, had not lifted his little finger to defend my cause. Was it out of jealousy or because he did not want my future to be different from his? And this while his own future did not satisfy him! For he too did not want to end his life as an accountant, or a travelling salesman, or a tie-seller in Lipscani Street, the Bucharest Mecca for small shop-keepers and other wheeler-dealers. All that just to get married, have children and raise them as a good family man...

The rain had just stopped as I strode into the deserted and silent courtyard. Silvery reflections of metal roofs and gutters shimmered in the rippling inverted mirror of rainwater on the still soaked alleyways. Distracted, I stepped into a puddle. There was so much water in the courtyard that it was as though the rain had swallowed the gravel. In the sky above, dark clouds raced, chased at high altitude by a wind absent on the ground.

From the leaves of the white mulberry tree at the corner of the Bercovicis' house, raindrops dripped on a patch of wet grass with the steady rhythm of a clock. It was cold. The cold rid me of my anger and I was returning home when I thought I saw the silhouette of a soldier striding past the Theodorecus towards the centre of the courtyard. It took me a few seconds to realise that the figure approaching was none other than Barbu Stanescu, Aurel's friend. I recognised him from his build, his thick neck, square head and his abundant black hair that covered his nape in the style of our national poets. Why had I first thought I had seen a soldier? No doubt because of the uniform. But the uniform he was wearing was not that of the Romanian Army. It was, to my astonishment, the uniform of the Iron Guard: the infamous green shirt with the Sam Browne belt tightened around the waist. Barbu was therefore a Legionnaire, a member of the Iron Guard of Corneliu Codreanu, the Captain. Nobody in Romania had hated the Jews with more ferocity than Captain Codreanu, the archangel wearing a peasant's sheepskin jerkin riding down from heaven on a white horse. Aurel's friend was therefore part of

44

this clan! So that was the great secret that Barbu and Aurel shared, the secret that had bound their mysterious friendship! Barbu strode down the alley of the old oak towards Aurel's house and disappeared from view. I was immobilized by the discovery and waited. Not long after, he reappeared, certainly without having found Aurel. He appeared upset and agitated and glanced around nervously several times, as if to make sure that no one had seen him. He had perhaps seen me and was bothered or more likely, he thought that he should never have set foot again in this place, stuffed as it was with Jews, and that was the last we saw of Barbu.

For some reason, I didn't mention this episode to Pouia. Did she know that Barbu – the close friend of the man she planned to marry – was a member of the Iron Guard? And, had she known, what explanation would she have received from Aurel to justify this relationship? Without doubt, the grave political events of the time and the fury with which the earthquake of 10 November 1940 struck Romania and its capital marked me infinitely more than the anecdotes of the courtyard of numbers 47-49.

At three thirty-nine in the morning, a terrifying rumble made my brother and I jump from our bed as plaster and dust rained down from the ceiling. The long wall of the living room bulged and bent like a drunkard and the earth rolled beneath our feet. The floorboards were heaving from one side of the room to the other and, for a moment, we thought the ground would open and swallow us up. My mother's dresser, containing her best china, went for a turn between the bed and the dining table, colliding with a group of chairs in its way. The heavy lion-claw chandelier swung dangerously overhead, threatening to crush us. As we ran to our parents'

45

room, the large mirror hanging near the window facing the Cassimatis' crashed to the ground, shattering into a thousand pieces. Speechless and trembling, our parents sheltered us in the doorway leading to the kitchen. At that moment, the cupboard doors burst open with a bang as several shelves flew out, breaking a windowpane. After a few minutes, the walls stopped swaying, the deafening noise ceased abruptly and an eerie silence set in. Our little house, like all the others in the courtyard, had absorbed the shock and sustained little damage. But we learnt later that the earthquake had caused thousands of deaths in the country and that in the capital the Carlton, a large building of fourteen floors on the elegant Boulevard Bratianu and the closest thing to a skyscraper that Romania had, had collapsed like a house of cards, burying its numerous inhabitants under a mountain of plaster, stone and twisted iron.

On 19 November, while the government was still trying to deal with the consequences of the earthquake, Antonescu went to Berlin to meet the Führer. The two heads of state got on marvellously and established an excellent relationship. On 23 November, at Berchtesgaden, in the Berghof, the Führer's personal residence, Antonescu signed Romania's entry into the tripartite axis of Germany-Italy-Japan. The die was cast. In secret, the general was committing to an alliance with Hitler to attack the Soviet Union and to participate in the establishment of a New European Order in which there would be no place for Jews. We were therefore sentenced to death in absentia. Even if for the Jews of the old kingdom, particularly those of Bucharest, the general reserved the right to suspend this sentence, at least for a time.

General Antonescu's visit to Berchtesgaden and the apparent personal friendship he struck up with the Führer put an end to his relations with Horia Sima, the head of the Iron Guard. Once their common aim of abolishing the parliamentary regime was achieved, their alliance died, for each wanted absolute power for himself. During the night of 26 September 1940, the Iron Guard murdered sixty-five dignitaries of the former parliamentary regime in the infamous prison of Jilava. The following day, Professor Nicolae Iorga, Romania's most eminent historian, suffered the same fate. In the past, Iorga had been one of the first adherents to the cause of Corneliu Codreanu, and had remained to his last days a convinced anti-Semite. But in the eyes of the Legion, he had become too liberal and to make the point, they stuffed a liberal newspaper down his throat and executed him in an open field near his villa in Sinaia, but not before tearing out his beard. The aim of these crimes, fomented by Horia Sima, was to challenge the authority of General Antonescu and to sow anarchy in the country in preparation for a rebellion that would not be long in coming.

Indeed, it erupted on 21 January 1941, when the Iron Guard, with villainous zeal, at the same time that it attacked government offices, army barracks and police stations, committed acts of terrifying violence in the Jewish neighbourhoods of the capital, in particular those of Vacaresti-Dudesti, near our home.

In the courtyard, we survived the rebellion and no one in our family was physically harmed. It was not, however, a moment for rejoicing, for as soon as we could return to the streets, the scale of destruction brought about by the Iron Guard on the Jewish centres of the city revealed itself in all its barbarism: numerous synagogues were seriously damaged or burnt down entirely; shops and artisan workshops reduced to ashes or smoking ruins; grocery stores smashed with hammers and axes, and their contents, if they had escaped the looters, scattered across the frozen streets.

By some miracle, our Jewish Cultural high school escaped the Legionnaires' attention. It was only in the following weeks, when the leaders of the Jewish community came to review the scope of the three days of terror, did we discover with horror that more than two hundred Jews had been murdered by the Iron Guard. At the municipal abattoir, the Legionnaires hung Jews upside down like flayed carcasses on meat hooks, their intestines wound around their necks, and a label 'kosher meat' slapped on each corpse. We had only remained alive by chance, for they were Jews like us, living in the same city as us and we could easily have been killed in their place. Our life in Romania under the Antonescu regime was no longer secure: from that moment on it depended on pure luck.

Under the orders of General Antonescu, the Romanian Army crushed the rebellion after three days of street fighting. The Iron Guard was disbanded and a large number of its members as well as its leader, Horia Sima, found refuge in Germany. The general had restored order and life seemed to return to 'normal', nevertheless, even if we had found a measure of calm, we had forebodings of other sinister ordeals awaiting us. The greatest source of unease since the new year was the massive concentration of German forces in Romania, particularly in Bucharest. Our capital became a place of transit for the Wehrmacht in its frequent and secret movements: following Italy's invasion of Greece, Germany was preparing to attack Yugoslavia, with which Romania had common borders to the West. War was drawing ever closer. Yet in the capital, the only ones to wage war were the children, loud and joyful, who battled each other in the streets with snowballs, under an occasionally blue winter sky and a biting, frozen sun. The embassy of the United States remained open and active, not far from the royal palace. There was still hope.

During this period of relative calm that followed the rebellion, the Marcovici and Halpern families announced the forthcoming marriage of Pouia and Aurel. The joyful ceremony took place before a reduced, but enthusiastic, number of guests in a synagogue that had escaped the Legion's fury. Our family was invited, as were Chichi and Rozica with their parents – in fact, the entire courtyard was invited, with the exception of our Christian neighbours, and Barbu Stanescu, naturally. But he had his part in the Iron Guard's rebellion, as had my father, for on that same 21 January 1941, he had not returned home at the time we usually expected him.

4

Two or Three Things About My Parents

My father was a handsome man, slim and of medium height, blonde and with beautiful blue eyes; his looks belonged more to what would be considered Aryan, than to those usually attributed to Jews. He was gregarious, loved by women and enchanted by them. In the courtyard and among his friends, he had the reputation of being a good storyteller, although he frequently spun his stories out too long. Too bad if someone was in a hurry to get to the point; he waved them away with the Yiddish word *Hapnisht* ('don't rush me!'). Over the years, *hapnisht* became the magic word my brother and I would use to make our poor mother laugh when she lost patience with us.

He was also a good dancer. He led his partners with brio to the rhythms of the tango, foxtrot and waltz. He adored adventurous nights out and exciting parties, having always had a taste for the unexpected and a disdain for the mundane. My mother, on the other hand, rarely went out for amusement and lived in the prison of the ordinary.

When in company, my father enjoyed drinking white wine, often a bit too much. The mix of dancing and alcohol made his head spin and he would vomit when he returned home. My mother cleaned up, cursing her misfortune. Overcome by guilt, he said nothing. Alcohol did not make him violent; he adopted a hangdog look, but he did not promise to change. When a row followed, always in Yiddish, my brother and I would escape to the living room, slamming the door behind us. We were deeply affected by these incidents for a long time after; discord between parents does not disappear easily from the memory of children.

Nevertheless, my father was a very good man: generous, honest, hard-working, devoted to his family and responsible, although his sense of responsibility often collided with a certain recklessness, the origin of which has always escaped me. He needed to be guided tenderly and with patience, so as not to bring back the demons from which he had freed himself. My mother was only good at relentlessly criticising him with rancour and bitterness. Without doubt, in the past, at a certain moment, a profound crisis had led them to live together, but disunited. Did they still love each other? He, certainly, loved her deeply, as much as he feared her. As for her, I doubt she still loved him, but she remained tied to him by the routine of family obligations and by that sort of affectionate camaraderie that a long life shared often seals in a couple. Conscious of her dependency, she had accepted the necessity of compromise, but could not forego the resentment that jeopardised it.

At the age of forty, they were still young, even for those times. In my eyes, my mother was very beautiful: she had a softness, a sparkle and grace that always touched me profoundly. But in relation to other women of her age in the courtyard, her body bore the marks of fatigue: her waist had thickened, her hands had lost their femininity after so many years of chores, one as thankless as the last, and her legs were frequently swollen. She got up at dawn and often her day's work ended only at midnight. She did the laundry by hand, cleaned the house, cooked for four, darned our socks, altered my father's clothes to fit my brother, then those of my brother to fit me and, on top of that, sewed dresses for a few well-off ladies of the neighbourhood to supplement my father's modest salary. I once heard my mother complain to Fanny (a cousin who was a pharmacist, not the prostitute!) that night was the only time she had for herself and bed her only refuge. Soothed by the silky freshness of the starched sheets, she could, she said, withdraw into herself and, once my father was asleep, meditate on her life and destiny.

For some time, Leo and I no longer heard the familiar sounds coming from my parents' bedroom when they were being intimate. To my great displeasure, my brother had told me one day that our mother had probably lost her sexual appetite while my father's had quadrupled. How had this idea got into his head? Had he, as my older brother, had intimate conversations with my mother? Did she confide in him?

One Sunday, while my father was playing poker at the home of our neighbour Nicu, the father of Rozica, I found my mother sitting on the bed, staring into the distance. I surprised her by asking what she was thinking about. As though woken from a dream, she was startled and turned her eyes towards me without saying a word. I insisted. Her expression softened and she answered, almost inaudibly, 'I was thinking of God'. 'You were thinking about God? Why?' She replied, 'I don't know why. I was also thinking about *Anna Karenina*, the book Pouia lent me.'

That she might think about God did not astonish me. She believed strongly in Him. But why was she thinking about Anna Karenina? I remembered that when she was reading the book, I had often seen her in tears. When Pouia came to take the book back, my mother told her that in her humble opinion Anna's tragic destiny came from a wrong choice, that of having fled a comfortable family home to surrender herself to a carnal passion that had no future. By leaving her husband for prince Vronsky, Anna had abandoned her child and defied society's moral codes. Before Pouia had time to reply, she added that, despite her abhorrence of adultery, Anna's suffering had touched her greatly, as did her courage to leave the man she no longer loved.

My mother had a passion for reading, but she only had an hour or two in which she could give herself to it, usually on Sundays, but rarely on a Saturday. Night was essential for her to rest in, to escape the daily hardships and to dream of inaccessible things. By chance I heard her confiding in Fanny one afternoon that she dreamed of having a bed to herself. Her only companion would then be the pale moon, hanging in the corner of the sky of the inner courtyard like some celestial lantern. But there was no place to add another bed in our home. And even if there had been, how would she have explained to us that she no longer wanted to sleep with our father? People thought more about the implications of their actions on their children in those days: The children can hear us, not in front of the children! My parents therefore continued to sleep together, but after having shared the same bed with my father for twenty

53

years (the only man of her life, the father of her two sons), she had decided, I don't know why and my brother did not know either, to shut him off from her body, refusing to respond to his desire. A wall of discord rose between them. Confused, he could neither understand nor accept her aversion. His refuge became his work as a fur salesman and his devotion to his employer, Paul Auerbach.

The entrance to the Auerbach store premises was through a grand wooden doorway embossed with bronze panels, from which a doorman, dressed in a grey uniform with gold epaulettes, escorted clients through a second, revolving, glass door into a vast salon, illuminated by sparkling baccarat chandeliers. Ensconced in a plush, Belle-Époque armchair, like a monarch settled on his throne, Paul Auerbach, the 'grand patron' appraised and rated his visitors, getting up only for the most important of his clients. And, in truth, in the kingdom of furs and furriers, he was a king: a modern king, wearing three-piece suits, white shirts and, depending on the day, a silk Windsor knotted tie or a bow tie. He was not handsome, but he had the advantage of a good head of silver-grey hair, arresting clever eyes and an imposing presence. His pocket watch was a magnificent gold timepiece, bearing the famous insignia of Longines, a seal of his status and consolidated place among the affluent echelon of Bucharest society. His aesthetic taste was reflected in the dazzling extravagance of the shop's décor, as well as in the sumptuous presentation of the furs. Velvet sofas, armchairs bolstered by silk cushions, chairs in mahogany and palm, all set the stage for the display of astrakhan and breitschwanz hats, beaver muffs, ermine collars and fabulous coats in mink and blue fox. Along the marble-clad walls, Lalique and Gallé vases adorned glass shelves and graced

Empire style cabinets, and at the rear of the salon, an elegant Art Nouveau lift rose to the workshop on the first floor and the vast area on the second floor where a dozen artisans worked on the pelts and skins. To the left of the lift, was a small recessed area where esteemed clients were entertained with champagne and delicacies from Capsha, the most acclaimed and fashionable provider of gastronomic delights in the capital. On the right was the fitting room, reached through a narrow mirror-lined corridor. With barely dissimulated amusement, the employees observed as the extravagant, gloved and hatted society ladies, squeezed into double corsets, their high-heels reverberating on the pink and green marble floor, surrendered themselves ecstatically to the sight of the countless images of their surprisingly slimmed-down silhouettes reflected to infinity.

Paul Auerbach's was renowned not only in Bucharest; many clients came from other big towns in Romania and even from neighbouring countries. It was therefore a great stroke of luck for my father to have been taken on as a salesman in this luxurious shop. In return, he adored his employer and charmed the clients, even if these men and women were for the most part huge snobs who swanned around exhaling smoke from their Lucky Strikes in vain perfumed spirals. Auerbach rewarded him by sending him the most difficult and capricious female clientele: 'George, will you take Madame Trandafir's measurements?' Trandafir translates as 'rose' in English and 'Madame Rose' – her full name was Elvira Trandafir – had had the chance to have snared the director of a major bank on Victoria Avenue. Elvira spoke very quickly, mixing French and Romanian and gesticulating in all directions, all the better to show off her beautiful bejewelled hands. Without exception, she ended her persiflage by asking in a condescending tone: Do you under-stand? '*Avez-vous compris?*'

Taking Elvira Trandafir's measurements, in fact taking the measurements of any other woman of her standing, was more of an art than a science. Pin cushion and tape measure in hand, prudence was called for around the contour of their bosom, their waist, their thighs and knees, and sometimes even as far down as their feet. Physical contact was often so intimate that he could hear the beating of their hearts and inhale the heady perfume of their bodies. Fortunately, my father had acquired the necessary agility to carry out his work without the slightest faux pas. Under his skilful charge, Elvira sighed and quivered and stamped her foot impatiently, like a nervous racehorse, but all the while letting herself be led; sometimes, she would even give him an ambiguous smile as her almond-shaped, chocolate-coloured eyes filled with a sort of affectionate irony. Serving these high society women day after day inevitably provoked a natural masculine desire to undress them in the imagination and from this urge developed a pulsing drive and physical appetite that needed to be satisfied.

As a result, on days that were particularly feverish, in order to regain his composure, my father took to spending his lunch break with the young and beautiful Florica, a '*fille de joie*' who made her charms available in a small private hotel near Lipscani Street, the lively bazaar in the centre of the capital. But the pleasure Florica occasionally provided could not tem-per his ardour. At night, in the conjugal bed, when his body brushed against my mother's, sexual desire fuelled by love and tenderness returned to torment and enflame him. But my mother was no longer willing to offer what he sought.

5

Fălticeni
and My Roots

My parents had met, in far from ordinary circumstances, in Fălticeni, a small town in the north of what was Romanian Moldavia. Fălticeni is in that region of north-east Romania, stretching along the river Prut, not to be confused with the Republic of Moldova (situated between the rivers Prut and Dniestr), which was also, under the name of Bessarabia, part of Romania before its annexation by Russia in 1812 and by the USSR, in 1940. That my parents came from Fălticeni was a source of humiliation to me, as in those days, the town had less than thirty thousand inhabitants, and in the eyes of Bucharesters, known for their arrogance, was considered the epitome of provincialism.

Once, during the summer holidays, my mother took my brother and me to visit Auntie Brana, my mother's sister, and her husband, Uncle Mosh Copel Leibovici. They lived with their son Bercu and daughter Sylvia in the village of Dolhesti, a few kilometres from Fălticeni.

Uncle Mosh Copel (in Romanian, Mosh is a term for 'old man') was a farmer, which was unusual for a Jew in those days. He kept a horse, a cow, chickens, turkeys and a few rabbits, as well as having a small plot where he grew vegetables to sell at the nearby market. He often made a bit of extra money hiring out, at a good price, his horse and cart for the transportation of goods or for any other occasional trade. Bercu helped his father with his work, while Sylvia helped her mother with hers. I loved Auntie Brana for her excellent cooking, and Bercu for his inexhaustible reserve of jokes and his impersonations that made me laugh until I cried. But the one I loved the most was Mosh Copel. I envied his strong, veined, tanned arms and his robust torso, which he revealed at the end of the day when washing himself in cold water at the tap in the back of the yard, right next to the little stable and cowshed. Mosh Copel was a man of few words who observed others carefully, approving or disapproving of them with just the iris and the pupil. In the evening, sitting at the dinner table, he swallowed, under Auntie Brana's reproachful look, two small glasses of tzouika[3] tempered by a chunk of rye bread. He had got used to this look during their marriage. After his meal, he placed his fists one on top of the other and leaned his chin into the hollow formed between the entwined thumb and forefinger. Gazing into space, he cut himself off from the rest of the world and entered a state of grace that no one dared disturb. According to Bercu, it was in this meditative posture that his father found the answers to all his problems, whether related to work, finances, or to the daily irritations coming from Auntie Brana.

3   Tzouika (ţuica): Romanian plum brandy.

Alas, the fleas and bedbugs made my time at Dolhesti intolerable. They infested our beds every night, sucking our blood, and mine in particular, as my mother and my brother did not suffer as much. And yet, Auntie Brana cleaned her home meticulously and beat the mattresses every day without exception. I suspected that the nasty creatures came from the cowshed. Feeling somewhat guilty, Mosh Copel produced what he swore was a miraculous ointment with which he covered me at bedtime, despite it not appearing to frighten the predators one bit.

I was only freed from this torture on the day we left Dolhesti for Fălticeni, where my mother's brother, Uncle Max, and my father's sister, Aunt Golda lived. It was also there that my parents were born and where they had met and married. At the end of the visit, we warmly embraced Mosh Copel, Auntie Brana, Bercu and Sylvia, hoping rather to see them next time in Bucharest. We also said goodbye to the fleas and the bedbugs and boarded the train to Fălticeni.

Leo and I loved Uncle Max and his daughter, Bianca, a gifted young girl, but not at all his wife, Dora, who, from her exalted position as German and French teacher at the local girls' secondary school, had adopted a disdainful attitude towards our parents and a frigid, if not contemptuous, indifference towards us, their delightful progeny. Unfortunately, or fortunately, just as we arrived for our visit, they left on their summer holiday, obliging us to spend the rest of our stay in the sad home of Aunt Golda and her husband, Maher, a butcher whose rough manners contrasted with the burlesque gallantry he displayed towards my mother and his lame efforts to win us over with stupid jokes.

At Aunt Golda's, we slept well but ate badly. Her cooking stank and the taste was even worse than the smell. Did we really have the courage, my brother and I, to throw half of what was on our plates under the table? As for Uncle Maher, with his bushy moustache and bovine eyes, having once seen him skin a lamb with an enormous knife, blood dripping from his hands, he terrified me to the point of giving me nightmares.

The house in which they lived was situated in a poor neighbourhood, near the market, where most of the Jewish population was crowded. It was an ugly neighbourhood of bleak houses constructed in wood or plaster along dusty, dirty streets. The upper town, a more recent development, seemed less miserable and more presentable, with large modern buildings. Certain streets, particularly the Grand Avenue, were wide and paved, and according to my mother, the paving stones had come all the way from far-off Galicia.

We visited the Great Synagogue and strolled in the park next to the Somuz River, but having once got lost in the crowds of the Grand Avenue, we thereafter kept to the same route back to Aunt Golda's, sticking to the narrow and gloomy back streets that we were familiar with, where rowdy, barefoot children chased each other along the broken pavements.

There was nothing about Fălticeni that impressed me particularly, except for its picturesqueness. Before leaving Dolhesti, Mosh Copel had told me that, according to chroniclers, the lands of Fălticeni were bought in 1490 by Isaac, the Jewish treasurer of Stephen the Great, famous voivode of Moldavia. Fălticeni, the burgh that would spring up later on these lands, attracted in its glorious past the rich merchants of Bukovina and Ukraine and was dubbed 'the Fair of the River Somuz'.

'Don't mock this little provincial town,' Mosh Copel chided, 'for, over the years, it has attracted almost as many writers, poets, painters and men of science as your pretentious Bucharest.' No doubt seeing the scepticism written on my face, he had added: 'Have you read Mihail Sadoveanu, who lived and studied in Fălticeni? He's the Romanian writer I like the most.'

I had not read Mihail Sadoveanu and, feeling a bit embarrassed, I changed the subject and asked my uncle if in his view my ancestors had gone to Fălticeni from Austrian Bukovina or from Ukraine. Shrugging his shoulders, he replied with a smile: 'From one or the other, or even from further away.'

My brother and I had not known our grandparents; they had all died before we were born. As for our great-grandparents, I did not even know their names. The little I had learned about my family came from stories, true or false, told to us by my father, my uncles and our cousins – notably Fanny the pharmacist. And since the deficient memory of all these close relatives failed to shed any light on the darker recesses of the past, the logic of the heart and the angels of intuition mercifully came to my aid.

Leib Davidescu, my paternal grandfather, was a baker. The only photo I found of him shows a handsome man with a calm and respectable demeanour. A top hat sits on his head, lightly pressing on his left ear. His thick, ash-grey beard starts from his sideburns, joins up under his nose and flows around the contours of his slightly parted lips, as far as the wrinkled collar of his coat. His shining, gentle eyes reflect a secret and lofty calm.

One summer afternoon, a mysterious fire broke out in my grandfather's bakery. Flames rapidly engulfed the old wooden building and, trapped in the cellar, he was unable to escape. He was only forty-two.

The police concluded that the fire was accidental, but the Jewish community thought it more likely to have been a deliberate, criminal act perpetrated by envious peasants or by anti-Semitic thugs. Being the eldest son, my father, whose given name was Ghershon, aged thirteen, scarcely two months after his Bar-mitzvah, had to take on the responsibilities of head of the family. He had to look after his mother, two sisters and three brothers. Diphtheria tragically made his task easier: in less than a year, he lost two brothers and a sister. Fortunately, he found work with Nachman Tuchner, one of the richest Jews in Fălticeni, the owner of a large grain company.

Tuchner was a skilful businessman and a well-known benefactor. There were too many poor Jews in the town and many of them could not have survived without the help of wealthy Jews. The tragic death of Leib Davidescu and the destiny of his family had moved him. It was for this reason that he invited my grandmother, Fruma, to bring her eldest son, my father, to his office in order to get to know them and see what kind of support he could provide. There are no existing photos of my grandmother Fruma; according to my uncle Pincu, she was of medium build and had the severe face of a peasant woman hardened by work and the misfortunes of life.

Immediately after presenting his condolences, Tuchner asked my grandmother to leave him with her son. When they were alone, my father noticed that Tuchner's left eye was of glass, but he did not flinch when this cold and inert eye stared at him. Tuchner realised this and was pleased; he asked if my father was sorry to be leaving school to start work in his business. My father replied that his only regret was having lost his dear father and the important thing for him was to start work as quickly as possible, for he was then, as everyone told him, the head of the household.

According to my father's description, Tuchner was fat and ugly, his kippah slid comically sideways over greasy, ginger hair and his nose reached almost to his mouth. His glass eye frightened his young nephews, whom he didn't care for in any case. He was irritated by their chubby, red cheeks and their fat thighs that rubbed against each other. They were too much like his sister, Shula, who also had red hair like he did, now thinning on top. Laughing loudly, to hide his embarrassment, he once confessed to my father that the day when he had first seen him, a sad orphan but firm and courageous, he had noticed in him the qualities that he would have loved to possess himself: strong, bold, and, especially, blonde!

Two days later, my father started work as an apprentice carrying sacks of flour for The House of Wheat. He told me very little about his first years working for Tuchner, nor of his adolescence and entry into the adult world. The fact is that from thirteen to eighteen, he slowly progressed in the business, under the protective wing of his employer, right up to the accounting department – a very enviable promotion, as once on the first floor, near the boss's office, one escaped the heavy physical work of hauling sacks of grain and flour and aspired to a higher and more respected level of activity, where men earned their daily bread in suits and ties, without being obliged to dirty their hands.

Everyone in Tuchner's business knew that the 'boy', who was no longer a boy, but a confident and sensible young man, was his protégé. The fact that Tuchner liked her son and appreciated his work naturally helped my grandmother to regain a taste for life, which had been lost after the tragic death of my grandfather. She was then able to do her shopping in the market with her head held high and a smile on her face as she acknowledged the hypocritical greetings of the stallholders who had treated her in the past with the contempt reserved for poor old widows. She was proud of my father who, in turn, was proud of himself. But what made him the happiest was that he had become the adored hero of his siblings to whom he gave a few coins nearly every day to treat themselves to doughnuts.

It could reasonably be said that life had finally looked kindly on my father and his family, but everything changed brutally for them on 28 June 1914. That day, the heir to the Austrian throne, Archduke Franz-Ferdinand of Habsburg, and his wife, Sophia, were assassinated in Sarajevo by a young Serb from Bosnia, Gavrilo Princip, member of the Serbian terrorist organisation, the Black Hand. The assassination served as a pretext for Austria-Hungary to declare war on Serbia, ally of tsarist Russia, its rival in the Balkans. In solidarity with Serbia, Great Britain and France aligned themselves with Russia creating the Triple-Entente, while Germany took the side of Austria in the aim of extending its conquests in France – this troublesome neighbour that it had already defeated in 1870-71, dispossessing it of a great part of Alsace-Lorraine. In this way, in August 1914, generals replaced diplomats at the negotiating table and men went off to kill each other on battlefields for four long years.

At the start of the conflict, Romania found itself in the difficult position of having to choose between two opposing camps: the Triple-Entente and Serbia on one hand, and the two central powers, Germany and Austria-Hungary, on the other. It was up to the King and his Prime Minister to decide what camp to ally with, or to stay neutral. However, due to a quirk of history, the then reigning king of Romania, Carol I, was a German of the famous Hohenzollern-Sigmaringen dynasty. Naturally, he wanted to rally to the side Germany.[4] He [i] believed in the invincibility of the German Army and in the moral and cultural superiority of the nation into which he had been born. However, Prince Ferdinand, heir to the throne, who was married to Marie of Saxe-Coburg – oldest daughter of the Duke of Edinburgh and grand-daughter of Queen Victoria of Great Britain – favoured alliance with the Entente, and was more willing to listen to public opinion and the government than was his uncle. In order to avoid a rupture between the King and the political parties, the government chose neutrality. This decision affected the health of King Carol and when he passed away on 10 October 1914, Prince Ferdinand became King Ferdinand I.

Although war had been avoided, it did not lessen the terrible fear of being called up that had gripped my father and his family. The absurdity was not lost on them that Jews, who did not have the right to citizenship, were not exempt from military service. My father was going to turn eighteen and like all the young men of his age had to imagine himself as a recruit: hair shaven like a convict; body wrapped up in the rough, repellent khaki wool of the military uniform; legs bound from boot to knee with greenish puttees and head stuck, as far as the eyebrows, in a metal helmet that rang like an old bell. The fate of my father and his family depended on the new king's decision: would he remain neutral or would he join Germany, land of his birth, in the war against the Entente?

It was surprising that King Ferdinand, hesitant by nature, had the courage to place the interests of his adoptive country

4   See end of book for endnotes with Roman numerals.

65

ahead of any feelings that bound him to his fatherland and the powerful Hohenzollern dynasty, to which he belonged. As soon as he received assurances from the Entente that in the event of victory the territorial demands of his country, especially concerning Transylvania, would be satisfied, he declared war on Germany and the Austro-Hungarian Empire.

Towards the end of August 1916, my father learned from the newspapers that the Romanian Army had invaded Transylvania, winning some stunning victories. But without the intervention of Russia, the great ally in the East, and with the arrival at the front of massive German reinforcements, Romania was doomed to defeat. On 10 December 1916, Bucharest fell and, abandoning almost three quarters of the country's territory, the Romanian Army had to regroup in the north, on the vast plateau of Moldavia, protected by a high mountain range that was difficult to pass. The government and the royal family took refuge in Iași, the former capital of Moldavia, one hundred kilometres to the south-east of Fălticeni. Due to its proximity to Iași, from where the war was now waged, Fălticeni acquired a great strategic importance and was transformed.

6

Fălticeni
During the First World War
—
Kolka the Cossack
—
My Father Commits an Act of Madness

One Sunday, sitting on the edge of my bed as I was resting during my convalescence from scarlet fever, my father described the atmosphere in Fălticeni in 1916 to me, as well as the unexpected detours that his life had taken because of the First World War. I listened to him fascinated by the vividness and the precision of his description. He demonstrated his gift as a storyteller that was so admired in the courtyard and in the family.

The carefree, peaceful streets of pre-war Fălticeni suddenly had to cope with an influx of people, carts and other vehicles. In the deafening hubbub of the town centre, soldiers on horseback or on foot, mingled with a mass of peasants, merchants, schoolchildren, priests, women in multi-coloured shawls and war widows, black scarves tied over their hair. On the great avenue leading to the railway station, it was astonishing to see both police and the military directing the flow of vehicles. Fălticeni experienced its first traffic jams as military convoys arrived continuously, whilst others departed for secret destinations and Red Cross vehicles made their way with difficulty through throngs of confused pedestrians. In a long sinuous line, heavy cannons, their wheels caked in mud, were being hauled on gun-carriages drawn by four horses. The panting and neighing of the overworked beasts were audible all along the stony, steep roads, together with the incessant shouting of the officers exhorting their men to quicken their pace. The streets simmered with the buzz of engines and agitated crowds. A cloud of dust and smoke filled the sky. The air was little more than a mixture of petrol fumes, dung, human and animal sweat, grilled sausages, grass and oats. On sunken pavements and in rundown and dirty streets, the crowd expressed itself in a multitude of languages and dialects. For the first time, Russian could be heard everywhere. The Tsar's Army being Moldavia's guest, Fălticeni had to get used to living with this influx of drunkards who had come in polished boots from the great steppe of the East to fight to the very last Romanian. The Russians' appetite for drinking and carousing had stimulated trade. Thus, Fălticeni became more prosperous during the war than it had ever been in peacetime. But this good fortune also brought chaos, epidemics, corruption and immorality.

Tuchner's business also benefited from the war, the price of wheat exceeding that of gold. 'But if money alone is not the source of happiness, it is even less the guardian who protects us from misfortune,' Touchner had said to my father. And misfortune struck him in the most unlikely way. His wife, Rivca, had a cousin, Lia, who lived in Vienna, married to a physician of renown. A year earlier, Rivca had gone to Vienna to receive treatment under his care for a liver problem and subsequently the two cousins maintained frequent correspondence, particularly in the weeks leading up to the start of the war. Carried away by a growing wave of anti-Semitism and xenophobia, that King Ferdinand did nothing to temper, the Romanian authorities decided to open an investigation into Jewish women who had epistolary relations with persons suspected of ties to the enemy. As soon as Rivca received a summons to present herself at the police station, Tuchner hastened to contact the mayor and the chief magistrate. Both promised to 'sort things out' and he took care to assure them that their support would be generously rewarded. Nevertheless, the affair did not cease to worry him and had an immediate detrimental effect on his health. He complained of violent headaches and tension above his prosthetic eye. His doctor prescribed pills and advised him to work less and rest more.

Meanwhile, despite Tuchner's help, all the efforts my father made to escape being conscripted were met with failure. The military did not believe for an instant that his family would be unable to feed itself without him and they were even less impressed by the medical certificate provided by Haimovitch, the family doctor, 'proving' my father's unfitness for military service. My father didn't know to whom to turn and with whom he could share his fears that the prospect of recruitment elicited in him. He went to the Jewish cemetery where his father had been buried five years previously in order to regain his composure at the grave. He had noted the number and the row where it was located. The marble slab, and the stela made of stone, were gifts from the generous Nachman Tuchner. He sat down on the marble, wiped the sweat from his brow with a crumpled handkerchief, and closed his eyes. He had been drawn to the cemetery to feel his father's love again, as if he were going to the bakery after school to help him with his work. One day, hugging him close, his father had said with tears in his eyes: 'You, my son, you will finish your studies. You will not be a baker like me, but an educated young man, with a great future ahead of him, just as people have said.' Once again, it was time to leave and separate himself from this father. He got up and was struck by the absolute silence enveloping the cemetery. Behind the last row of graves where his father lay, a soft wind stirred the dark branches of a dozen trees that, in the late afternoon half-light, looked like majestic, grieving silhouettes. Suddenly an inner voice instructed him what path to take: 'If they call me up and teach me to carry arms, I will do it, and I will do it well. But if they send me to the front, at the first opportunity, I will wound myself, as though by accident and with a bit of luck and the grace of God, I'll get out of it. If not?' The question terrified him. With a last look at the stone carrying his father's name, he whispered under his breath: 'When you were burnt to death, I had to take care of the family. If I die, who will? Have I any choice?'

Not far from Ionitza Sandu Sturdza Street where my father and his family lived, the Cossacks of a cavalry unit of the Tsar's army had just moved into old barracks. The Cossacks, I had read, were descendants of the Tatars of Central Asia and of serfs who had fled Poland and Lithuania. Ferocious warriors and unrivalled horsemen, they were granted the Tsar's permission to settle in the south-east of Russia and Ukraine, on the condition that they defend the frontiers of his empire. The Cossacks' arrival in Fǎlticeni sowed terror among the Jews of the town. Who had not heard the terrifying accounts of their savage customs and the acts of cruelty they had committed, not only against the Tsar's enemies, but also against the peaceful Jewish communities of Russia and Ukraine? [ii] During the Cossack riots of 1648, one hundred thousand Jews were slaughtered and the name of Bogdan Khmelnytsky, the Cossacks' hetman in Ukraine, was more reviled by the Jews than the name of Haman, the venomous vizir of the Persian king, Assuerus.

According to an old saying, the exception confirms the rule. And if my father is to be believed, the exception among the Cossacks was Kolka Vassilovitch; their meeting could only have been the work of Providence...

One fine quiet night at the end of summer, my father was disturbed by someone banging on the front door. Sitting at a small table lit by an oil lamp, his head buried in a pile of invoices from a wheat merchant, he rose and left his bedroom. In the corridor leading to the front door, he met his mother Fruma, lamp in hand, coming from the kitchen where she had been busy ironing a mountain of laundry. Her worried look signalled caution. Silently, my father approached the corner of the vestibule where, hidden against the wall, between umbrellas and old boots, was the wooden cudgel that my poor grandfather had prudently kept. Dogs barked in the distance, breaking the calm of the night. Weapon at the ready, my father demanded: 'Who goes there at this hour?' While Pincu and Golda suddenly appeared as backup, a melodious voice replied in rudimentary Romanian: 'Deschide va rog... Ofitzer armata russa, Kolka' ('Open please... officer of Russian Army, Kolka').

'Ashteapta!' ('Wait!'), my father ordered. He set down the cudgel and turned to the reinforcements, ordering them to withdraw from the front. Refusing to obey, Pincu took the oil lamp from his mother's hands, stepped back a few paces and stood firm. His sister Golda fled to her room and Fruma hid in the kitchen. Ghershon turned the key in the lock and opened the door. He saw a bloodied head and gleaming white teeth in a mouth that was trying to crack a smile. A white rag, serving as a bandage, was wound around the head. The wounded left arm was supported in a sling made by a scarf. My father could see that the 'visitor' had a wide moustache, but the rest of his face was difficult to make out in the faint light of the new moon. The officer introduced himself: 'Kolka Vassilovitch'. '*Pozhaluysta*', my father replied in Russian, and, with a friendly gesture, invited the Cossack to follow him into the house. Kolka took a few steps, crossed the threshold, and stopped. Shutting the door, my father turned to examine him: he was young, dressed in an officer's uniform, dark brown hair, dark eyes and a hooked nose like a bird of prey. He incarnated a strange mix of eagle and crow. His jutting cheekbones certainly came from his Tatar ancestors, his suave mouth inherited – who knows? – from one of their poets or musicians. Overall, Kolka's appearance reassured him. They shook hands and my father introduced himself as 'George', the name he aimed to take and keep for the rest of his life, providing he survived the war...

He offered the Cossack a chair and sent Pincu to fetch doctor Haimovitch, who lived nearby. Grandmother Fruma lit two additional oil lamps in the sole big room of the house and went into the kitchen to prepare some tea. A mischievous wind sneaked into the room through the gaps around the front door, causing the candles to flicker on an end table. All the while, Golda remained locked in her room; my father having forbidden her from showing her face, fearing she might give the Cossack ideas.

The doctor arrived before the tea was served, expressing what an honour it was to treat a Cossack officer in 'flesh and blood'. The wounded arm was not broken, but it was necessary to snip some hair here and there to treat the head wound. Half an hour later, his ministrations completed, with hand on heart and refusing payment, he wished everyone a good night and, his country doctor's medical bag tucked securely under his arm, hurriedly left the house relieved that he was too old to be sent to the front.

And, indeed, on the front the military situation continued to worsen. If, at the start of summer, the Romanian Army had won glorious victories at Marasti, Marasesti and Oituz, to the north of Moldavia, the Germans had managed to retake Czernovitz, the capital of Bukovina. Reeling from the abdication of Tsar Nicolas II in March 1917, entire units of the Russian Army deserted their positions, confronted by the accession to power of Kerensky's provisional government and the increasing influence of Lenin's Bolshevik Party. This phenomenon was also seen among the Russian troops stationed in Romania, as the ideological confrontation between units still loyal to the Tsar and sympathisers of Kerensky or the Bolsheviks often turned into bloody brawls.

That explains how fate arranged the meeting between Kolka and my father. The night when he knocked on the door, Kolka had gone to get drunk with other Cossacks in a tavern run by Hershl Singer, an old bald and bearded Jew who was scorned by his community. When the Cossacks entered, the place was packed with a mass of soldiers, drowning in clouds of tobacco smoke, each shouting louder than the other. Hardly had the new arrivals time to sit down than a religious silence took hold, like the moment an orchestra conductor raises his baton. Scores of alcohol-enflamed, hateful eyes, settled on Kolka and his companions like so many gun barrels aimed at the heart of a man condemned to death. Without warning, the Cossacks found themselves face to face with sailors from Sebastopol, fervent supporters of Lenin, and infantrymen from Voronezh, partisans of Kerensky. The sailors did not like the Cossacks, who were faithful to the Tsar, while the Cossacks hated the disciples of Lenin just as much as Kerensky's apostles. A long piercing whistle through two fingers opened hostilities. Broken chairs and tables, glasses and shattered bottles flew through the beer and vodka saturated air. Hershl Singer managed to escape to alert the military police and save his seedy establishment from annihilation. It was not every day that Fălticeni or elsewhere, was treated to the spectacle of the Cossacks of Krivoi-Rog confronting the sailors of Sebastopol and the infantrymen of Voronezh. It must be said that the battle was as unprecedented as it was unequal. A Cossack without his horse is more lost on land than a sailor without his ship. But finally, those who inflicted the biggest losses on the Cossacks were not the sailors, but the infantrymen. The infantryman's savagery is fed by rancour, the infantry being the least respected branch of the army, despite the fact that in war the foot soldiers provide the majority of corpses.

Kolka had managed to flee before the military police arrived and spent the night in my father's bed. My father, as a good host, but also to keep an eye on the Cossack, had chosen to sleep on the floor outside the bedroom door. The following day, fresh and rested, after a good meal prepared by Fruma, Kolka returned to the barracks, but not without having concocted a solid alibi.

When the day came, my father presented himself at the recruitment centre. He travelled in a train filled to capacity by equally depressed recruits, which took them to a large military camp on the banks of the river Siret, near the town of Roman. Undergoing the numerous and absurd formalities, so indispensable in the army, each recruit took his place in desperately dark barracks with damp and freezing walls. The life of a recruit, as we know, is sad and miserable. There was no other choice but to get used to it and obey blindly; in the end, beaten down by the drudgery of barracks' life, my father gave in and, like the other recruits, accepted it...

At the same time, in Fălticeni, while Tuchner was at work, despite all the guarantees and promises, the police came to arrest his wife, on the charge of having exchanged regular correspondence with the enemy. In a group of forty women, Rivca was put on a goods train in which she endured several days in the most abject conditions before it stopped on the edge of an isolated wheat field where a dozen sadistic policemen forced the unfortunate women off the train, ordering them to walk as far as the town of Pascani, south of Fălticeni. Several women died of exhaustion and despair during this long march, but after nearly three weeks of wandering, Rivca and thirteen other survivors were permitted to return to Fălticeni. On arriving home, she learned from her old servant that her husband, the generous Nachman Tuchner, had died of a brain tumour twelve days earlier.

Tuchner had promised to look after the family during my father's military service, but this promise was now worthless. The Tuchner family, engaged in an inheritance dispute, sold the business in order to share the fortune and leave the town. Tuchner's House of Wheat ceased to exist.

How would my father get by in the future without the man who had been his guide and benefactor? He had no diploma, and was qualified for no trade. His experience was limited to what he had learned under the protective wing of Tuchner in the administration of the House of Wheat. Who would he turn to for employment? And who would offer him a comparable wage? In the silence of the dormitory, amongst the other recruits, he swallowed his tears, with a lump in his throat, as he had done in his childhood when his father punished him unfairly for something he had not done. That night, he thought of dying and fleeing the uncertainties of the future and the responsibilities towards his family, but he pushed such thoughts away with distaste. Since the age of thirteen, the duty to help his family had been the engine of his existence, the force behind each of his accomplishments. Immersed so brutally in the universe of adults, he had not let himself be intimidated by them. He had confronted with courage and steadfastness the challenges of senior employees, taking their insults without complaint, and thus winning the respect of everyone, including those who envied him because he was 'the boss's protégé'. In the face of such difficulties, he had never thought of suicide: why would he kill himself now, before even experiencing the great love he dreamed of?

Shortly before he went off to the army, Kolka had taken him to a brothel in Suceava, a city close to Fălticeni. The madam, Serafina, was a boisterous brunette whose generous backside could barely fit in the narrow corridor as she sashayed from the reception to the girls' bedrooms. She called her girls 'my white roses of Bessarabia'. My father told me how the sweet memory of a 'white rose' who had taught him how to give and take pleasure had helped him to tolerate the hard military exercises under a scorching sun or in torrential rain. His white rose's name was Irina and many were the nights he fell asleep with the memory of her laying her head on his shoulder, caressing the silky hairs on his chest, after making love.

Pincu and Golda wrote to him regularly. Their letters reassured him: the Cossack had kept his promises beyond my father's hope. Without Kolka's support, the family could not have survived. Every week, he passed by to bring them food and sometimes even money. And, according to Golda, he never forgot to ask for news of his *golubshik*, his 'brother', as he liked to call Ghershon. However, a letter from Golda soon came with the disheartening news that the Cossacks had to leave Fălticeni in a hurry. The Bolsheviks had taken power in Petrograd, Kerensky had fled, and Kolka's unit was being sent to join the Cossacks of Ukraine in the civil war against the Bolsheviks. He had promised to see them again before his departure, but he had not returned.

◇◇◇◇◇

On 11 November 1918, at Compiègne, Germany signed a humiliating armistice and the war came to an end. My father began to count his remaining days of military service, thanking heaven for having escaped the horrors of the battlefield. The rejoicing was vain and brief, for on 21 March 1919, Bela Kun, an apostle of Lenin, took power in Hungary, installing a communist regime inspired by the Bolshevik revolution. Lenin, who after the war, had had difficulty accepting Bessarabia's return to Romania, hoped that Bela Kun's success in Hungary would prepare the ground for the liquidation of the Romanian monarchy and the advent of a communist dictatorship under his authority. In order to escape Bolshevik encirclement and safeguard the monarchy, King Ferdinand put the Romanian Army back on a war footing. My father's regiment was sent to the north of Transylvania and crossed the Tisza River into Hungarian territory. Foreseeing the grave danger that the consolidation of a communist regime in Hungary would represent for Europe, the Supreme Council of Paris recommended Marshal Foch to encourage the Romanian and Czechoslovakian armies [iii] to launch a simultaneous offensive against Bela Kun on 20 July 1919. My father learned that his regiment was being sent to the front line. All at once, luck had deserted him. He had to act quickly, if not, he risked finding himself in the battle for Budapest.

His regiment was camped near the city of Debrecen and he was on night watch guarding a network of trenches that had been dug hastily during the previous day. A plan had been in his mind for some time: before dawn, he would fire a bullet into his thumb; he would say that he had dozed off, a noise startled him and in the confusion, he had fumbled with his rifle and had pulled the trigger.

It must have been just before five in the morning when my father inspected his rifle and, trembling with cold and emotion, placed it on the edge of the trench. He slowly moved the butt so that the barrel was pointed at the thumb of his right hand. The index finger of his left hand brushed the trigger. He was conscious of what he was doing, without being completely sure that it was really he who was doing it. Surprising himself, he ordered the index finger to pull the trigger. The shot was fired. His scream echoed in the emptiness as the bullet tore away the end of his thumb, but he had time to understand that

78

he had just alerted the entire world of his act of madness before he lost consciousness.

His finger was saved by a surgeon of the division, but though a military tribunal did not refute the possibility of an accident, a hastily convened court-martial sentenced him to forty lashes before his regiment. The sentence was carried out one morning on a Saturday, the sacred day for Jews. My father's lacerated body, unrecognisable, but still alive, was sent back to his family like damaged goods that could no longer be of use to the army and could perhaps not be of use to anyone. The war was well and truly over for Private Ghershon Davidescu.

7

My Father Meets Sheina

My father struggled for three months to survive his wounds. He recovered thanks to his family's devotion and the good care of doctor Haimovitch. Some deep wounds close to the ribs, neck and back, had threatened to damage ligaments and muscles, but Doctor Haimovitch had watched over his patient, making sure that his wounds healed, avoiding gangrene and any physical disability that might follow. When his recovery was complete, the Jewish community of Fălticeni made sure to give him discreet support. Zalman Zilberman, the rabbi of the synagogue where my grandmother occasionally went to pray, approached Baruch Goldenberg, owner of the *Nouvelle Mode* men's shop to get my father taken on as a salesman. Remembering the fondness Tuchner, bless his name, had for my father and his family, Goldenberg thought that taking the unfortunate young man under his wing was a mitzvah to please God. He offered him a 'tailor-made' job: bookkeeper and deputy salesman for a modest starting salary. My father did not hesitate to seize the offer; the pressing needs of the family demanded that he begin to earn money as quickly as possible.

At that time, the cold and leaden skies suited him better than joyful sunny days. He left for work early in the morning and when he finished late in the evening, he returned home as quickly as possible, taking less busy streets, avoiding familiar faces and encounters with old friends. His physical wounds were almost completely healed, but those of the mind did not cease to torment him. A deep sadness, such as he had never experienced before, became his daily companion. He started going frequently to the cemetery to pray and lay flowers on his father's grave and that of Nachman Tuchner, his unfortunate benefactor. When he went to enquire after his widow, Rivca, he was told she had gone to live with her family in Bacau.

Two years passed. At the end of the 1914–18 war, official anti-Semitism encouraged or, at least, tolerated by the King, was in retreat. Under the pressure of members of the Peace Conference and especially of America, Romania gave Jews the right to claim citizenship. The country was emerging from the war triumphant. Its territory and population had almost doubled. Its riches, notably oil resources, attracted investment by the biggest international companies. It was a time for optimism all around, including in Fälticeni. Trade at *La Nouvelle Mode* was flourishing again. Baruch Goldenberg – an asthmatic, ageing, childless widower – had practically relinquished all daily responsibilities of the business to my father, keeping the administration of finances to himself. Despite always being short of money, because he lost a lot at poker, he had agreed several times to increase my father's salary, fearing that he might leave to work elsewhere. The Davidescu family lacked for nothing anymore. Pincu, my uncle, having decided to learn carpentry, was taken on as an apprentice by one of Goldenberg's cousins. Golda, pressured by my grandmother, agreed to get engaged to a butcher, Maher Zusman, whom a matchmaker had introduced to her. Marrying his sister to a butcher would not have been my father's choice and he reprimanded my grandmother for having 'arranged' this commitment without his consent. For the first time in his life, he shouted at her. But mothers know how to take revenge... Hurt, my grandmother sobbed for hours, after which she no longer spoke to him for a whole week. Nevertheless, during this time, she did not fail to carry out her duties towards him: preparing the meals, washing and ironing his shirts, making his bed, ensuring that his pyjamas were folded away under his pillow, all that in silence and holding back the tears. Not being able to stand these theatrics, and particularly his mother's expression of martyrdom, any longer, my father ended up by asking for her forgiveness. He promised to agree, in due course, to having a butcher as brother-in-law.

In short, it seemed that everything was going well, and yet my father was not happy. He had only work in his life. He avoided everyone, even his former friends. He had chosen to live in isolation, whilst knowing that it was one of the reasons for his unhappiness. He persuaded himself that all his misfortunes flowed from Fălticeni, from this town where he had been born, but which he had turned against. Unless he left it, he would never escape his past, would never erase the stigma of the humiliation inflicted on him, or rather which he had inflicted on himself.

82

He was frequently sent to Galati to meet suppliers and liked the hectic energy of this great port on the Danube. As grain was one of the major exports of Galati, he had the opportunity of meeting several of the Jewish merchants he had first met when he worked for Touchner. He became particularly attached to Zissu Feinberg, the furrier who supplied Goldenberg's shop with winter coats. Zissu had recently been divorced from his wife of Bulgarian origin, suspecting her of having cheated on him with an officer of the merchant navy. On finding himself a bachelor once again, he invited my father to accompany him on an exploration of the nightlife in the bars of the port. My father thought that after Golda was married, he would leave Fălticeni to find adventure in this bustling and cosmopolitan port.

One day, *La Nouvelle Mode* received a strange client: a tall man with a clipped, dark moustache and a kindly expression, who it seemed to my father was someone he had known in the distant past. The effort he made to remember froze him for an instant and it was then that the visitor cried out in a voice to waken the dead: 'Ghershon Davidescu, what a nice surprise! I can't believe it...'

Astonished, my father replied, 'But to whom do I have the honour? Who are you?'

The stranger extended his hand and introduced himself, 'Max Davidescu... Don't you remember?'

My father shook hands and said hesitantly, 'As far as I know, there is no Max in my family.'

'Of course not! We have the same surname by sheer coincidence! I've looked into it...'

Dispassionately, my father looked at the stranger without moving. But Max had no intention of giving up. 'I'm going to refresh your memory...' he continued. 'Third infantry

83

regiment... the Dimitri Cantemir division, don't you remember? Your battalion joined us after we crossed the Tisza... I was sergeant in the company, but not in yours... in... in that of Captain Dragan. Now do you remember?'

The colour drained from my father's face. He felt a stab in his heart. Max approached him and added sadly, 'I was there when they punished you... I'm glad to find you in such good health.'

What did this man want from him? In a bitter voice, my father replied: 'Excuse me, but I am employed here to sell, not to relive unpleasant memories.'

Max smiled at him, visibly embarrassed.

'Listen, we are between Jews here. Why are you angry? I'm just happy to see you again. Sincerely...'

'Between Jews, as you say, how can I be of use to you?' my father insisted.

'I have come to buy shirts and a suit. I've been lucky enough to have obtained a visa for America. What better dream is there than that! However, the thought of leaving my family in a fortnight is making me ill.'

Frosty, but courteous, my father led his client to the shirts and suits section.

'You are going to set sail in winter, so you will need some flannel shirts. And it would be good to have two suits, one for the winter, and one for summer... Do you have a nice warm overcoat?'

'No, I've nothing new,' said Max. 'We're scheduled to arrive in New York on the 18 November. The Statue of Liberty will no doubt be covered in snow.'

Once Max had bought the clothes he needed, the two men shook hands and my father wished him a safe journey. Max was going to open the door when he suddenly turned around, put his purchases on a stool, and cleared his throat before saying in a very emotional voice:

'I am embarrassed to open up to you so much, but I have to act quickly. I've only two weeks before I leave. I ask you to listen to me patiently... After the war, once I had returned to my family, I could not erase what they had done to you from my memory. For a long time, I heard, even in my sleep, the cracking of the whip on your back, lacerating your flesh... Nor could I forget the courage with which you stood up to them. I spoke about you to my family. They know your story. We settled in Fălticeni only just recently. In Dolhesti, where we come from, my father and I were in the timber trade. The business was going well until the day war broke out and I was called up. Aged nineteen, I had hardly begun to shave, and found myself in the bloodiest battles: Neajilov, Argesh, Marasesti. From the grade of corporal, I was promoted to that of sergeant and I even received a medal, which I keep in a drawer, for it serves no purpose. I got out of that hell, praise be to God, without the slightest scratch, apart from the wounds to my soul. Today, I'm another man. I want to know the world, America. That's why I'm leaving. My father will look after the business while I meet my destiny beyond the ocean. I'm getting to the point: I can see you're impatient.'

Of what interest is this story of Max's to me? Even though the oddness of the situation intrigues me, my father thought to himself. 'No, no, I'm listening,' he assured Max.

'I have four sisters, Ghershon... Mina, Brana. Malca and Sheina. Brana married in Dolhesti to a farmer, a fine man. But my sister Mina lives in Bacau with a goy, a lieutenant in the artillery. A goy! Can you imagine what that's been like for us?

85

That's why we all left Dolhesti, my father, my mother, Malca, Sheina and me... To escape from all the malicious gossip! Brana and her husband did not want to leave Dolhesti. As for Malca, she has a fragile nature, timid and taciturn. Of all my sisters, Sheina is my favourite, the one I love and admire the most. She was born with a gift for sewing. During the war, her talent brought in almost as much money as the timber.... But I don't know why I'm telling you this. It's not money I want to speak to you about... It's something else... I'm hugely attached to Sheina and I would like you to meet her. In all sincerity, up until now we've been unable to find a man worthy of her. Would you agree to have tea with us this Saturday?'

My father did not know how to hide his embarrassment. He had to reply, but his mind was empty. After a short while, he heard himself speak, as if his voice came from someone else, 'Sure, why not?'

Max smiled widely. 'I thank you. I can see we're on the right path.' He took a piece of paper out of his pocket, wrote down his address, and handed it to my father.

On the Saturday afternoon, without telling my grandmother where he was going, my father called on Max's family as planned. He put on his finest suit, the one that Tuchner had given him, his favourite striped blue shirt, and the beautiful tie he had bought in Galati. Black or brown shoes? He opted for brown.

Max and his family – Salomon, the father, Zelda, the mother, Malca and Sheina, the sisters – were waiting for him, visibly tense. Salomon apologised for having such a poorly furnished house. He recounted, as Max had done before, that they had only just recently moved to Fălticeni. He was a man of medium build, with a round face and a very pale complexion. His lips,

86

of a pronounced pink, stood out in the whiteness of his face and of his beard. One might have mistaken him for a rabbi who had never left the confines of his synagogue and seen the sun. Zelda, the mother, wearing a vivid, floral scarf over her hair, chewed her lower lip nervously, her suspicious and severe expression betraying a difficult nature. Malca, slender and pale, with green eyes, scrutinized Ghershon from under her long lashes, as though she had never seen a man in her life before. She did not seem to my father to be as shy as Max had described her. There was an arrogance in her face and he thought that at any moment she might interrupt with a provocation or challenge. He wondered whether jealousy might be the source. And Sheina? He found her more beautiful than Malca, and certainly nicer. He was particularly impressed by her eyes, whose colour was neither green nor blue, but between the two. He told himself that the secret nature of these three women was defined by their mouths, by the language of their lips. Sheina's spoke to him of love, kindness and tenderness.

The following Sunday, Max took Sheina and my father to the patisserie *Le Petit Paris* in the centre of town, where 'high society' came to taste their delicious profiteroles. They then walked in the Mihai Eminescu park, talking about everything except Max's journey to America. Before they left each other, as they were saying goodbye, Max entreated my father to join his family at the railway station the following Thursday evening at six, the day of his departure. My father agreed and kept his promise.

At the station, he felt that Sheina's parents had accepted him as one of their own. The parting gave rise to a moving scene: while Zelda wept in Max's arms, Malca and Salomon, standing on their right, had tears running down their faces.

Next to my father, embarrassed, or intimidated by his presence, Sheina discretely wiped her eyes with a little lace handkerchief. Gently freeing himself from his mother, Max went over to embrace his father, then his sisters, hugging Sheina longer than Malca. The sad farewell ceremony ended with Max kissing his father on the mouth 'Russian-style' – a rather unpleasant custom unless you are Russian! As the train disappeared out of sight and Max could no longer be discerned waving goodbye out of the window, my father consoled Sheina, assuring her that everything would work out for her brother in America. On saying that, he took Sheina's hands in his and noticed that she did not resist and he felt a shiver of happiness pass through him.

After Max's departure, my father decided that it was time to tell my grandmother of his meetings with Sheina and her family, even daring to reveal how much he liked the young woman. My grandmother listened in stony silence: she had her doubts about this woman, she feared losing her son and, in any case, she didn't hold with the notion that people could like each other, just like that, at the drop of a hat.

My father and Sheina continued to see each other every week. She frequently invited him to join her family for dinner and on one occasion, the Davidescus on Sheina's side went to dine with the Davidescus on my father's. All they talked about was Max. He had written a letter from Istanbul and another from Athens. He promised he would send the next one from Valette, Malta being the next port of call. His letters were not jolly. Travelling by boat had turned out to be a bad experience, as he suffered terribly from seasickness and spent most of his time shut up in the narrow and suffocating cabin he shared with another traveller. He missed his family to the point where he questioned whether leaving for America had been the right decision. Sheina thought she detected tearstains on a page of his last letter.

During the meetings between the two families, Sheina did her best to get close to my grandmother, but without much success. One day, grandmother told my father that she would have preferred Malca to Sheina as a daughter-in-law. Irritated, he retorted that if Malca pleased her so much, she had only to marry Pincu, his young brother, to her as soon as he was old enough!

The lyric theatre of Iaşi was on tour in Fălticeni and Sheina asked my father if he would like to accompany her to see Chekhov's *The Three Sisters*. He happily agreed and it was the first time in his life that he set foot in a theatre. The experience enchanted him, though he had difficulty understanding why the three sisters were so deeply unhappy and wondered whether they were a bit unstable. He noticed that Sheina cried a lot during the play and he often held her hand to comfort her.

Walking her home, my father took her arm and felt the pleasant warmth of her body. They talked about the play, and Sheina told him that, after the experience of the war, Max's desire to leave Fălticeni to build a life elsewhere was similar to that of the three sisters who wanted to escape provincial life and live in Moscow. But she also wondered if there were other reasons. My father replied that he did not know Max well enough to be able to understand his decision, but that he too was thinking of leaving Fălticeni. He told her that he was patiently building up contacts in Galati, but that finally his real aim was to live in Bucharest. And he dared admit to her that ever since she had come into his life, that would also depend on her.

She listened to his confession in silence, trembling with emotion. Near her home, my father stopped suddenly to tell her that he loved her, that he had never loved another woman, and that he wanted to marry her and start a family. If, by the grace of God she consented, and her parents too, the engagement could happen as soon as possible. He took her hand, brought it to his face and gently kissed it. Then, keeping her hand in his, she spoke to him in a firm but troubled voice:

'I have feelings for you, Ghershon. I feel close to you. Max told me about what happened in Hungary, the sacrifice you made for your family. Others took it for an act of madness. When I saw you for the first time, I was not disappointed, I thought: Sheina, luck has perhaps made you meet a man you could love. Now that you have had the courage to express your feelings for me, I think that we should take our time. At this moment, I am too worried about Max. I think only of him arriving in America safe and sound. You must understand me.'

That night, my father kissed Sheina, hugging her so hard that she cried out and he feared she might faint. A letter arrived from Valette where Max's ship had a twenty-four-hour stop-over. He had fallen ill, but gave no details. He let it be known that he was thinking of giving up his dream of America and was going to decide at Oran or Tangier whether to continue the journey or return home to Romania. A postcard arrived a few days later from Marseilles. Max had left the ship at Tangier, no longer having the courage to cross the Atlantic and planned to return to Romania by train, if possible. To lighten his load, he had sold most of his belongings in the market at the main harbour. Back on dry land, he felt physically and psychologically stronger. He shamefully admitted to his weakness, but did not want to linger on failure. Not having succeeded in reaching the

New World, he wanted at least to discover the great cities of old Europe. With the money he had left, he would visit Paris, Berlin, Vienna and Budapest. Then, via Bucharest, he would return to Fălticeni. He signed off by sending his love to his parents and sisters, without forgetting to add my father to the list.

Max's family was both upset and relieved. Malca found her brother's behaviour totally ridiculous. She too would have liked to visit the great cities of Europe, but what chance did she have of ever doing that? Surely none! Had the passion Max showed for America just been a subterfuge? Sheina defended her brother with conviction: 'What do we know about the horrors of war on the battlefields? Can we understand the effect that they could have on the mind of a young man who had just left school?'

My father, witnessing one of these spirited discussions, unreservedly supported Sheina's point of view. Finally, the family calmed down. Like an ocean wave, the love they all felt for Max, the errant son, swelled and carried them all forward, driving away all doubts and suspicions in anticipation of the moment when kind and gentle Max would step down from the train and rush towards them with tears in his eyes.

The big moment arrived a few weeks later. The train from Bucharest stopped in Fălticeni at eight in the evening. Thin as a rake, Max was among the first to get off: he was carrying bags which, they would soon discover, were more loaded with gifts than personal belongings. With eyes glistening with tears and making wild shouts of joy, his nearest and dearest ran to meet him, holding each other by the hand so as not to get separated in the crowd. They embraced each other for a long time and began to talk, laugh and cry until a dozen cleaners in dirty yellow uniforms moved them along from the station platform.

My parents' wedding took place on 19 November 1922. Two years later, the young couple left Fălticeni to settle in Galati where my father found work with the furrier Zissu Feinberg. It was then that he finally changed his first name from Ghershon to George and my mother changed hers from Sheina to Jenny. In 1927 my brother Leo was born. In 1931, I followed, always behind him from the very start! In 1936, on Zissu's recommendation, my father found a job as salesman in the prestigious fur shop of Paul Auerbach in Bucharest and our family moved to Triumph Street, numbers 47-49.

8

From
One Encounter
to Another

In the afternoon of 21 January 1941 (the day my father did not return home at the time we expected him), the fur shop where he worked closed its doors unusually early. Paul Auerbach had personally overseen it. A week earlier, his friends at the Ministry of the Interior and the police prefecture had alerted him that serious riots were threatening the capital in the days to come. They promised him that the shop would be under permanent police surveillance and protection, but Auerbach did not set much store on men's promises. He decided to quickly secure the front door and the two big display windows with the help of double iron shutters. However, his friends did indeed keep their word: three policemen patrolled the pavement opposite, smoking cigarettes to keep warm and stopping from time to time to observe the closing-up procedure with idle curiosity. However, the capital seemed to go about its business in the usual calm of an afternoon like any other. Low clouds drove out the daylight and as soon as my father took leave of his colleagues, he checked his watch, saying to himself that he had just enough time to buy a few things on his way home. He went down Sfanta Vineri Street, then continued down Calea Moshilor where he stopped at Costacke's, the grocer. My mother loved cheese, especially telemea and cashcaval,[5] as long as they came exclusively from Costacke's. It was the same for apples: she only liked the Domnesti variety, and it was at Costacke's that you found the best. He added to his list ham, Portuguese sardines, some lakerda,[6] Greek olives and bars of Suchard chocolate, that Leo and I adored. Just as he was about to leave, Costacke took him by the arm and whispered: 'It's time to go home, Monsieur George. The Legion is preparing a surprise for us tonight. I know this from a reliable source. Be careful!'

Outside in the street, my father felt snowflakes on his face and decided to take the tram as far as Calea Vacaresti, finding it almost empty. He sat by a window, right in the middle of the carriage. The bags were not heavy, but they were no less a burden. From a distant seat, a fat woman wrapped in a heavy hooded cloak sent him a hostile look. With his fur hat on and his winter coat buttoned tightly, he was suffocating in the heat and decided to get off at the next stop. After walking for a few minutes, he was beyond Dobroteassa Street. Snow swirled in

5 Telemea is a Romanian cheese made from cow's, buffalo's or sheep's milk, which is made in a very similar way to Greek feta. Cashcaval, which arrived in the Balkans from Sicily, is a semi-hard cheese made from cow's or sheep's milk or a mixture of the two, lightly smoked and with a sweet or spicy taste.

6 Lakerda is a mezze of pickled bonito.

the frozen air. As he was about to cross Boulevard Marasesti, he noticed a group of three members of the Iron Guard standing in front of a tobacco kiosk and he felt that laden with packages he had called attention to himself like a magnet. The Legionnaires were wearing heavy sheepskin coats over their green shirts. My father accelerated his pace to cross the boulevard and felt a trickle of cold sweat run down his temple, his hair soaked under his hat.

Calm down, he said to himself: if they sense your fear, they'll be on you like a pack of wolves. He slowed down, thinking that this way he would control his emotions better. Supposing that they were following him, crossing the boulevard like he was, they could not be very far behind. About thirty metres, he estimated.

Very quickly, he had proof that he was being followed. He heard a man's shout, immediately followed by an explosion of oaths and roaring laughter. He understood that one of the Legionnaires had slipped on the icy pavement, landing comically on his backside. The struggle for Razvan – for that appeared to be the reprobate's name – to get back up on his feet, set off another wave of laughter and swearing before silence returned to the street. My father resisted the temptation to look behind him, acting as if he were unaware of any threat. They are playing cat and mouse with me, he thought.

At that moment, the group of three Legionnaires split up. He saw, out of the corner of his eye, that two of them had stepped off the pavement to overtake him whilst the third came up from behind. In a heartbeat, the two were now facing him and he felt the third man breathing down his neck. He was obliged to stop. In silence, the two Legionnaires sized him up from top to toe, as the third one skirted around him and stood between the other two. Tall, menacing and imposing, he asserted his position as their commander. After a moment, he addressed my father abruptly in a booming voice: 'Good evening. I hope Monsieur is not in a hurry.' He had a fur ushanka hat pulled well down on his head with the flaps completely covering his ears. His eyes were fixed on my father, whose features were indiscernible in the twilight that even the whiteness of the falling snow barely illuminated. With a gesture of the head, my father indicated the packages under his arm: 'As you can see... I am expected at home,' he explained.

'Who's waiting for you?'

'My family. My wife and children.'

'Put your things down!' This time, the voice was uncompromising and my father obediently complied. 'Do you know who we are?'

'Yes... I know,' my father's hesitated. Straightening up, after placing his parcels on the snow-covered pavement, he didn't fail to see the butt of a pistol revealed as the leader drew back his sheepskin coat.

'Who?' The man shouted the question, letting the coat fall over the gun.

'I don't live on the moon. You are the Iron Guard, the Legion.'

'Are you scared of us?'

'Scared? Why would I be scared? I don't do politics, me. The King, the parties, the ministers, they do politics. What do I know? I just work to feed my family.'

The two Legionnaires sniggered.

'We've found ourselves a wily bird,' said one.

'A philosopher,' added the other.

The commander gestured with his hand for them to be quiet. Then he said ironically: 'Well thought-out and well expressed, citizen! And how many children do you have?'

'Two... two boys.'

The legionnaire on the left said in a mocking voice: 'The race of Moses is reproducing like rats. I learned that in biology...'

A short caw-like laugh came from the legionnaire on the other side of my father and then he outdid his comrade with a joke of his own: 'That explains why we have such a population explosion. I learnt that in sociology, I even repeated the final year!'

Their guffaws rang out in the empty street. Surely, they must be students, my father speculated: the more they talk, the less likely they are to kill.

'Show me your identity card!' Suddenly, in a loud voice, the commander had spoken to him with the familiar *tu* form in Romanian. My father took out his identity card. He was amazed his hand was not shaking, as he wondered whether he would see another day or whether this was his last on earth.

The commander opened it, studied his photo, flicked the pages and then stopped like the roulette ball does on a number that can ruin a life. In a relaxed voice, he began to read: 'George Davidescu... Married... Domicile.... Triumph Street, 47-49... But we're just a few metres away from your home! I know the street well, the courtyard too...'

He has certainly seen the page with my religion, but he is more interested in my address. What is his plan? my father wondered. In the distance you could hear rifle and machine-gun fire.

The legionnaire to the commander's right, the one who wore a woollen hat and seemed numb to the bone, lost his patience: 'What the hell, Barbu? It's crystal clear he's Jewish. Why are we wasting our time in this deserted street?'

Barbu... Barbu.... the name sounds familiar... and he knows the courtyard, my father thought.

'Clear for you, but not for me, Chivu,' Barbu replied.

Chivu kicked the snow on the pavement. The other legionnaire, who was fat and sported a moustache, had to be Razvan, the one who had slipped. He shifted his weight from one foot to the other and shot Barbu an incredulous look.

'Let's take him to headquarters, Barbu!' protested Chivu. At the same time, he lowered his hat to protect himself from the cold. 'We'll strip him naked and then we'll see if his cock is Jewish or Christian.'

'And who's in command here, you or me?' Barbu snapped back.

Chivu looked down and fell silent. Cannon fire could be heard now in the distance. The cold and the cannonade dispersed a small group of bystanders who had gathered on the other side of the road. A taxi went by at speed and turned into Alexandru Vlahutza Street, its brakes screeching. The cannon fire became more intense. Barbu looked at his watch and said to his comrades: 'Let's go. I don't give a damn about this man. We have to get back to headquarters. You can hear the music.' Chivu and Razvan looked stunned as he handed the identity card back to my father: 'Take your parcels and get the hell out of here!'

'Thank you,' my father said mechanically.

'It's God you should thank!' Barbu replied.

98

As he buttoned up his coat and picked up the packages that were dusted with snow, my father heard Barbu say: 'Lads, every man has the right to a second chance. I gave him his. Who knows if he'll ever have another?'

Chivu spat loudly and Razvan addressed an obscene insult to my father's second chance. Then the three Legionnaires crossed the street, their shadows silhouetted on the snow.

The streetlights had been lit for a long time, illuminating the evening with a bluish pale light. It seemed that everything was freezing, except for this light. My father picked up his pace. He thought how miracles were unpredictable and undecipherable. He owed his life to this Barbu, who could only be Aurel's friend, the one who had entered the courtyard dressed as a legionnaire. He murmured the prayer Shema Yisrael: 'Hear, o Israel, the LORD is our God, the LORD is One. Blessed be the name of His glorious kingdom for ever and ever'....

Reaching Triumph Street, he stopped for a moment, not knowing for what reason, in front of the courtyard of number 37. On the pavement, opposite the wide-open gate, lay some logs and a few frozen potatoes that nobody had bothered to pick up. He did not know the people who lived in that courtyard. He slipped a hand inside his coat and felt his panicked heartbeats.

A wave of happiness flooded over him when he entered the alley, so familiar and welcoming, which led home. Lights were on at the Theodorescus', but it was completely dark at the Cassimatis'. The curtains were drawn at the Bercovicis'. Somewhere, a radio was broadcasting a military communiqué followed by the national anthem. He tapped five times on the kitchen window with his ring – his special code.

Leo and I ran to open the door and helped him with his packages. My mother came out of the bedroom with tears in her eyes. Loud explosions could now be heard along with the artillery and gunfire. The Iron Guard rebellion was beating the drum. My father took off his coat and sat down on a chair next to the big cooker where dinner was heating up in the oven. I took his coat and went to lay it on the bed in the next room whilst my mother put water on to boil to make him some tea.

It felt good in the kitchen. Slowly and in his own convoluted way, he recounted the events that had occurred since he left the shop. When the tea was brought to him, he quickly took the steaming cup and raised it to his frozen lips. The wound of 1919 that the bullet had dug through the flesh, bone and nail of his right thumb, had long since healed and been yellowed by tobacco.

The legionnaire Barbu Stanescu had saved my father's life, but we never heard of him again in the courtyard. Was he killed on the last day of the rebellion? In my heart I hoped that he had stayed alive, that fate had also granted him a second chance. Was he not, after all, a sympathetic and valiant young man who had chosen, like so many others, to rally to a bad cause in the grip of a religious and nationalist mysticism that was singularly and pathetically Romanian?

9

Romania Enters the War
—
Cornelia My Aphrodite
—
The Neighbourhood of the Stone Cross

On 12 June 1941, during his visit to Berlin, General Antonescu signed agreements with Germany that ensured Romania's participation in the war against the USSR. Ten days later, on 22 June, Hitler invaded the USSR along a three-thousand-kilometre front and General Antonescu joined in, committing the Romanian Army to the attack with these historic words: 'Soldiers! I order you to cross the Prut! Crush the enemy in the East and the South! Liberate your brothers from the red yoke of Bolshevism!'

A month later, the 'holy war', as the general had called it, rapidly achieved its initial goal: recovery of the territories of Bessarabia and Bukovina, ceded to the USSR after the Molotov-Ribbentrop agreements. But Antonescu, on whom King Michael conferred the title of Marshal, was not content with this brilliant success: the Romanian Army advanced into

Ukraine as far as the river Bug and played an important role in the taking of Odessa. Dreaming of an even greater Romania, the Marshal hoped that by continuing the war against the USSR, Hitler would reward him with this great port on the [iv] Black Sea.

The war alliance of Hitler and Antonescu turned me into a Russophile! It was the end of my political disarray. By choice or by force of circumstance, the Soviet Union was fighting Hitler's Germany. I no longer hated Stalin, because for us Jews, he embodied, along with the eccentric Churchill, our only hope of survival. We knew that if Nazi Germany emerged victorious from this Second World War, no Jew would be left alive in Europe. Alas, at this stage in the war, the military situation on all fronts gave us very few reasons to hope. Indeed, after scarcely two months of combat, the Wehrmacht controlled the Baltic States and the part of Ukraine west of the Dnieper. And, in the Atlantic Ocean, German submarines increasingly threatened Great Britain's supply lines, while the Luftwaffe inflicted heavy damage on its industry and terrible losses on its civilian population. Fortunately for Churchill, Hitler decided to delay the invasion of England, choosing to concentrate his military effort on the Eastern front. Blitzkrieg, his doctrine of lightning war, was to complete the annihilation of the Red Army before the arrival of the pitiless Russian 'General Winter'.

Our little community in Triumph Street sent only one soldier to the Russian front: a young man by the name of Ion Paraskiva, whom we knew since he courted Maria, the Theodorescus' servant. The son of a peasant, Ion had left his village in Oltenia aged twenty-two to try his luck in Bucharest. He had found a job as a stonemason and rented a small room in the poor neighbourhood of Vitan. On one fine summer Sunday, walking in Carol Park, he met Maria and fell in love at first sight. He invited her to take a turn in a rowboat on the lake, she didn't refuse and as a result they continued to see each other in the park or in the courtyard for more than six months, before announcing their engagement. Not long afterwards, in March 1941, Ion Paraskiva was called up and, when war broke out, he bade farewell to his sweetheart and left for the front. He was the only one from the courtyard, for Jews were not admitted to the army under the regime of the dictator Antonescu, while the two goys, Theodorescu and Cassimatis, committed patriots in the comfort of their homes, did not wish to die for the fatherland or any other cause.

Romania's entry into the war did not prevent the arrival of the summer of 1941 in Bucharest, on time, in a sweat and without a tie. Nature reminded us that it ignores the dramas of men and sticks to its own agenda. But anxiety had put an end to the joyful Sunday gatherings in the courtyard, the sunbathing sessions, poker and feverish political discussions. From then on, we spent Sundays and public holidays in the shelter of our homes. Nobody risked putting their nose outside any more, not even to take some fresh air on a deckchair. What's more, as soon as night fell, in anticipation of eventual air attacks, the authorities had imposed a complete blackout on the city. We therefore had to obscure the windows with black cloth or paper, and criss-cross the panes with tape to prevent flying shards of glass that exploding bombs may cause. Whether we liked it or not, during the moonless nights, the 'camouflage', as we called it, obliged us to feel our way through the darkness to find the doors of our homes. And, as trouble never comes alone, the authorities had given the task of keeping an eye on the blackout to an army of sadistic inspectors who, every evening, went up and down the streets in the hope of detecting any luminous signal sent, so they imagined, by spies in the pay of the Bolsheviks.

However, at the start of the war, the capital was not really in peril. Soviet bombers only appeared two or three times in the Bucharest sky, blindly dropping a few isolated bombs which, in most cases, did not even explode. On the days following the raids, the citizens of Bucharest, in relief and with sardonic wit, joked that the bombs had fallen upside down. The clumsiness of the Soviet pilots, of whom I would have liked to be proud even if my life was put in danger, worried me, for I had placed all my hopes in the Red Army, in the courage and skill of its soldiers. By reading the Romanian newspapers regularly and listening to the radio, I had learned the names of the most important Soviet generals, my new heroes: Zhukov, Rokossovsky, Koniev, Yeremenko, Malinovsky, Tolbukhin... I spoke about them during our meetings between Jewish neighbours. Since the start of the war, these took place in the houses of Bercovici and Herescu, or more rarely, our own. During these meetings, we took care to speak softly, often in whispers, like genuine conspirators.

War had dimmed Pouia's absence for me. After their marriage, Pouia and Aurel had moved into a modest apartment in the north of the capital. They came to the courtyard just to visit their parents and so I only met Pouia by accident. She had lost a lot of weight. Her black hair covered her forehead with a fringe that made her big brown eyes even darker, adding to them a note of sadness and melancholy. Was she not happy with her little Aurel, or maybe the war and other worries tormented her? Only a year had passed since the time when, sitting close to her on her sofa, I often kept her company, marvelled at her luminous face, bewitched by the exhilarating perfume of her body, so young and vibrant. But now she was a married woman and for her I was just another boy. The flower of spontaneity and innocence no longer gave beauty to our fleeting encounters.

However, as it is said, 'Nothing is lost, nothing is created, everything is transformed': it was during this period that my attraction to the pretty form of Cornelia Cassimatis emerged. The fact that, since war broke out, the Cassimatis had chosen not to be friendly with us anymore incited me to look at Cornelia in a different way from the times when I would see her cling amorously to her ungrateful husband, while he played poker with his Jewish neighbours thinking only how to get their money. Opposites attract: as she withdrew from us, I was drawn to her, furtively spying from behind the large living room window a few meters from her kitchen. Fringe curtains, which came, I suppose, from my mother's trousseau, made our living room invisible from outside. In summer, on the days when I was alone in the house, or only with my mother, hidden behind these curtains and also protected by the foliage of the plum tree, I waited for Cornelia Cassimatis to emerge from her kitchen doorway. She would appear in the sultry afternoon heat to water the flowerpots on the cement steps leading to the courtyard's roundabout. The kitchen door would open loudly and, like on a silver screen in the cinema, Cornelia would appear, dressed in a short, light shift that was moulded to her voluptuous curves. My eyes examined her body as if with a magnifying glass: the firm and pointed breasts, the svelte waist, the full and vigorous buttocks. As she moved from plant to plant, bending over each one, her breasts, in response to the movement of her body, frequently escaped the confines of the low neckline of her dress and as she rarely wore panties, when she crouched down to tend to a particular rose, I glimpsed between her shaded thighs golden and gleaming hair that made me think of a ripe harvest of summer wheat. When finally she turned her back to me and leaned down to pick up the hose unfurled on the ground, I could not take my eyes from the back of her knees, where fine veins traced the intimate convergence of calf and thigh. This only lasted a few minutes and Cornelia, my Aphrodite, went back into her kitchen, slamming the door in my face. A tired breeze, all the way from the Danube, lightly stirred the branches of the plum tree. On the damp steps, all that remained of Cornelia was the print of her bare feet evaporating in the over-heated air. I remember the feeling of abandonment that filled me then...

Leaving my observation post, I would go into the hall. I knelt on our thick Persian carpet with its short, dense wool pile. I could hear my mother working in the kitchen and through the door and the windows came the chirping of sparrows pursuing each other from tree to tree.

My father was at work. My brother was with his friends until late afternoon chasing girls on the banks of the Dambovitza, a narrow river that crosses Bucharest, dragging apathetically its muddy and greenish water to the Danube. I was facing towards the front door with its blue, opaque glass. Through the curtain of the small window, I saw a square of the courtyard bathed in red by the setting sun.

I murmured the name of Cornelia, with the 'forbidden to minors' photographs in mind that riffraff from my brother's class sold surreptitiously in the high school. I imagined I was kissing Cornelia on the mouth. I could feel the blood flowing through my veins. A burning, intense and mysterious pleasure seized me, and suddenly a short and violent surge lifted me into an ecstatic and sublime state of joy. But soon after, an inexplicable sadness overwhelmed me with anguish. Would I go mad, as I had read in one of my brother's books? I mumbled: 'I'll never do it again, I'll never do it again.' And yet, at the first opportunity, I was back behind the living room curtains, on the lookout for the appearance of beautiful Cornelia and, as soon as she went back into her kitchen, I found myself again kneeling in the hall at the altar of my pre-adolescence.

Of course, when I happened to come across Cornelia in the street or in the courtyard, I greeted her courteously and she smiled at me, still calling me Bébélush. Without exception, a flow of blood then rushed to my head and my face turned scarlet, for she would not have smiled at me like that had she known that I spied on the secrets of her enticing body from my window and that I used glimpses of her charms to initiate myself into the mysteries of sexuality; that force, as sidereal as it is earthy, which makes no distinction between age or religion.

To return to Pouia: I often felt guilty about my infidelity to our old friendship, but with time I learned to feel sufficiently at ease with my contradictory attractions. I noticed that on the occasion of the Jewish New Year festivities – which was always celebrated at the Bercovicis' house – my head spun when Chichi and Rozica sat just opposite me, their legs lasciviously apart. Perspicaciously, the two she-devils quickly readjusted their skirts, sending me half-angry, half-mocking looks. My whole face went red and, to hide my embarrassment, I hastily began an incoherent conversation with the adult sitting next to me. But that did not rid me of my embarrassment and, overjoyed, Chichi et Rozica nudged each other, clucking like hens. In reprisal, late at night, while the adults were saying their goodbyes, I would sneak through the crowd to pinch their breasts, after which I would flee, leaving them fuming with rage.

I leave the job of shedding light on my sexual behaviour at the age of ten or eleven to the Freudians. I offer them as a subject for meditation the fact that I spent my childhood near the neighbourhood of the Stone Cross, Bucharest's notorious red-light district, situated between Nerva-Traian Street and Calea Dudesti, a short distance from our Triumph Street. When I was still at primary school, I only ventured through there with my brother. In fact, the 'district' was just one street and about thirty mostly ugly small houses. Some of the more opulent in appearance welcomed a well-off clientele and were pro-tected from prying eyes by high fences and shutters. Early in the morning, the neighbourhood was deserted, but, during opening hours, it swarmed with men of all ages and social posi-tions. Dozens of girls crowded at the windows like bouquets of flowers squeezed into a vase, while, in the doorways, har-dier courtesans furtively opened their negligees, offering the browsers a brief but eloquent glimpse of their charms. Those passers-by who had already gone up and down the pavement a dozen times finally gave in to their all-consuming desire and ventured inside, hiding their faces to avoid being recognised.

I was too young to frequent those 'houses of tolerance', as they were called. On the other hand, Leo, to whom my father provided a modest sum, from time to time, to encourage him, 'visited' the district quite regularly, often in the company of Sergiu and Nellu, and occasionally with his other friends, Dica, the son of a very rich man, and Hershcu Wasserman, son of the local grocer. When his pockets were empty, Leo searched those of our father, who had the habit of leaving his jacket on the back of a chair as soon as he returned home. He always found some coins or a small banknote that my father deliberately 'forgot'. An additional, though less generous, source of revenue was the small change that we in turn 'forgot' to bring back to our father when he sent us out to buy cigarettes on a Sunday.

I learnt quite a lot of things about the brothels of Stone Cross on the days when my brother and his friends allowed me to attend some of their secret meetings. I remembered the names of the girls and the madams, and I took in numerous details about the reception rooms and the small private rooms where clients received their 'treatment'. The introduction ritual during which the visitor made his choice from a dozen naked nymphs, sitting on chairs or little sofas of worn damask, stimulated my appetite and my taste for the unknown. I obtained another precious piece of information by listening-in on the conversations between my brother and his friends: the sexual act could be performed in different positions, the man not having only to lie down on top of the woman.

Dica, whose pockets were never empty, was the only one among my brother's friends who had had the privilege of frequenting The Casanova, the most famous and expensive brothel in the district. According to him, there reigned a luxury equalling that of the harems of Turkish sultans. The day I asked him how he came to know about the harems of Turkish sultans, I received a slap from my brother. The walls of The Casanova brothel were painted light blue and its shutters yellow. There was a guard permanently in front of the door dressed in a tuxedo, like a fat director of a Polish circus. Dica's father himself being a frequent client, his son enjoyed special attention.

Mariouara, the beautiful young girl Dica favoured, was one of the most popular. Whether they actually happened or not, I would not have dared share with anyone the sexual exploits that Dica said he had enjoyed with her.

10

The Iaşi Pogrom

The Deportations of the Jews

The Struma

Awful news came to us of a pogrom carried out in Iaşi on the 28 and 29 June 1941, a few days after Romania entered the war. The pretext was a Russian air raid on the city, during which bombs had fallen with great precision on important strategic targets. The Romanian authorities accused the Jews of having signalled targets to the Russian pilots, and, in reprisal, on 27 June, Marshal Antonescu ordered the commander of the Iaşi garrison to 'cleanse the city of its Jewish population'. More than thirteen thousand Jews were killed during this 'cleansing', in which, not only the army, the police, and the gendarmerie participated, but also the anti-Semitic crowds incited to bestial acts by the authorities.

One of the most tragic episodes in the pogrom occurred when thousands of Jews were locked into livestock cars on a journey that lasted several days and nights. Crowded in groups of over a hundred in each wagon, they had begged the soldiers escorting them to remove the planks of wood nailed over the openings, but all perished from suffocation or of hunger.

The Italian writer Curzio Malaparte described the fate of these Jews in his book *Kaputt*.[7] In the company of Italy's representative in Iaşi, the Consul Sartori, he bore witness to these scenes as a war correspondent passing through northern Romania. At one small station where the train had stopped, Malaparte, in his Italian Army captain's uniform, ordered the Romanian guards to open the doors of the trucks. His orders were carried out and he described what happened next:

Suddenly the door of the cattle-wagon burst open and a mass of prisoners hurled itself at Sartori, knocking him down as they fell on top of him. The dead were fleeing from the train. They fell out in groups, landing with all their weight and a dull thud, like concrete statues. Buried under the corpses and crushed by their enormous, cold weight, Sartori twisted and struggled in an attempt to free himself from under that dead burden, from under that frozen heap, but he disappeared beneath the pile of corpses, as if under an avalanche of stones. (...) The soldiers climbed into the wagon and began throwing out the bodies one after another. There were a hundred and seventy-nine of them – all suffocated, heads swollen and their faces blue.

We in the courtyard feared, like the whole Jewish community of Bucharest, that we would suffer the same fate as the Jews of Iaşi. And not long after the Romanian Army had re-conquered the provinces of Bukovina and Bessarabia, the victorious Marshal shocked us with another brutal decision. He demanded that the regained provinces also be 'cleansed' of Jews, accusing them of having received the Soviet occupier

7 *Kaputt*, author's translation.

with open arms in 1940 and even of having initiated attacks against Romanian soldiers. At the Council of Ministers held on 8 July 1941, Mihai Antonescu, Minister of Foreign Affairs, made this terrifying declaration:[8] 'At the risk of not being understood by traditionalists... I am for the expulsion beyond the frontiers of any Jewish elements in Bessarabia and Bukovina... You must show them no pity... I do not know how many centuries will pass before the Romanian people will again have such freedom to act, such an opportunity for ethnic cleansing and national revision... This is a moment when we are masters of our land. Let us seize this moment. If necessary, fire your machine guns. I will not care if history remembers us as barbarians... I take formal responsibility and tell you that no law exists... So, no formalities. Total freedom.'

On his orders, in October 1941 and January 1942, one hundred and twenty thousand Jews from northern Romania were deported to Transnistria and forced to live in ghettos and improvised camps in fields. It was in these camps, either transition, labour or punishment, that almost all the deportees died. This explains why thousands of Jews, from Bucharest and other cities in Romania, risked their lives, at the height of the war, by boarding dilapidated ships in order to reach Palestine.

In the courtyard, we had feverishly debated this desperate choice when travel offices opened up lists for sailing on the *Struma*, which was to leave Constantza on 8 October 1941, its destination Palestine. The man behind this project was a Greek shipowner, Jean Pandelis, who had secured the support of an American Jewish philanthropic organisation, the Joint, as well

8   Mihai Antonescu, Wikipedia (Ancel, Jean: Archival sources on the 'Holocaust in Romania'; minutes of the meeting of the Council of Ministers, 8 July 1941, doc. 3).

as that of the Zionist Organisation of Romania. Hundreds of Jews sold everything they had to pay the astronomical sum demanded by Pandelis.

However, the provenance of this ship hardly inspired confidence. It had initially been used to transport cattle on the Danube and, having become too run-down, it was turned into a barge. Purchased by Pandelis in the name of a Panamanian shipping company and refurbished in the docks of Constantza, the vessel was equipped with a new engine, the hull was reinforced, and tiny cabins were improvised with wood from orange crates covered with wallpaper. The ship, which was to welcome on board nearly eight hundred passengers, measured only forty-six metres by six metres wide.

None of this seemed to be of concern to Chichi's father, Aron Herescu, who wanted to put his family on the list. In his opinion, whether we stayed or went, our chances of survival were the same: we had to act as quickly as possible instead of waiting passively for the fate that Antonescu and the Germans had prepared for us. No one else in the courtyard agreed with him, except me, albeit silently. The ideal of a Jewish national State in Palestine attracted me. Making a long sea journey added the excitement of adventure.

My father did not like Aron Herescu whose eagerness to put his family's lives in danger irritated him. 'So long as Paul Auerbach, with the relations he has with Wilhelm Filderman, is not worried, then I'm not worried either!' he argued during one of our meetings between neighbours. Rumour had it that Filderman, the president of Romania's Jewish community, had been friends with Marshal Antonescu since they were at high school. Thanks to this relationship, he had frequent meetings with the Marshal, before whom he courageously defended the cause of the Jewish population. Filderman, my father insisted, basing himself on what he had heard from his employer, was sure that the Marshal did not intend to hand the Jews of Bucharest over to the Germans. If the war turned badly for Romania and it was forced to end its alliance with Hitler, the Jews would serve as a bargaining chip. Finally, as no one else in the meeting rallied to his cause, and as Sonia, his wife, and Chichi, his weeping daughter, had opposed the plan to leave from the very start, Aron gave up and no longer spoke about it.

This is how, without any of us on board, on 12 December 1941, the Struma – with a Bulgarian captain and crew – left Constantza and began its crossing of the Black Sea to Istanbul, carrying seven hundred and sixty-nine passengers, including one hundred and three children. We heard that, despite a few engine failures, the old ship had taken its passengers, safe and sound, to Istanbul after three days' journey. But, in the following weeks, we had only fragmented news. We did not know the reasons why the Turks and the English had prevented it from continuing its journey to Palestine, and, even less what its fate would be, until the day when the tragic news reached us [v] and made us freeze in horror: during the night of 24 February the Struma exploded in the Black Sea, outside Turkish waters. Only one man survived the disaster and, after twenty-four terrifying hours spent clinging to a wooden section of the deck, was saved by brave Turkish fishermen from the village of Sile, on the Black Sea coast, near the Bosphorus. The survivor's name was David Stoliar. The villagers took good care of him but, after two days, soldiers arrived in the village and took him by bus to Kadikoy, a district on the Asian side of Istanbul. There, a host of journalists were waiting for him, as the Struma tragedy had found a great echo in the international press and on the airwaves, which obliged the Turkish officials to behave courteously. David Stoliar spent several days in hospital, where doctors treated the frostbite his hands and feet had sustained in the freezing water, but on discharge from the hospital he was promptly arrested and thrown into prison, accused of having 'entered Turkey without a visa and having stayed without permission'![9]

In Bucharest, death notices appeared in the synagogues and several other institutions. In our Cultura high school, lessons were interrupted for an hour, and we were all gathered in the big sports hall ('mens sana in corpore sano') to pay tribute to the *Struma's* victims, that included pupils and their families. Our esteemed history teacher, Marcu Weintraub, was at the centre of the ceremony. He accused Great Britain and Turkey of insinuating, in Machiavellian fashion, that the passengers had themselves provoked the explosion, thereby washing their hands of all responsibility. At the subtle play of cynicism, cruelty and farce, the Turks had shown themselves masters, he said, but the English, he added, didn't even come up to the Turks' knees when it came to cruelty and farce, but they stood head and shoulders above them in the art of cynicism...

At the end of his eulogy, addressing the teachers of literature and their pupils more than us, the incurious and ignorant from the commercial branch of the school, he quoted the words of Oreste in Racine's *Andromaque*:

> *What unjust power for all time*
> *Persecutes innocence and comforts crime*

9   David Stoliar was released from prison after six weeks. He reached Palestine via Turkey and Syria and joined the British Army to fight the Nazis.

Aron Herescu apologised to my father for having treated him so harshly in the debate as to whether or not to sail on the *Struma*, and admitted he had been wrong. He even ended up hugging my father, believing sincerely that he owed him his life and that of his family as well. I too should have asked my father for forgiveness, for in the debate, despite my silence, I had been of the same opinion as Herescu, ready to board the ship blindly. My father had been right, while I had shown a predisposition for reckless adventures.

One thing seemed very clear to me: the English had stood in the way between the land of Eretz Israel and the Zionist dream. But it was not the moment to hate them. Our enemy was Hitler and not Churchill! However, a strong feeling told me that soon I would be confronted with the English, for the Promised Land was calling me.

11

Life Among the Wolves

In the month of December 1941, news broadcast by the Romanian press and radio implicitly confirmed to us that the Germans were not going to win the battle of Moscow. Arriving prematurely (snow had begun to fall in early October and the temperature fell to minus 30° C in November), the fearsome Russian winter forced the Wehrmacht to become bogged down in the mud and the snow, lacking warm clothes, fuel and food supplies. The Red Army, well equipped to face the cold, went on the counter-attack and, in late January 1942, the German forces had been pushed back from Moscow. This news warmed our hearts. The Russian capital had not fallen into their hands. The Germans were not invincible!

What's more, I was encouraged by unexpected testimony that came directly from the front. I was in the kitchen doorway one afternoon when Maria, the Theodorescus' servant, who had always had great affection for my mother, read her a letter, freshly received from her fiancé Ion Paraskiva. In tortuous writing, Ion recounted the horrors of the war and the fear that had settled in his soul like a constant, incurable pain. Maria wanted to share her anxieties with my mother, as during the first months of the war, her fiancé's letters had been rather euphoric when the Romanian Army was winning victory after victory and the exhilaration had eclipsed his fear of death and even the desire to be back in the arms of his sweetheart. Now it seemed that Ion was no longer the same man.

From this letter that Maria so wanted to read to my mother, I understood that what terrified Ion in particular was a Soviet rocket called 'Katyusha'. The name of this weapon came from a popular song about the love of a girl, Katia, for a young Russian soldier gone off to war. Made up of about forty rocket launchers clustered together, its appearance had prompted the Germans to dub it 'Stalin's organ'. With their pounding barrages, wrote Ion, the infernal noise of the Katyushas' roars, screeching and wailings, demolished the men's morale and obliterated their will to fight. Under their nocturnal attacks, the sky was set alight ten times per second, giving at each blink of the eye, a glimpse of the luminous trail of the army of meteorites raining fire on the panic-stricken troops. In vain the soldiers threw their hands about their heads, tearing at their hair, trying to block their ears with anything they could find: neither man nor nature could escape the terrifying onslaught of the Katyushas. One night, when his company and a German reconnaissance unit were resting in the shelter of a forest, a rain of Katyushas poured down on them. In an instant, the ancient forest lost all its splendour. As the shrieking rockets skimmed the forest canopy overhead, the trunks of the trees bowed down towards their roots protecting their crowns; their branches, violently shaken, creaked in pain and their foliage dispersed like green hailstones in a gale. Even the presumptuous and 'infallible' soldiers of the Wehrmacht dragged themselves across the ground on their knees, crying like children. In the grip of fear, they made an unprecedented and pitiful spectacle of themselves, though their misery aroused in Ion less pity than derision. In order to improve the morale of its troops, the German high command had given the order to shoot on the spot all prisoners belonging to Katyusha units.

Out of compassion, my mother was able to find some words of encouragement and support for Maria, and I was very proud of her when she reassured her that her fiancé would return from the front safe and sound, while adding soberly: 'Whatever the outcome of the war.' Naturally, poor Maria did not realise what happiness her fiancé's letter had brought us. In all sincerity, although we did not personally wish Ion any harm, for he had not gone off to war out of conviction nor of his own free will, we rejoiced at the misfortune of the Germans and the Romanian Army.

Unfortunately, a year later, Ion Paraskiva died from the cold at Stalingrad, according to what a soldier from his unit, returning from the front with one leg amputated, told our luckless Maria. She had loved him with all her heart and took a long time to recover from this loss. Who among us could have dared tell her that Ion had been another innocent victim of the Marshal's folly, just like thousands of other peasants' sons sent to fight for a land that was not theirs?

Keeping abreast of the most recent news concerning the military situation on all fronts was much more than a passion for me. Our very survival depended on the nature of this news, our chances of having a future on earth, of escaping the fate that awaited us inexorably if the Germans triumphed in the war.

The victories of Rommel and his Afrika Korps worried me in particular. If the British line of defence in Egypt collapsed, nothing could stop his army conquering Palestine. That would lead, as in Nazified Europe, to the extermination of its Jewish population and it would have been the tragic end of the dream of creating an independent Jewish State there. But the victory of General Montgomery at El Alamein, on 11 November 1942, saw the Germans out of Egypt, saved the Jewish community in Palestine, and marked the beginning of the end for the Afrika Korps.

That's where we were on the military front in 1942. And we, the Jews of Bucharest, where were we at this time? At the end of 1941, a government decree condemned the Jews of the capital to forced labour: clearing snow from the pavements and public highways, cleaning the streets, carrying out chores for the Romanian Army or the military industry. Another law obliged them to supply the State with tons of clothes – suits, shirts as well as men's and women's coats – and even, periodically, large sums of money, gold and jewellery. To this end, the authorities had divided the Jewish population into seven categories, beginning with those with a modest income and ending with the wealthiest.

However, between one oppressive decree and another, between a new eruption of anti-Semitic hatred and the next, we managed to go on with our usual activities, forgetting the threats that weighed on our heads. What would have been the point of worrying too much? Our fate was already in the hands of benevolent providence. We still benefited in Bucharest from the privilege of being able to walk freely in any street, to frequent the theatres, cinemas and restaurants and do our shopping like any other citizen, without having to display in public the degrading yellow star imposed on the Jews in other regions of the country. With time, we got used to the paradoxes of our situation and to the fact that each paradox brought another, even more inexplicable than the one before.

For example, in September 1940, while a decree prohibited Romanian theatres and orchestras from employing Jewish actors and musicians, at the same time banning the use of the Yiddish language on stage, six months later, the Jewish Yiddish language theatre, Baraseum, was authorised to reopen its doors as a Jewish theatre in the Romanian language! The title of the inaugural show was 'What are you doing this evening?' a rather mediocre musical revue, but its popular success went beyond expectations: the audience was, it seemed, made up as much by Christians as by Jews!

In short, we still remained proscribed Jews, but those among us whose nose was not long and hooked like in the caricatures of Der Stürmer[10] could walk down Victory Avenue without fear of being bothered. They would have risked nothing in lighting a nice cigarette in front of the King's palace, just like any Romanian of pure race and orthodox Christian religion.

Of course, the Germans were not ready to passively accept Marshal Antonescu continuing to grant us privileges. While they would have liked to devour us on the spot, the Marshal promised to hand us over a little later. Hoping that Antonescu would fold to their demand under pressure from the grass roots of his supporters, the Germans had recourse to their propaganda machine, including the press and cinema, to sow a

10 *Der Stürmer*: virulently anti-Semitic Nazi weekly publication.

blind hatred of Jews in the population. Goebbels, the Minister for Propaganda of the Third Reich, was passionate about cinema and believed in its influence on the masses. My brother and I discovered this power of the cinema when Veit Harlan's film, The Jew Süss, was released in the capital. We decided to go [vi] to a matinee at the Scala cinema on Bratianu Boulevard.

Early in the afternoon, the cinema would not be too full and we ran less risk of meeting anti-Semitic thugs in such an elegant and reputable place. On entering, Leo signalled the presence of a few groups of louts in the back rows and told me not to look in their direction. We sat down in a row quite close to the screen, amongst a few elderly people, and we also made sure that the seats behind us were empty. Without delay, the lights went out and darkness enveloped us in an icy silence.

Over an image of an interior of a synagogue, the wail of a heart-wrenching Jewish prayer broke the silence. The opening credits began to roll slowly, while the plaintive voice of the hazan[11] melted into a rising, solemn, even mournful, orchestral theme punctuated by short, triumphant bursts of trumpets. The date 1733 was superimposed on the map of the Duchy of Württemberg and its capital, Stuttgart, denoting the end of the credits.

The Jewish prayer provoked the audience's first reactions: scornful laughter and whistling that stopped abruptly when Duke Karl-Alexander, a flabby and repellent character, appeared on the screen. He victoriously announced his re-election, swearing to uphold the Constitution and to bring prosperity to the Duchy. The duke's counsellor, his daughter, Dorothea, and her fiancé then toast the duke's health and the

11 Cantor in a synagogue.

123

State of Württemberg. The duchy being in debt, the extravagant ambitions of Duke Karl-Alexander (eager for the city of Stuttgart to have an opera, a ballet and, not to forget, a personal guard de corps for himself) demanded means that the treasury did not have at its disposal. His counsellor and the Council of State were fiercely opposed. As a result, the duke decided to send an emissary to Frankfurt to meet the Jew Süss Oppenheimer, known for his financial skills.

In a miserable alleyway of the Jewish quarter, the duke's emissary presents himself at the door of a house on which 'Trading house for coins and jewels' is engraved on a plaque. A small, timorous Jew, with a goatee and wearing a skullcap, opens the door and announces that Süss is expecting him. Leaning out of nearby windows, bearded and ugly old men, caricatures of old Jews, exchange comments on the nature of this strange visit in a deliberately grotesque accent. Süss receives the duke's envoy wearing a black kaftan, white silk scarf and a black skullcap from which some curls escape onto his forehead. His physical appearance, with his pointy beard, big hooked nose, side-locks down to his shoulders, embodies all the stereotypes of Jews. Süss opens a safe and takes out a crown encrusted with precious stones, reserved, he says, for the duke, as well as a necklace of enormous rare pearls for the duchess. 'The price is high, but we will come to an agreement in Stuttgart,' he adds. 'Jews are forbidden entry into Stuttgart,' the emissary reminds him, studying him contemptuously from head to foot. 'If he wants to do business with me, the duke will find a solution,' Süss replies drily. In the cinema, people started to heckle and shout anti-Semitic insults, and my brother and I felt fear penetrate right to the marrow of our bones.

On the screen, a transformed Süss cuts a striking figure: gone are his beard and ringlets, a dandyish wig covers his curly hair and he is wearing fine clothes of the latest fashion. From one scene to another, we follow his meteoric rise from the trading house in that poor alleyway in Frankfurt's ghetto to his position as Minister of Finance of the Duchy. At the height of his power, he becomes the most feared man in Württemberg. He grows rich and the duke with him: he taxes houses, roads and bridges; he ruthlessly exploits and mercilessly punishes the good and honest Christians who cannot pay the crippling taxes; he sends innocents to their deaths, perverts morals, corrupts Christian women and girls, but despite everything, he secures immunity from the duke before the law for as long as the duke is alive. He even manages to force the duke to abolish the ban on Jews entering Stuttgart.

Nevertheless, he is unsatisfied, for he desires Dorothea. He wants to marry her, but her father, who opposes the union, marries her off in haste to the young Faber, with whom he is fermenting a popular revolt against Süss. Faber is then arrested for treason on Süss's orders and tortured to reveal the names of his accomplices. Dorothea begs Süss to free her husband, but before doing so, he rapes her brutally. Shame drives Dorothea to suicide and in the scene in which Faber carries her body, brought from the river where she has drowned herself, the angry shouts from the audience shattered the numbed silence that had followed the rape scene: 'Death to the Jews, death to the Jesus killers!' But the majority of the audience remained silent, in its outrage not saying a word. In our row, women took out their handkerchiefs. Leo and I, sitting on the edge of our seats, impatiently counted the minutes, because we could not take any more of it. 'I know that at the end of the film he will be hanged,' Leo whispered in my ear. Indeed, after a heart attack, the duke dies and his death annuls the immunity given Süss, thus allowing his arrest and death sentence. To drumrolls, Süss is hanged. In the final scene, it is announced that all Jews were given three days to leave the duchy of Württemberg.

As the audience got to its feet with thunderous applause and hurling anti-Semitic slurs, we too stood up and made believe to applaud, hoping that in the commotion no one would notice as we hastened to join the tumultuous flow of people to the exit before the house lights came up.

What a joy it was to be back on the boulevard facing the caressing sun! My brother and I loved this wide Bratianu Boulevard, lined with tall modern buildings, some of the tallest in the capital, in the beautiful architectural style of the thirties-forties. The weather was fine, as it often is in the month of November in Bucharest, and we decided to return home on foot to get some fresh air. The portrayal of the Jews in the film had shaken me. As I walked, a disturbing thought troubled me that I finally dared share with Leo.

'You know... the film, as horrible as it is, portrays an image of the Jew which does not seem to me to be entirely invented by the anti-Semites. It shows some aspects of certain Jews that do not lack authenticity, like their physiognomy, their customs, their behaviour...'

'What do you mean by that?' Leo asked, turning suddenly towards me. We stopped to cross Rossetti Street, a street we did not frequent often.

'I know it's not easy to accept,' I said, 'but have we not ourselves met Jews like that? I'm talking precisely about their physiognomy, their behaviour, the way they dress, certain character traits.'

'For example?' Leo queried.

'For example, the dirty and miserable Jews that we see in the film entering Stuttgart, with their carts loaded with their belongings like gypsies with their caravans, or the Jews in the synagogue scene, where they pray before launching into demonic dances.'

'And where have you seen them?' Leo asked me provocatively.

'Well, I've seen them just like you have in Fălticeni, in the streets and at the synagogue, or even, but more rarely, in Bucharest. You think I'm making it up?'

We were near the beautiful Italian church that made the single storey building of the Sanitas company took like a Lilliputian at Gulliver's feet. 'So what?' Leo asked.

'So what, so what!' I exploded. 'You remember that Jew, Hershl!... I've forgotten his name... the one who had the tavern in Fălticeni? Father spoke to us of him.'

'Singer... Hershl Singer,' Leo shouted at me impatiently. 'What's he got to do with this?'

We approached University Square, which was big, noisy and difficult to cross.

'Yes, Singer, bravo! In my eyes, the description of Hershl fits that of Levy, Süss's associate, perfectly: small, wearing a skullcap, hooked nose, protruding ears, goatee beard. Except that Hershl didn't have sidelocks. That wouldn't have gone down well with his customers – peasants and merchants he got drunk and cheated when handing back their change. Fortunately, Jews did not frequent his establishment.'

From where we were, the way back to Calea Vacaresti and Triumph Street was still long and we sat down at the terrace of a kiosk to have a drink, a glass of grape juice for Leo, lemonade for me. He took a sip, then said to me, 'I think you're rushing into a stupid theory, little brother. I must note in your defence that it is not the first time. This film has made an anti-Semite of you: hesitant, cautious, but an anti-Semite all the same.'

'You don't understand me,' I retorted, exasperated.

'Stop a moment. In your view, where did they come from, the miserable Jewish refugees you saw in the film walking along the streets of Stuttgart, or those who went to Moldavia, and Bucharest, for more than a century? Were they not fleeing pogroms in Poland, Ukraine and Russia? Do you think they intended to become Minister of Finance or corrupt the Christians' women? It was in order to survive that they came. They were not oppressors, but victims of oppression.'

'I know all that...'

'You know it... I'm delighted... But in the places where they arrived, they were not welcomed with open arms, and, in the Middle Ages, in nearly all the countries of the West, professions were organised into guilds. If you weren't Christian, you couldn't be admitted into a guild. So, what could the Jews do? They were excluded from all the professions, except...'

'Commerce!'

'*Hapnisht!*' He exclaimed, using the Yiddish word my father used when someone interrupted him. 'Yes, commerce, and especially money-lending! The church forbade Christians from practicing this dirty trade, so the well-off Jews, who for sure weren't many, became usurers... Kings and nobles needed them in order to build their grand castles and to wage war. If, to survive, a poor Jew occasionally duped a Christian, on their side, the kings, the nobles and the Church stole from their people a million times more than the Jews.'

He observed to see what effect his demonstration, good or bad, but based on historical fact, had on me. I nodded in agreement to make him happy, but added to needle him: 'You say *hapnisht* to me like Father, and make a long speech to me on things I have already heard a thousand times.'

'You heard them with deaf ears. You who always know what I mean before I even say it, did you know that in the 12th century the Church decreed that as part of what Jews were obliged to wear, to distinguish them from Christians, was the colour yellow?'

'No, why?'

'Because according to the New Testament, Judas liked wearing yellow and then there was also the round yellow badge that symbolized the 30 pieces of silver Judas received for betraying Jesus. Judas became the greatest traitor among traitors in the anthology of traitors!'

I had finished my lemonade and would rather have liked to have another. In all truth, I did not know this story about Judas being the origin of the yellow star. What incredible luck to have been able, in Bucharest, to escape the humiliation of having to wear one!

I broke the silence that had settled on us as we sat in the reddish glow of the setting sun and I told him that what he had called my 'theory' was just a simple thought, neither stupid nor anti-Semitic, which corresponded perfectly to the historic facts he had used. I explained to him that my argument was based on aesthetic aspects and that in the ghettos, aesthetics had been sacrificed for survival. The ghettos were not beautiful. The houses and the synagogues were not beautiful. The clothes imposed on them were not beautiful either.

What characterised the Jew's physiognomy went hand in hand with the degrading appearance of his clothes. As for life, it was not beautiful either, neither in the *shtetl*[12] nor in the ghetto, where beauty survived and took form only in Jewish spiritual life. I had learnt from a book that it was during the French Revolution that Jews were first emancipated and ghettos abolished in France. And, with the revolutions of 1848, the emancipation and abolition of ghettos spread, especially in Germany, under the dissemination of liberal ideas. Leo, who had listened to me patiently, and even with some interest, up to that point, cut in: 'But the big change took place in Germany with the birth of the *Haskalah* movement, which modernised Jews' lives, striving to integrate them into society, often through assimilation and even conversion.'

[vii]

'In the big cities of Germany, yes,' I replied, 'but in Eastern Europe, the *shtetl* and the ghettos have remained a world apart.'

'Come on,' he said suddenly, 'it's time to pay and go home. But, in a few words, tell me why that vile film has turned you into an anti-Semite.'

I took my time before replying: 'Neither the *Haskalah* nor Zionism have radically changed a certain image of the Jew of the Diaspora which I dislike and which disturbs me. Besides, I think that you were no less shocked than I was by that portrayal. I think that Zionism must change not only the economic and social pyramid of the Jewish people, but also those Jewish traits I'm talking about. I well understand that it is born from the suffering the Jews have known since they lost their country, but it facilitates the work of the anti-Semitic caricaturists and I would like it to disappear. Is that being anti-Semitic?'

12 *Shtetl*: Yiddish word for a Jewish big village or small town in Eastern Europe before the Second World War.

Getting up, Leo said to me with a smile: 'Yes and no.' Hardly had he said it when his smile vanished and he added: 'But you know what? That horrible film makes me more Zionist than Theodor Herzl: what we need as a people, if we survive Hitler, is a state of our own!'

◇◇◇◇◇

Cinema was my other great passion, after politics. This explains why, by getting my brother to go with me to another Hitlerian production, *The Adventures of Baron von Munchausen*, at a cinema on Elisabeta Boulevard, I subjected myself again to the torture of the harsh and guttural inflections of a language I had come to detest, since it was no longer the language of Goethe and Heine, but that of Hitler and Goebbels.

At the start, the film thrilled me. I forgot the presence of my brother sitting next to me and, speechless, admired the colours, decors and costumes. In the scene of Munchausen's journey to the moon, the special effects amazed me, yet the plot left me cold and I disliked the actors, knowing each worked for the National-Socialist propaganda machine. The fact that, at the end of the film, Munchausen gave up his immortality to grow old with his faithful wife, did not change my indifference. In my eyes, Munchausen, like Hans Albers, the actor playing him, was just a repellent advocate of the pure race. What's more, in the role of Count Cagliostro, who offers Munchausen eternal youth, I even recognised Ferdinand Marian, who had played Süss in Harlan's film!

I felt filthy when I left the cinema that rainy Sunday. On the boulevard, cars had already turned their headlights on and drove by slowly, almost silently, like muted shadows. We walked quickly in the direction of the National Military Palace. On the other side of the street, a group of young German soldiers, laughing loudly, hesitated as they left a patisserie, not knowing which direction to take. Ah! The Krauts! For months we had been living with them, among them. They were the wolves, and we were their prey. Our paths often crossed. We did not greet each other, but our eyes met. Sometimes we even brushed up against each other. They scrutinised us with cold curiosity, their nostrils seeking out our scent. But it was not yet the time. They were trained to behave like docile wolves, policed, taught not to devour their prey as long as the order had not been given. They would transform into killers once the time came. For the moment, we lived in their company, the company of wolves, in a sort of precarious peace, in this Bucharest that had become strange and incoherent.

The Krauts were still on the pavement, crowded together under the awning of the patisserie, protected from the rain. There were four of them, making the best of their luck to be in Bucharest rather than on the Russian front. They had surely all stuffed themselves with chocolate cakes drowned in café crème. I had seen officers of the SS indulge this penchant in a patisserie of our neighbourhood where I bought trigone baklavas, with nuts and honey syrup, which my mother liked so much. A thick coating of cream covered the lips of the SS and they laughed stupidly, pointing at each other's cream-covered mouths. Interrupting my train of thought, my brother asked me if I had liked the film. 'No,' I replied, 'I feel soiled.' He looked at me as though I had landed from another planet. 'Not even the girls in the harem?' I shrugged my shoulders with indifference. Suddenly, a speeding car drove through a puddle near the kerb, sending up a spray of rainwater. The jet of cold water on my clothes made me angry. I'd had enough: the German soldiers, my trousers soaked by dirty and icy water, my brother and his annoying questions. I felt the sensation of having spent hours in a circus and I saw pass in front of my eyes an army of clowns in tears, bare-chested dwarf acrobats, women of Herculean build, their faces hidden behind hideous and grimacing masks.

The group of German soldiers had disappeared. Thinking of them, my mind lit up at the idea that the film I had seen was the cinematic equivalent of the chocolate cake drowned in café crème: a cinema manufactured to entertain the widows and children of the Schutzstaffels[13] dead or missing on the Eastern front.

We took the tram as far as Vacaresti Street then we strolled home, breathing in the pleasant smell of the refreshed asphalt. The heavy rain had given way to a light drizzle. I had almost rid myself of my anger when my brother whispered in my ear, 'Those bloody Krauts, they still know how to make films!'

I stopped and turned to him, exasperated. He also stopped and snapped at me: 'What a calf's head you are!'

... Head of a calf, or of some other beast, the gala premiere of Munchausen, presided over by Goebbels, took place in 1943, in Berlin. The event celebrated both the tenth anniversary of Nazi cinema and the twenty-fifth anniversary of UFA – the powerful industrial and financial cartel grouping together all branches of the German film industry.

I did not see another German film until the end of the war. But, I went to see Italian films, which were less polluted

13 The Schutzstaffel ('protection squad'), more commonly indicated by its SS acronym, was one of the main organisations of the Nazi regime.

by fascist propaganda. I took my mother to see comedies and melodramas, and my brother to period dramas. My mother had adored *Vivere*, with the famous tenor Tito Schipa. We had also seen several comedies by Mario Camerini, in which Vittorio De Sica played the leading role. Among the period dramas, the one which had impressed me the most was *The Iron Crown* by Alessandro Blasetti. Apart from De Sica, I admired a whole host of great Italian actors: Alida Valli, Amedeo Nazzari, Gino Cervi, Massimo Girotti, Osvaldo Valenti, Rossano Brazzi, Paolo Stoppa, and Anna Magnani.

My father went to neither the cinema nor the theatre, except on rare occasions. However, theatre stars often frequented the fur shop where he worked. The shop was able to stay open during the entire war thanks to their loyalty, but also thanks to Maria, Marshal Antonescu's wife who, according to rumour, patronised it secretly. My mother adored the theatre as much as the cinema. She attended in the company of our unmarried cousins – Adela, Clara and Paulina – and Fanny the pharmacist. They loved dramas and I remember that they had seen Henrik Ibsen's *Ghosts*, Eugene O'Neill's *Mourning Becomes Electra* and William Shakespeare's *Hamlet*, with the famous actor Ion Manolescu in the role of the troubled young prince.

I had read nothing by Shakespeare, but who did not know that his *Merchant of Venice*, like *The Jew Süss*, provided anti-Semitism with the cape it needed to clothe itself in artistic respectability. I had accepted therefore that the play was anti-Semitic simply because anti-Semites made use of it so frequently.

In Romania, a deeply Christian and traditionally anti-Semitic country, *The Merchant of Venice*, better known under the title *Shylock*, played an important role in the propagation of anti-Jewish racism. We learned from Neta Marcovici, who had heard it from Pouia, that at the time when Shylock was staged at the National Theatre of Bucharest, the Administration had been worried that the play included passages which risked portraying Shylock as too human and sympathetic for an 'uneducated' audience. The passage that worried them the most was: 'Hath not a Jew eyes? (...) If you prick us, do we not bleed?' According to her, when Liviu Rebreanu,[14] the director of the theatre, was asked if the passage in question did not pose a problem 'given the circumstances', he replied, 'No, because it will be acted in an anti-Semitic way!'

I pressed my brother, who had read the play, to tell me if, in his opinion, *The Merchant of Venice* was a comedy, like most specialists categorised it, or rather a tragedy? He replied with a wry smile, 'Comedy for the Christians, tragedy for the Jews...'

14 One of the greatest Romanian novelists.

12

The End
of the War

On 30 September 1943, a great ruckus from the street interrupted all those present at the fur shop, Paul Auerbach, the
employees and a few clients who had arrived early to avoid
the heat forecast for that day. Newspaper sellers, running in all
directions like a panicked flock of sheep, were shouting in their
hoarse and jarring voices: 'Daily News, special edition. Daily News,
special edition!' A barefoot young paperboy hurriedly dropped
a few copies off to the doorman in exchange for some small
change and vanished in the blink of an eye. A copy of the paper
was soon in the hands of Auerbach, while the clients and the
staff, including my father, got hold of others. What could cause
such a commotion? No, it was not the end of the war that this
special edition was trumpeting. It concerned an unexpected
and unprecedented event that went far beyond an anodyne
joke. The Daily News had published a virulent pamphlet by one
of the most important Romanian poets of the time, Tudor

Arghezi, addressed to the German ambassador in Bucharest, Baron Manfred von Killinger. Apart from direct personal insults to the ambassador, the pamphlet, entitled 'My Baron', also accused Germany of stealing Romania's natural resources. In so doing, Arghezi brazenly signalled to his compatriots that the war was turning against the Germans and that their power was fading like a star at daybreak. Arghezi's pamphlet was like a cold shower for Auerbach and the morning clientele, which included a famous doctor and a few high dignitaries and their wives. To openly attack the German ambassador was unthinkable! Von Killinger was the most important personage in the diplomatic corps, the Führer's spokesman, the symbol of the Third Reich's power and global domination.

Auerbach read the text rapidly and, as a precaution, chose to say nothing; my father and the other salesmen did the same, while the clients just expressed their stupefaction and fear for the safety of Tudor Arghezi.

In the evening, when my father returned home with the page from the special edition, we learnt from the radio that the poet had been imprisoned and that the newspaper had been banned from publication! However, the message that Tudor Arghezi was sending the Romanians could not be imprisoned or banned. Just like our father, Leo and I were amazed by what we read. Two paragraphs impressed us in particular:

'You have stunk out the mattress that I gave you to sleep on and you have fouled the water I gave you to drink and which you used to wash. Your feet have bathed in the Olt[15] and, ever since, its water stinks as far as Calafat,[16] noble filth!'

15 Olt: river in Romania which has its source in the eastern Carpathians and flows into the Danube.
16 Important Romanian port on the Danube and crossing point to Bulgaria.

'... A flower bloomed in my garden, like a red bird with a rounded tail with a grain of gold. You have destroyed it. You put your paws on it and it withered. My ears of wheat in the ploughed field grew like a dove and you ripped them out. You stole the fruits of my orchard and took them away in your cart. You plunged your beak, with its thousands of nostrils, into the rock of my springs and sucked their depths until they were empty. There remains after you only mire and slime in the mountains and yellow and arid drought in the plain. And of all the song birds, you leave us with only squadrons of crows.'[17]

After we had read it, we discussed the pamphlet during and after dinner and, as was the custom in a Jewish household, when discussing a poet, a musician, a painter or a little-known politician, the first question was whether he was Jewish and, if not, whether he was anti-Semitic. But spotting a 'philo-Semitic' Romanian poet at that time turned out to be more difficult than finding a needle in a haystack, while the anti-Semitic poets were legion, Mihai Eminescu, the national poet, being the most famous among them. In the case of Tudor Arghezi, how could we know where he stood in relation to the Jews? In truth, neither Leo nor I had read the work of Arghezi, a modern poet who was not on the curriculum of a commercial high school, but Leo promised to get me a book of Arghezi's poetry via his brilliant classmate, Dorel Baraban. My father concluded the discussion by telling us that, according to Paul Auerbach, Arghezi's audacity signified that the Germans were not going to remain in Romania for long and that Marshal Antonescu's days were numbered.

Indeed, at the end of January 1943, Germany had suffered its greatest defeat at Stalingrad: what remained of its 6th

17   Tudor Arghezi, *Pamflete*, Editura Minerva, Bucharest 1979.

Army had laid down arms, and its commander, Field Marshal Friedrich Paulus, surrendered to the Soviet forces. More than a hundred and fifty thousand soldiers of the Romanian Army, we learnt later, had been killed, wounded or taken prisoner at the Battle of Stalingrad. After this crushing defeat, the press and radio fuelled our hopes on an almost daily basis by regularly announcing successful German retreats to 'pre-established positions...'

Antonescu, as well as Maniu and Bratianu, leaders of the country's two biggest traditional parties, understood that Germany was going to lose the war and that the national interest demanded that the Romanians prepare an historic volte-face. In the spring of 1944, the group of agrarian, liberal, social-democratic and communist opposition parties, encouraged by King Michael, demanded the opening of serious peace negotiations with the western Allies. With the agreement of Marshal Antonescu, meetings took place in Madrid, Ankara and Stockholm with representatives of the United States and the USSR.

Rumours reached Paul Auerbach about these talks and according to him, it was precisely there that we, the Jews of Bucharest, had an important role to play. How could the Marshal, and all those who advocated a break with Germany, justify the liquidation of the Jews of Bucharest while they begged the Allies for a magnanimous armistice? The Marshal's obstinate refusal to hand us over to the Germans was to guarantee Romania a certificate of good conduct at a future peace conference. And that explained why we were still alive!

The Allies demanded that the Romanian Army lay down its weapons unconditionally. In the month of March, Soviet units crossed the river Prut and entered Romanian territory.

In April, other units reached as far as the Carpathians and captured the towns of Botosani, Radauti and Suceava. For their part, the Americans and British, who the Marshal had hoped would liberate Romania before the arrival of the Soviets, appeared in Bucharest, not as liberators, but as angels of death and destruction. From their newly established bases in Foggia, in southern Italy, their bombers now had the range to reach targets as distant as Bucharest and the oil fields of Ploiesti.

On the morning of 5 April 1944, shining high up in the sunny sky about a hundred B-17 and B-24 four-engine planes, flying in triangular formations of seven or twelve aircraft, dropped a rain of bombs of terrifying power on the capital. Their main objective was the Gara de Nord railway station, a communication centre of great military importance, and, in order to ensure its destruction, a thick carpet of bombs fell on all the surrounding streets. The neighbourhood of Grivitza, which included the station, workshops of the CFR (the Romanian railway company) and workers' homes, was almost totally destroyed. In this neighbourhood alone, more than one thousand five hundred victims were counted. However, the station only suffered minor damage... Three further bombing raids, on 15, 21 and 24 April, left more than three thousand dead and two thousand wounded.

In the raid of 24 April, bombs fell on the neighbourhood of Filantropia, quite far from ours. The rumble of the planes as well as the furious fire from the anti-aircraft batteries went on longer than during previous attacks, although the explosions seemed to me less frequent and more muffled. I was a bit disappointed; I loved the raids and wished them to be savage and dramatic. For my pleasure to be complete, I did not take refuge in the cellar and refused to go into the public air raid shelters; I went out into the courtyard at the very instant when the howling of the sirens stopped, leaving the gloomy task to the barking dogs.

The roar of the flying fortresses rapidly took hold of the city, shaking buildings as though under the deafening rumble of an earthquake. Flying in tight formation, the heavy bombers appeared like a cloud of fearless birds sweeping its shadow over the city. I held my breath, feverishly scanning the sky. Around me, houses began to sway, distressed from floor to ceiling. Suddenly, the first bombs fell, disembowelling the earth. I could taste the acrid air tainted by the anti-aircraft batteries and the powder of explosive bombs. Oxygen began to rarefy and a smell of smoked metal, carried by a scorching wind, quickly spread through the deserted alleys of the courtyard. Seeking protection under the little roof of an awning, I could observe, alone and sovereign, the theatrical immensity of the sky, against which the silver birds dropped wave after wave of death, until they disappeared over the horizon. The infernal noise of the engines, explosions and cannon fire gradually diminished and, finally, a deathly silence fell, as if the world had ceased to exist. Soon the sirens sounded the return to life. Fascist Romania was punished! An extreme joy filled me; one I had never felt before. 'Joy and sorrow are sisters, and both are holy,' Romain Rolland had written. My joy was vengeful, stupid, evil, ferocious and shameful, for the bombs had killed thousands of innocent souls, Christian as well as Jewish. Death makes no distinction.

In the month of May, to the daylight raids by the Americans were added those of the British, always around midnight. The pilots of His Majesty flew in four-engine bombers of British make, the Lancasters. Their roar and their ability to sow death were no less terrifying than those of the American bombers. There was only one difference, but an important one: they had a preference for incendiary phosphorous bombs while the Americans used explosive ones.

Explosive bombs were death in prose. You were either killed or not according to the nature of the sound you heard: a long and acute whistling meant that the bomb, even though it was near, would fall further than the place where you were. I heard right into the depths of my being the whistling of a one-ton bomb as it fell and dug, without exploding, a huge crater, a hundred metres from where we lived, at the house of Doctor Steinhard, an unkempt physician whom we did not frequent. On the other hand, a frightening high-pitched whistling, followed by an enormous gust of air and a strange noise like the tearing of a thousand bits of fabric – barring a miracle, the bomb was headed straight for you!

Incendiary bombs were death in poetry. Dozens of luminous parachutes slowly descended from the sky, casting an indecent red halo on the city still in its pyjamas. Crates dropped out of the planes' bellies and, by way of a mechanism that made them open like petals, each one scattered a hundred blind bombs. The earth burst into flames on contact. The long white tails of the reflectors, intertwined with the orange of the fires and the curling smoke created a surreal apocalyptical vision.

Standing in the kitchen doorway, or occasionally at the back of the courtyard, from where the view of the sky was bigger, the nightmarish beauty of this haunting nocturnal spectacle fascinated me. I could not rid myself of its image for a good while after the sirens had announced the end of the raid. Often, I only went to sleep shortly before it was time to go to school and early in the morning, walking with my brother through the deserted streets, some of them still enveloped in the smoke from the fires, we wondered if the bombs had spared the lives of our teachers and classmates.

The large presence of the Red Army in northern Romania, and its advance on Iași, scared the Romanians, for whom bolshevism was even more terrifying than the plague. That they be rid of the German soldiers, that war should end and peace return to earth seemed perfectly conceivable to them, but not at the price of a Soviet occupation leading to the bolshevisation of the country and with disrespect of the Church and the name of Jesus Christ.

On the contrary, for us, the Jews of Bucharest and for those in the rest of the country, the Red Army's arrival marked the end of the threat of deportation to the death camps and the hope of winning back our rights as free and equal citizens in Romanian society. Hershcu Wasserman, my brother's classmate and son of the grocer at the corner of Nerva-Traian Street, was perhaps the first Jew of Bucharest to dare express his right as a free and equal man in this society. Here is the story of his courageous endeavour.

Near our Cultura school was situated, in Matei Bassarab Street, the Romanian Craciulescu school. It was inevitable that in the mornings, when going to class, or in the afternoons, when it was time to leave, the boys of the two schools came face to face in the surrounding streets. The encounters offered the Craciulescu boys the chance to attack those of Cultura with their fists and satchels. A swaggering history teacher had probably inculcated in them the warrior exploits of the knights Godfrey of Bouillon and Baldwin of Flanders, the heroes of the first and fourth crusades, exacerbating Christian fervour in their imagination to such a point that hatred of the Jew had replaced that of the Muslim.

Naturally, we tried to avoid the fights, as in defending ourselves we ran the risk of seriously hurting an assailant, which would have led to our expulsion from school, or even prison. On the other hand, knowing that the law was always on their side, the pupils of the Craciulescu secondary school had no scruples about beating up a Jewish boy from Cultura. Hershcu Wasserman, who was small and chubby, with a slightly hooked nose – an adolescent, and therefore with a 'miniature' hooked nose – offered an easy target.

One day, in the month of May, Hershcu, my brother and I were hurriedly crossing Matei Bassarab Street in the direction of Anton Pan Street, spurred on by hunger. It was already very hot and our shirts were soaked with sweat. Suddenly, four 'crusaders' blocked our path: two boys with a malevolent expression in their eyes, a third, slightly hunchbacked, and a fourth one who was a tall and skinny beanpole, with eyes that rolled from left to right. My brother ordered me to run away as fast as I could.

I ran about twenty metres, missing the start of the action, but then stopped abruptly and turned around looking for my brother. The two malevolent boys were fleeing at a gallop with Leo pursuing them at a trot. He did not seem to be making a great effort, for obviously those two no longer counted as a fighting force. I saw him stop, turn his back on them and approach the leader of the gang, the beanpole, who was stretched out on the pavement, clutching his groin. 'I'm in pain, Mummy, I'm going to die,' he wailed. On his knees next to him was the hunchback whose neck Hershcu was squeezing in the crook of his arm, in a tentacle-like grip, whilst twisting the hunchback's wrist with his other hand, wringing out a spluttered 'I'm sorry, sorry'.

All of this had lasted only three or four minutes, for, despite his tubby appearance, Hershcu hid muscles of steel. He had developed them in the grocery shop run by his parents, as well as from training as an amateur boxer. His idol, the famous Max Baer, son of a German Jew who emigrated to America, had built up his muscles by lifting heavy meat carcasses as an apprentice butcher. In 1933, Baer won the match of his life against the German champion Max Schmelling, a protégé of Hitler. In a gesture of solidarity with the Jewish victims of Nazi persecution, Baer had a Star of David printed on his shorts.

A week after the fight, Hershcu, the 'beanpole', and their respective fathers were summoned to the police station on the corner of Mircea Voda and Olteni Streets. The beanpole's father, Bogdan Timbru, had lodged a complaint against the Jew Hershcu Wasserman, accusing him of perpetrating 'a dangerous act of brutality' on his son, also providing the police the names of a few classmates ready to testify.

The superintendent charged with the affair was called Viorel Frunza, *frunză* meaning 'leaf' in Romanian, though he was bigger than a beer barrel. Zigu Wasserman, Hershcu's father, expected the worst.

The policeman's office was small and stuffy. A ventilator snored on a shelf and drowsiness reigned everywhere. Sitting on an old padded chair behind a wide table cluttered with paperwork, the superintendent sighed and put on his thick glasses. He furtively rummaged in the papers spread out in front of him and, not finding what he was looking for, sighed again, exhausted by so much effort in vain. A half-stubbed-out cigarette slowly burned in a metal ashtray, stinking of cheap tobacco. His audience, anaesthetised by the terror of the wait, was suddenly startled by the sound of his deep and powerful voice like an alarm clock ringing in the early morning. He addressed the beanpole's father, Mr Timbru:

'So you are telling me that three Israelite thugs beat up your son, is that it?'

'Yes, Inspector.'

'And why, in your view, would they dare to commit such an act of aggression?'

'You would have to ask that question to the Jews, Inspector!'

'Yes, yes, certainly... And there were three Israelites, is that correct?'

'Yes, there were three of them... I mean, there were rather two of them, Inspector. The third one, a little boy, ran away before the fight.'

'So there were only two of them... Well, I'll note that down... Four Romanian high school pupils, descendants of Stephen the Great and Mihai the Brave, I'll pass on the date, entered into physical conflict with two Israelites of the neighbouring Cultura high school... Are we agreed on this preamble?'

As Mr Timbru nodded reticently, his son raised his eyes to the ceiling in bafflement. Zigu Wasserman coughed drily and offered a faint 'Yes', while Hershcu ventured a shy, misplaced smile. The superintendent wiped his forehead and lit another cigarette.

'Well, I see that everyone agrees that I can continue... The Israelites, as we all know, are the descendants of the tribe of Moses, the prophet with the long beard who, according to the Old Bible, received from God the Ten Commandments on Mount Sinai.... Being an unbowed and ungrateful people, the Jews contravened the laws of their God, while claiming to be the chosen people. Punished for having killed Christ, the living son of God, they were expelled from their land, and have become a wandering tribe of petty thieves, usurers, merchants, grocers, liquor and tobacco vendors, but also, it must be said – musicians, doctors, lawyers and intellectuals...'

He stopped and scrutinised the frozen expression of Hershcu and his father, sitting rigid on their chairs.

'I notice that Mr Wasserman and his son do not embrace my version of history, something that doesn't surprise me... I'll go on.... Ever since the time they have wandered from one land to another, the Jews have never had a great reputation as brawlers... They are rather renowned for being afraid of their own shadows... I am talking here of an unquestionable truth, no?'

The policeman glared at his immobilised and silent audience, and paused again. Then an idea came to his head, which brought a cunning smile to his lips.

'I must tell you one thing... This legend that the Jews drink Christian blood at Easter... Who can truly believe it? Do you believe it, Mr Timbru? I certainly don't believe it! Which leads me to the following question: how do you want to make me, Superintendent Frunza, believe that Jewish boys would, at their own initiative, attack four Romanian lads of pure race?'

'I'm sorry, Mister Superintendent, but the Jews had clubs hidden under their shirts!' Timbru exclaimed, leaping from his chair.

'Come on, come on.... I wasn't born yesterday. Blows from clubs can be seen, they leave traces. And the Jews, do you seriously believe that the Jews would have dared to attack Romanian boys with clubs? In their dreams, maybe, and even then, I have my doubts... so, dear Mister Timbru, this is how I figure things really happened. During the fight, your son received a punch to the stomach followed by a boot to the testicles. That explains the nature of the pains described in his complaint. Kicks to the testicles are, I admit, hardly fair play. But the Jew was defending himself, he was not attacking! Besides, it's visible from the naked eye that he is two times smaller than your son. I don't need a measuring stick! And to be frank with you: also being of small build, I've broken the balls of guys much bigger than me. Why do you think I chose the job of policeman? For the money? No way! It's because I like a fight, Mr Timbru! But careful, with an important nuance... I only fight for just causes!'

Timbru, still standing, tried to protest, but the superintendent cut him short, 'No point in insisting, Mister Timbru. The case is closed. Justice has been done, full stop!'

This version of events related by Hershcu Wasserman proved to us that a new breath of air was blowing through the capital. Granted, it was very possible that superintendent Frunza counted Jews among his friends or that he had been cleverly infiltrated into the police by the communists. In any case, it appears he had taken his precautions: his 'verdict' was clearly favourable to Hershcu, but at the same time, and no doubt to escape any suspicion, his description of the Jews was in no way flattering.

On 6 June 1944, the Allies landed in Normandy. For us, the twenty Jewish families of courtyard number 47-49, the announcement of this news provoked an explosion of ecstatic joy, even expressed only in the privacy of our homes. Theodorescu and Cassimatis, more worried than joyful, also understood that the Normandy landing marked a decisive turning point in the war. Proof of this was that they became more approachable again and ready to have friendly conversations with us. Even Madame Filotti reappeared at her window one day and stopped me to say that she had never liked Adolf Hitler and that Romania was in much better shape when it was friends with the English and French! Knowing that old Filotti was more cunning than a fox, I had no intention of falling into the trap she was surely setting for me. Rather than subscribing enthusiastically to her view, I prudently replied: 'We must trust the Marshal, Madame Filotti...' She promptly said: 'Bah, the Marshal, the Marshal... Who got us into this trouble if it wasn't the Marshal? It seems he's now going off to Germany again to meet his big friend Hitler.'

The old woman was well informed, for, in August 1944, Antonescu went to Germany to meet Hitler at Rastenberg. Hitler, no doubt aware of the negotiations that Romania was holding with the Allies, wanted his 'friend' to put his cards on the table: did he plan to remain the faithful ally of Germany right to the end, or had he decided to betray it by signing a separate armistice with the USSR? As the two protagonists are no longer here to testify, we can speculate that the Marshal's replies to Hitler's questions were not devoid of ambiguity. In the short term, neither the Führer nor the Marshal wished to assume the consequences of a total break just at the moment when Soviet troops were advancing rapidly towards the frontiers of north-east Romania.

Towards the end of August 1944, we learned from the radio that the Red Army, under the command of generals Rodion Malinovsky and Fyodor Tolbukhin, had attacked the Romanian defence line with enormous forces. On the following Sunday, in the courtyard, we rejoiced, in hushed tones, at learning that the defence line had rapidly collapsed. Several

Romanian and German divisions were encircled and laid down their weapons, and Iaşi, where thousands of Jews had been killed in the pogrom of June 1941, fell. One day, those responsible for that massacre were going to pay for their crimes!

I still carried out my duties as political commentator and I had predicted that this defeat could lead to the fall of the Antonescu regime. And that turned out to be true. From then on, I was known as the 'prophet Bébélush', for on 23 August, invited to the palace by King Michael, the Marshal was arrested in humiliating fashion by a group of military men of much lower rank and, that very day, the King chose General Stanescu as Prime Minister of a new government that brought together the royalist and left-wing parties. During the night, the King received the German ambassador, Baron von Killinger, expressing his hope that the German Army would leave Romania promptly in a calm and orderly manner. Returning to the German embassy, von Killinger committed suicide. Nobody shed a tear for him in our courtyard.

On 25 August, Romania declared war on Germany! We would have been happy to go out into the streets to sing our joy, except that on the same day the Romanian Army began a fierce fight to clear the capital of the Nazi forces, while German aviation launched savage attacks on civilian targets in the capital. As the Stukas took off from an airport very close to the city, the bombs fell before the air raid sirens had time to alert us. Hundreds of buildings were destroyed, among which the National Theatre, the Opera, the new wing of the Royal Palace, the Telegraph Palace, but also churches, ministries, hotels and factories. But one thing was sure: wherever I found myself during these bombings, at home or at school, I did not stick my nose outside to 'admire' the Stukas' steep dives or to relish the sound of their terrifying sirens. The idea of getting killed by Luftwaffe pilots when Hitler's defeat was no longer in doubt was hardly appealing.

Fortunately, Allied aviation liquidated the Luftwaffe's air bases at the edge of Bucharest and obliged the last remaining German troops to withdraw towards the town of Ploiesti and finally to capitulate. Six days later, near the King's palace, lost in the midst of a raucous crowd, I watched the tanks of a Soviet vanguard unit parade along the Avenue of Victory, each carrying around its open turret a dozen soldiers covered in dust and holding the hypocritical bouquets of flowers that they had been given. I was filled with joy, but I did not dare express it in front of a crowd that inspired no confidence in me. I returned home that day with the striking image of one of these soldiers engraved on my heart: a *pilotka*, the Russian armed forces' boat-shaped cap, with its little red star fastened to the centre of the prow, sitting drunkenly lop-sided on the head of a Mongol, as bald as the moon, who was wearing a *gimnasterka*, a tunic that was no more than a shirt with an upright collar, belted at the waist and worn over trousers that ballooned out absurdly around the thighs. An automatic weapon, with a round magazine stuffed with bullets, hung from his shoulder like a mandolin. Two dried herrings were stuffed into his boots like bayonets in their sheaths: his frugal meal on the turret of a T-34.

◇◇◇◇◇

Germany surrendered unconditionally on 8 May 1945 and Japan followed suit on 15 August of the same year, after the terrible carnage at Hiroshima and Nagasaki. The Second World

War, of which I had been a young witness, was over. It was also the end of my career as a political commentator, or more precisely as a clandestine war correspondent. Romania again lost Bukovina and Bessarabia and had to face economic, ideological, political and cultural submission to the USSR for decades to come.

The Jews of Romania had triumphed over fear. The nightmare years of Antonescu were now behind them. But, for me and my family, the joy was short-lived.

13

After the War

Poverty, poverty, poor poverty! Who would have thought that, after the war, life would be more difficult for our family than during it? In the past, we had never been short of food, nor suffered from the cold in winter. And now that the long-awaited peace had arrived, Nazism defeated, a new Romania born, we fell into the darkest misery! And all without anyone in the courtyard realising it...

This reversal of fortune surprised us like a thunderbolt from a cloudless sky. Paul Auerbach, anticipating the communist takeover, decided to leave Romania to join his brother and his family in England. One day, without notice, he gathered his employees, offered each of them a considerable amount of money as compensation, and wished them good luck for the future. A week later, he left the country with his wife and three sons, and the shop closed its doors. His lawyers and two of his cousins took charge of the liquidation of the merchandise and current business.

Ill-advised by Sandu Grossman – an old friend of the family I called 'Uncle Sandu' – my father, rediscovering his youthful taste for adventure, threw himself into business with a group of furriers he knew and invested a large part of the money received from Auerbach in a very risky business: importing silver fox fur from Siberia. One of the associates had found a 'connection' through a high-ranking civil servant, allowing the import of furs – 'at dream prices'. But the merchandise was stored by a trader in Kishinev, the capital of Moldavia, now back in Soviet hands, and bringing it to Romania proved more difficult than foreseen. The war was hardly over. Chaos reigned throughout the country. At nightfall, gangs of robbers, who had pillaged the arms dumps left behind by the retreating German military, became masters of road and rail. The transport of merchandise by train or lorry was subject to their daily raids, often with the complicity of the police. The foxes of Siberia never arrived in Bucharest, or, in any case, not at the right address. Faster than a fox fleeing its predators, my father lost all his investment. The associate who had started the business disappeared without trace. He turned out to be the main suspect, but given the rather seedy side of the business, neither Sandu, nor my father, nor any other associate dared alert the police to find him. While the other partners had the means to recover, my father came out of this adventure ruined, dragging us into poverty and distress.

For months, we survived thanks to the little money that remained from the compensation given by Auerbach. When this money ran out, my mother asked for a loan from her brother, Uncle Max, who had left Fălticeni with his wife and daughter to work in a nationalised timber enterprise in Bucharest. My father was not against the initiative. It was as though he had lost all self-esteem and nothing concerned him anymore. Every time we tried, for the sake of the family, to have a calm discussion about our situation, he drove us to exasperation with his rambling and muttering. He soon stopped talking to us altogether and spent his days in brooding silence. From these long ruminations came the absurd idea that he would find the money needed by selling off my mother's possessions. First it was her blue fox collar, then a beaver muff and a mink hat and as a last resort, once all my mother's furs, which he had been so proud to give her, had been turned into bank notes, he moved on to the jewellery. However, my mother hardly had any: two rings set with little stones, a pearl necklace, a few pairs of earrings, a brooch and an old gold watch. Like the furs, all they served was to wipe out the most pressing debts, covering the costs of firewood, electricity, school fees and our rent. Even worse, my father claimed he was totally ignorant of the circumstances of their disappearance. Where did this money come from which appeared miraculously after each theft? From his successful business deals, he asserted, while insisting that we remain ignorant of their nature.

We were very angry with him for lying instead of opening his heart and admitting that he was no longer able to support us without stealing from our mother. On our side, we had been unable to curb his madness by means of understanding and affection. At seventeen, my brother considered himself old enough to demand an equal say in all that concerned our family life and had adopted a rebellious attitude towards my father, whom he thought had lost his bearings. In my presence one day, he said to our mother that Father needed to see a doctor because, according to him, you could not act like that without having some form of mental illness. He analysed our father with objectivity, as though he was not his own kin. Furthermore, in his view (I had found a copy of Sigmund Freud's *Introduction to Psychoanalysis* amongst his books), the closure of the shop, followed by the mortifying failure of his business enterprise, had revived in my father the dark and painful memory of the humiliation he had suffered in front of his regiment during the war of 1914–18. By losing the job in which he found the true measure of his worth and by getting mixed up in a seedy enterprise, without even consulting us, he had discredited himself in his own eyes; once he had lost self-esteem and confidence in his own qualities, shame had returned to trouble his soul.

One day, Leo explained to me that Father could never be a model father for us. Because of his meagre education, he did not possess, Leo told me, the ability to help us in our studies and, even less, to guide us through the labyrinth of life. As if that did not shock me enough, he added that Nellu, Sergiu, and Dica, his close friends, were lucky to have educated and prosperous fathers, willing and able to encourage the talents and aspirations of their sons. My eyes filled with tears as I listened. Leo looked at me in astonishment and told me that crying does not change anything in life, that I had to accept this reality as part of who I was, who we were, a handicap to turn to our advantage in order to become better and stronger than the others. This final remark set off more tears, when he suddenly put his arms around me. Pulling myself from his embrace and wiping away my tears, I replied to him that I loved our father; to see him so humiliated and miserable broke my heart, it was not his fault if he could not be a model father, in the past he had done everything to satisfy our needs and ensure we were well looked after! 'So, what do you want me to do?' Leo asked. Looking him straight in the eye, I replied: 'Are you not the cleverest specimen on the planet? Find out yourself what has to be done.'

Indeed, as our father's authority had eroded and Mother had neither the ability nor the strength to take his place, Leo took it upon himself to decide how we should live our daily lives and plan our future. He was older, had more schooling and, of course, was more muscular than me. I would see red when he frequently quoted the first line of La Fontaine's fable *The Wolf and the Lamb* at me: 'The reason of the strongest is always the best' rolling his 'r's in the manner, he claimed, 'of Edith Piaf and the Parisians'. He was not always joking; when I got on his nerves, he demonstrated to me with a slap what the wolf in the fable proved to the poor lamb when he devoured it. Despite that, or rather despite everything, I loved my brother and, since he had become a sort of substitute father to me, I revered him. For Mother, he was a close confidant, to whom she often opened her heart.

Pressured by Leo, Mother went to plead her case to the school's deputy headmaster, Mr Littman, in order to obtain a bursary for me, without which she would have no choice but to send me to a trade school. Littman explained to her that he wanted to count me among his pupils, for I was a 'good element', but the institution was going through financial difficulties. Refusing to give up, Mother insisted on the merit of my prize in the free composition competition organised by the school a few months previously, for which I had chosen the subject 'Moses the prophet, liberator of the Jewish people and founder of Judaism'. Littman replied curtly that free composition had nothing to do with accountancy, the essential subject in a commercial school. He brought the meeting to a close by repeating that he was unable to offer me a bursary.

A fortnight later, Leo again put pressure on Mother, this time to go to the headmaster, and despite having told me that crying doesn't change anything in life, he advised her to resort to tears if the circumstances demanded it. As the headmaster was a kind man, honest and sensitive to women, my mother managed to obtain a substantial reduction in my tuition fees.

By chance, at the same time, my father got a job in a shoe factory and that brought a better atmosphere to the home. The thefts ceased, though there was nothing of value left to steal, and rows became less frequent. My mother started to sew dresses again for a pittance from the well-off women in the neighbourhood. With the few coins earned as a seamstress adding to the meagre pay my father brought back from the factory, we at least managed to cover our biggest outgoings, particularly the electricity; our greatest fear was having the supply cut, which the neighbours would surely notice. Unfortunately, once we had paid our debts, we did not have enough money left for food. From morning to evening, hunger tormented Leo and I. My father suffered less, because he benefited from two free meals at the factory. As for my mother, she nourished herself with prayers. And whether one is a believer or not, the fact is that her prayers did sometimes find an attentive ear in the Kingdom of Heaven, where they must have been heard.

Leo learned from a friend that Ciocanul ('The Hammer'), the vocational school belonging to the Jewish community, had opened a canteen providing free meals five days a week to schoolchildren from needy families. We had two meetings with the school administrator, filled in infuriating forms, and after a long wait, to our great joy, we were accepted as members.

Surprisingly, my father was against it: since he had found work at the factory, his self-esteem had risen from the ashes. But for Leo and me, hunger had priority; my father's shame at 'begging for welfare' was not going to prevent us from benefiting five days in a row from a free hot meal. And what a pity the canteen was closed on Saturdays and Sundays!

As soon as we were through the doors of the canteen, we opened our school bags and took out our tin bowls that were so clean we could see our reflections in them and, not without some embarrassment, took our places in the queue opposite three wide serving pans that spread the odour of barrack food as far as outside in the street. Our sad faces were in direct contrast with the thirty-odd other boys who, though as famished as us, were happy and jovial. A fat lady with spectacles perched on a nose that looked like a potato, dished out invariably unequal portions with the cruel detachment of a croupier. I regularly received more carrots than potatoes and more bones than meat. Nevertheless, we returned home with full stomachs, and when, very rarely, the fat lady made an error in the portion that was in our favour, we kept a piece of meat for our mother.

Now that I suffered less from hunger, I could apply myself to my daily maths and physics homework better. Mr Isaac Shechter, a burly middle-aged man with a slight paunch, taught us the former, while Miss Rozenzweig, young, tall and beautiful, persecuted us with the latter. We called the mathematician 'Isaac the Furious', because he entered the classroom with a violent kick to the door with the toe of his shoe. He then proceeded to announce the subject of the lesson, explained it at the blackboard in a virtual whisper with his back towards us and then asked whether we had all understood. Whoever dared to say no was called an imbecile or a cretin, depending on the day.

Miss Daniela Rozenzweig, on the other hand, entered the classroom all sweetness and smiles, but her beauty and her lovely legs were too provocative for pubescent boys. Facing us from the podium in front of the blackboard, her curves invariably led our thoughts to stray from Ohm's law. Should she accidentally drop a piece of chalk and bend to pick it up, the sniggering from the back of the class signalled that her skirt was a bit short, but she took her revenge by giving us low marks. High or low marks, having overcome hunger, I rediscovered my interest in politics at a time when Romania was undergoing transformations, the impact of which was going to change its destiny and mine. A year after the war, the USSR's vice-minister for Foreign Affairs, Andrey Vyshinsky (amongst ourselves, we called him 'The serpent with glasses') arrived in Bucharest and forced King Michael to form a new government by bringing together the two old royalist parties and the communist party, in order to prepare the latter's progressive takeover. France, the United Kingdom and the United States did not intervene. At Yalta, we all knew, the West had accepted the Stalinist doctrine according to which the security of the USSR should be guaranteed by a cordon of countries belonging to its sphere of influence.

These events, along with the historic changes that they announced, brought about an unprecedented politicisation of intellectuals, academia and the advanced classes of the secondary schools, especially those in the capital. Marxist-Leninist ideology could, from then on, flourish in total freedom, attracting certain layers of the working class and a minority elite of intellectuals and students. Politically as well as ideologically, Romanians were divided into the old royalist right and the socialist left revitalised by a communist party benefitting from the Soviet Union's decisive influence.

In the Jewish community, the ideological divide was of a different kind. Poor or rich, the Jews could not give their support to the right-wing parties of the old regime, for the Romanian right, be it fascist, Anglophile, or Francophile, had always been ferociously anti-Semitic. We Jews had really only two options available: assimilate into Romania with the hope that socialism would offer us a better future, or emigrate to Palestine and found, with the existing community and Holocaust survivors, a national home where we would no longer be prey to discrimination because of our religion and our race. We therefore had to choose between a Zionist movement of the left or of the right.

My brother and I chose to join the movement Hashomer Hatzair ('the Young Guard'). Its ideological platform brought [viii] together Zionism, socialism and scouting to prepare the young Jews of the diaspora to become *halutzim* ('pioneers') in the egalitarian agricultural communes – the kibbutzim. What's more, Hashomer Hatzair was also the only one of the left-wing Zionist movements to embrace Marxism-Leninism and the idea of creating a bi-national State for the Jews and the Arabs in Palestine.

Once becoming members, we attended the local ken[18] regularly. It occupied a modest two-storey building where the members, divided into groups (*kvutzot*) of male and female young guards (*shomrim* and *shomrot*), gathered regularly for various activities. Each group had its instructor (*madrich*) who was assisted by 'adults' (*bogrim*), the members aged sixteen or over. All the activities – group meetings, lectures, cultural and sporting events, political and ideological discussions, songs

18   Ken: nest, in Hebrew. Meeting place for members of Hashomer Hatzair.

161

and dances – were supervised by the movement's emissary (*shaliah*), who came from a kibbutz established in Palestine by members of Romanian origin.

Scarcely had we joined the movement than my brother became a 'star' thanks to his talent as a graphic artist. Leo, whom I thought I knew well when in reality I knew him very little, took on the role of editor and designer of the weekly newspaper we posted on the central wall of the *ken*. I had never seen Leo drawing at home. From where, and since when, had he acquired this particular skill? The wall of news was the first stop on entering the main room of the ken; by creating imaginative and original letters, Leo had made the most anodyne announcements attractive. And his caricatures of the instructors, of the *shaliah* and various aspects of the *ken*'s daily life earned him the admiration of all the members of the movement in Bucharest, and, of course, of the girls ...

But, being of a solitary and shy nature, I did not shine like he did. I diligently attended my group's meetings, taking part in all the cultural and political activities, but avoided the song evenings and fled the dances, like you flee the devil and specially the she-devil. In short, I fled the girls.

The *ken* and my involvement in the movement changed my habits and my centres of interest. I definitively freed myself from the influence of historical and adventure novels and turned towards writers more interested in social reality, like Maxim Gorky, Mikhail Sholokhov, Emile Zola, Romain Rolland, Roger Martin du Gard, Sinclair Lewis, John Steinbeck and Upton Sinclair. I read a lot, but quickly. I began to read a book and occasionally abandoned it before the end to rush into another. Between school, the *ken*, the problems at home and my continued keen interest in politics, I did not find the time and serenity to plunge into a work that was too voluminous. I had even begun to read Karl Marx's *Capital*, but I jumped from one chapter to another in search of something less difficult to understand. Talking of Romain Rolland and Roger Martin du Gard, I must confess that I had had neither the time nor the patience to get through the ten volumes of *Jean-Christophe* or the twelve tomes of the *Thibaults*. On the other hand, I had read, without jumping pages, *Germinal*, *The Jungle*, *The Grapes of Wrath* and *Babbitt*. I would add to this list Karl Marx's *Manifesto of the Communist Party* as well as Joseph Stalin's writings on the national question, knowing full well that the 'Father of All Peoples' – a nickname, among so many others, that Stalin had given himself with the help of his sycophants – did not recognise the Jews as a nation.

Leo was interested in different things from me. Approaching the last year of secondary school and the age of eighteen, he was entirely absorbed in his imminent baccalaureate exams. He had proven his talent for drawing, but dreamed of becoming a surgeon. However, the diploma from a commercial high school could not open the doors of the faculty of medicine. He would have to get a scientific baccalaureate and that obliged him to sit extra exams in anatomy, chemistry, physics, mathematics and... Latin! Under our bed, where Leo kept most of his books, I one day discovered among the Latin, physics and chemistry textbooks, the *Treatise on Human Anatomy* by Leo Testut and André Latarjet, a classic work for medical studies. Broke as he was, he could only have borrowed it from Herman, our Trotskyist cousin, who, after years spent in the prisons of King Carol II and Marshal Antonescu, had returned to his trade as a bookseller in a little kiosk on the quayside of the river Dambovitza.

Indifferent to my brother's personal ambitions, considered by the movement to be of a 'petit-bourgeois' nature, the *shaliah* wanted him, come the autumn, to follow preparatory agricultural training (*hachshara*) at a farm in Iaşi – a prelude to his *aliyah*[19] to Palestine and his joining a kibbutz. I envied him whilst also fearing that once again, he would be ahead of me: he would reach the shores of *Eretz Israel* before me, would be a *halutz* before me, would work the land and learn to use a firearm to defend himself – all these marvellous things, before me. And as for my opportunity, I wondered when it would present itself.

It came at the start of the summer holidays in the name of *Shomria*, the big summer camp gathering of young members of the movement, representing *kens* from all the country's big towns. That year, it had been decided that the *Shomria* would camp near the famous Gorges of Bicaz, a narrow rocky passage separating Transylvania from Moldavia in the north-east of Romania. All the *kvutzots* had feverishly prepared for this event, which included athletic competitions and sports games like volleyball, table tennis and chess. On the day when I learned that no member of my *kvutza* wanted to take part in the sporting competitions, I decided to volunteer. If my brother was preparing to become a *halutz*, then I was going to distinguish myself in the sporting competitions! The name of my *kvutza* was *Lapid* ('flame'). I would therefore be the torchbearer of my *kvutza* and my *ken*!

I hurried to contact the sports *madrich*, Moshe, told him my desire and he agreed to help me. On a small piece of ground

19 *Alya, Alyah* or *Aliyah* is a Hebrew word literally meaning 'going up' or 'spiritual elevation'. This term refers to Jews' act of immigration to the land of Israel (*Eretz Israel* in Hebrew): the Holy Land. Jewish immigrants are called Olim ('ascendants').

near the ken, he made me endure a series of physical tests, notably running and jumping, after which, despite his scepticism, he thought I had a chance at the high, long and triple jumps, because of my long legs, so I started my training with him in these three disciplines. Thanks to his relations with Maccabi, a Jewish sports club, Moshe procured the necessary equipment for the high jump: the pair of poles, the ropes, the bar, the uprights on which the bar rests and the landing mat. For the long and triple jump, Moshe and I, with two members of my kvutza, had to build a runway, construct and paint a take-off board, then cover a landing area in sand to make it soft enough to protect my bones.

As soon as everything was ready, my training began in earnest. I had a burning desire to prove myself, but Moshe dampened my enthusiasm by telling me: 'It would be useless to jump before learning to run, to run truly and properly.' And without a doubt, he made me run – and suffer! – for days before teaching me how to build up to the jump and how to slow down just before it. But, at the beginning, he would not allow me to jump. 'The run-up to the bar, like in all jumps,' Moshe explained, 'determines the result. The secret is in strength, speed, suppleness and coordination.' I had to acquire a bit of each. I was doing my best and, after several days' training, I dared to point out that he had not taught me how to overcome my hesitation in front of the bar, nor the fear of breaking my back, or my limbs, when I fell. My remark amused him. With a smile, he replied that courage could not be taught: you were either born with it or you were not.

It was not easy. At the high jump, when my right leg passed above the crossbar, I did not manage to lift the left without making the bar fall. At the long jump, I would frequently step on the foul line, a fault that in competition disqualifies the jump. When that happened to me, and it did many times, the jump did not count, and the effort was completely wasted. I shook the sand off my body in the landing area, removed the grains that got into my eyes and ears, and noticed in shame the look on poor Moshe's face. I regretted causing him such irritation, but I suffered as much or more from my own. How many times was I afraid of breaking an arm or a leg? And how many times, between two attempts, did my knees not bleed, did my bones not groan? And yet, although with every fall I lost another ounce of confidence, I immediately rediscovered the will to start again with added determination. Moshe liked this trait in my character. One day, he tapped me on the shoulder and said: 'You are obstinate, you're ambitious, and you have a ton of pride. That's what I like about you. We'll do our best to win a medal, but in Palestine, dear Bernard, in Palestine, I think we'll need you to do something other than jumping.' I took it as a compliment and blushed. The spirit of competition was burning in my blood. The desire to be better than the others, to be first!

Of course, Leo was aware of my activities and referred to them ironically and meanly as 'rather curious sporting ambitions'. The only thing that really counted for him was his baccalaureate at the end of the month for which he had begun to work furiously, day and night. He passed the commercial baccalaureate without difficulty. On the other hand, in the exams for the scientific baccalaureate, he received the humiliating mark of 2 for Latin. The examiner and the jury found his ignorance more than unacceptable. It was: IN-SULT-ING! But he excelled in anatomy and physiology, thanks to the textbook Herman had lent him and his drawing talents. At the blackboard, he made a demonstration of the nervous and respiratory systems that astonished Professor P. Dumitrescu, a luminary in Romanian medicine, who was chairing the jury. Impressed and influenced by this eminent professor, the jury gave Leo the chance to re-sit Latin a month later. This time, out of pity, the examiner admitted him: my brother obtained the diploma that was to open up the path of a medical career, on condition that he pass the entrance exam of the faculty of medicine.

When Leo announced that he had passed the scientific baccalaureate, our home lit up with happiness and pride. My father kissed him on the cheeks (when was the last time he had done that?) and my mother threw herself on him like an enamoured young girl. As for me, shy, hesitant, relieved and jealous all at the same time, I was waiting for him to approach me first. I wanted him to encourage me to adore him. I liked his tender smile when he caressed my cheek and gave me a fraternal kiss on the forehead, though he did not do that often, as he rarely got emotional, but the rareness made me even more happy and confident.

The courtyard also rejoiced at my brother's success, Sergiu and Nellu a little less: they had been enrolled at a scientific senior school while Leo was at a commercial one, and that had encouraged them to look down on him. In one fell swoop, Leo had reached their level. Sergiu, like his friend Dica, was waiting to be admitted to the Polytechnic, as they both aspired to become mechanical engineers, and Nellu, like my brother, dreamed of entering the faculty of medicine.

14

Herman

Herman, the Trotskyist cousin who had helped my brother pass the scientific baccalaureate by procuring for him the French anatomy textbook, was – along with Bianca, Uncle Max's daughter – the 'intellectual' branch of the family. Sadly, they were the only ones to occupy this enviable position. Bianca spoke seven languages and her perfect knowledge of Russian allowed her, after the change of regime in Romania, to obtain a post as secretary at the Romanian embassy in Moscow. She had inherited her unusual linguistic talents from her mother, who had taught languages and literature at a secondary school for girls in Fălticeni. The young Uncle Max had met his future wife in the train taking him from Budapest to Bucharest, when she was returning from Vienna where she had been visiting a cousin, and they found themselves in the same compartment. They talked during the journey and liked each other straight away. Max was a handsome man of big build and with a pale complexion, like that of his father, Salomon. His big black, sparkling eyes and his small virile moustache under a twitching nose attracted looks wherever he went. Dora was no beauty, but she had grace and charm. Her elegant manners and the svelteness of her body did not fail to escape Max's attention. During his extravagant journey, he had had occasion to see many beautiful women in the streets and cafés of the great cities of Europe and had been intoxicated by the sophistication of women's fashion and the excesses of their plunging necklines. Dora reminded him of the refined elegance of European women. Her very presence opposite, her knees so close to his, inebriated him. Dora's parents were for a long time opposed to the marriage, convinced that their daughter deserved better than a timber merchant as husband, but they too ended up being conquered by Max's kindness and charm.

Bianca was born two years after their marriage. She had her mother's elegance and her father's black, sparkling eyes, but she was too tall and thin for men's taste. An ink-black fringe covered her forehead in a straight line, almost touching her eyelashes. Before she left for Moscow, she had paid us a brief visit, but her studies and the demands of a promising diplomatic career did not allow her to bond with us like Fanny the pharmacist, or our other cousins. And we rarely saw her mother, Dora, at the house; she had, with time, become a cold, distant and haughty woman. In Bucharest, she had stopped teaching at the secondary school, contenting herself with giving private French and German lessons to students from rich families. Bianca had not inherited her mother's character. She was kind like her father, and, on occasion, showed a certain attachment to Leo and me. She had congratulated me when

I won my composition prize and, on another occasion, had encouraged Leo to sit the scientific baccalaureate to be able to study medicine. However, Zionism did not fill her with enthusiasm. Her career destined her to remain in Romania, and her career had priority.

Herman was 'the black sheep of the family', a sad privilege he shared with Fanny, the prostitute, who was its 'shame'. Early in his youth, his rebellious temperament, passion for books and thirst for knowledge had led him to read banned socialist publications. Later on, he joined the Trotskyist movement, which during the monarchy of King Carol II, then under the fascist dictatorship of Marshal Antonescu, was illegal in Romania. For Herman, only one thing distinguished the two regimes: under Carol II, between each period of imprisonment, he temporarily rediscovered his freedom and returned to his kiosk, whilst under Antonescu he had remained incarcerated for three years in a row, until King Michael's coup d'état and the amnesty he granted all political prisoners.

One evening in summer 1939, therefore before King Carol II's abdication and the seizing of power by Antonescu, Herman, freshly released from prison, came to join us for a family dinner. My parents had also invited his brother Moritz, his sisters Adela and Clara, as well as his cousin Pauline. Unless it concerned what seemed to them 'good' or 'bad' for the Jews, my parents were not interested in political ideologies, but both of them had big tender hearts, sensitive to human suffering. Trotskyism and Leninism went through one ear and out the other, but Herman's fate touched them. The fact that he had sacrificed his happiness, his personal life for an ideal, for his faith in a more just, more egalitarian world, had won their respect. That evening, they wanted to show him that he was

170

welcome in their home and to offer him the warmth and family love that he had lacked in that horrible place that he had just come out of.

Thin, with sparse blonde hair, stained loose teeth and prominent cheekbones set above sunken cheeks, Herman scrutinised us – taciturn, suspicious, disbelieving – from where he was sitting, between my brother and Clara. His eyes were only half open, as if the living-room light, the light of freedom, was partially blinding him. God knows what he thought of us. Maybe he wondered who his real family was: his fellow prisoners or us, the strangers bearing the same family name as his, who were showing him the kind of tenderness that they would to a dog that had just come out of quarantine? Whatever he was thinking, he observed us, while swallowing what was on his plate. He was surely building up reserves for his next prison term. As always, my mother's cooking was delicious and Adela, eating slowly, told funny stories about the young doctor who had a room in the apartment she shared with Clara and Pauline, all three of them unmarried like him. Overall, the evening was going reasonably well up until the moment when Moritz, who was sitting opposite Herman, began to criticise his brother's table manners.

'You're no longer in prison with pickpockets and Bolsheviks. Eat like a civilised man,' said Moritz provocatively, while an inane smile played on his lips.

Herman froze for a second, his fork suspended in mid-air, his tense face drained of colour. Then a mad fury seized him, his eyes bulged from their sockets and his teeth chattered as though he was having an epileptic fit. A deathly silence fell on the table. Moritz, petrified in his chair, was no longer smiling. Scarcely had my mother time to open her mouth to utter some calming words than Herman leapt up with a dexterity that he could only have acquired in prison, and spat across the table, the contents landing right between Moritz's eyes. Nobody dared move or say a thing. Herman glanced around him, as if to assess the damage, then knocking his chair over, he ran out of the house, slamming the door violently behind him.

During the three years of imprisonment spent under Antonescu, Herman had abandoned Trotskyism. He forged relations with members of the communist party, which, like all the other communist parties in Europe, was affiliated to the Komintern and obeyed the orders of the USSR. Although Trotskyism was considered by Stalinist orthodoxy to be a deadly heresy, the party leaders, detained in the same prison as Herman, had forgiven his Trotskyist past, because, being incarcerated together, they shared the same suffering and also, they liked to call upon his encyclopaedic knowledge. Besides, the conditions of detention in prisons and prison camps like Doftana, Jilava and Târgu Jiu, encouraged camaraderie and solidarity between all the detainees, be they 'politicals' or just common criminals. As soon as the communist party took power, at the Red Army's 'liberation' of Romania, it seems that a large number of these criminal 'comrades', who had converted to Marxism-Leninism in prison, obtained important positions in the Securitate, the new regime's dreaded secret police. It was hardly surprising that they particularly excelled in extorting false confessions under torture, even surpassing in bestial zeal the interrogation methods of the fascist police.

After the fall of the Antonescu regime, Herman married Margareta, a beautiful Romanian of gypsy descent, who gave him an adorable boy. Although he did not join the party, during the first years of the communist regime, Herman benefitted, thanks to friendships forged in prison, from a certain number of material favours, including a modest apartment near the centre of the capital and reserved seats at the theatre and Opera. Alas, he suddenly lost his privileges when the party entered a serious internal crisis provoked by disagreements between the native faction and the imported 'Moscow bureau'. The natives came mainly from the working class and they did not look kindly upon the Muscovites. They had spent the war years in prison camps, or hidden underground to escape the claws of the secret police, while those from the Moscow bureau, the great majority of whom were of Jewish origin, had, before the war, taken refuge in the USSR, where they benefitted from a reasonable standard of living and had been prepared there to take control of the party on their return to Romania. Tito and 'Titoism' (in communist jargon 'nationalist deviationism'), as well as Zionism (otherwise known as 'cosmopolitanism') led Stalin to favour the leaders from the country's working class, to the detriment of the intellectuals and Muscovites, sidelining the Jews in particular.

In the logic of the party's new political line and in accordance with the 'humanist' norms of 'proletarian justice', Herman, a Jew and former Trotskyist, had been predisposed since birth to embrace Zionist cosmopolitanism or any other form of anti-revolutionary deviationism. He could therefore no longer benefit from the protection of his former prison mates. They ceased to contact him and even crossed to the other side of the street to avoid him. Herman hardly cared. Margareta was earning a good salary as secretary in a big industrial complex, so he did not have to worry when the sales of old books did not bring him enough money. He felt happy to be a good husband and a good father.

One day, Herman did not come home from his kiosk. He had been arrested by the Securitate for possession of *The Revolution Betrayed* by Leon Trotsky, described in the indictment as 'the agent of capitalism in the workers movement'. He returned to prison, but, this time, his cellmates were his past jailers: politicians, policemen of the old regime, and, even worse, former members of the Iron Guard. Soon after, he had a heart attack and died in prison. My brother and I loved him. I saw in him a model of the permanent rebel, against the world and against himself.

15

My Brother Will Not Become a Doctor

My brother's dream of getting into the faculty of medicine, a dream that he had passionately believed in and in which he had invested so much work and energy, was not to be fulfilled. He had failed the exam, his marks being below the entrance requirement. This failure broke his heart, all the more so as he was convinced he had answered the questions well, all except the Latin. To his anger was added the fact that Nellu, less strong in anatomy and physiology, had been accepted, and with good marks! A strange thing also bothered him about that day; and he saw something suspicious in the fact that he and Nellu had been convened at the same time. Nevertheless, before the exam, a member of the commission had separated the candidates into two groups, according to name, and Nellu had been guided to another room. Leo recalled that, for a fraction of a second, he had wondered about the logic of such a separation, but, as soon as he entered the room, he had not thought about it again, focused as he was by the importance of what was at stake.

Disappointed by his failure, Leo thought about contacting Professor Dumitrescu, in the hope of finding a sympathetic ear. Not knowing how to get his address, he called on his gifted ex-classmate, Dorel Baraban. Thanks to his uncommon literary talents, Dorel had just been hired as a journalist by *Scînteia*, the official newspaper of the communist party, the most important and most widely read newspaper in Romania. Dorel had deserted the commercial secondary school to sit the baccalaureate in letters, just as my brother had done in science. From the age of seventeen, he had published poems, theatre and cinema reviews and translations of French and Russian poets in several important publications. A member of the Hashomer Hatzair in the past, but for a brief period only, he changed direction at the right moment, joining the UTC (Union of Communist Youth), which enabled him to obtain a post in the official organ of the communist party.

Dorel provided my brother with precious information. Due to what the party judged to be his 'reactionary mentality', professor Dumitrescu had just recently been removed from all baccalaureate and higher education commissions at the national level. And his case was not an isolated one: hundreds of other renowned teachers had fallen victim of the purge preceding the great 'education reform' later decreed by the party. According to Dorel, the party had decided to impose, in a new education system, the Marxist-Leninist principles in use in the Soviet model. He told Leo with a smirk: 'Eradicating the old concepts of teaching and removing anti-Marxist elements from the professoriate is indispensable for reaching our objective of assimilating Soviet science, which is, as you know, the most advanced in the world...' He paused briefly, pierced Leo with an inquisitorial look, and went on forcefully. 'But, Leo, what planet are you on? Can't you feel that change is in the air? Aren't you sensitive to the strength of this wind from the East, which is certainly refreshing, but also glacial and pitiless? Don't you see the finality of this change?' My brother listened to him without saying a word. 'Leo, comrade Leo,' Dorel said impatiently, visibly irritated by his comrade's silence, 'in your case my diagnosis is the following: you are still suffering from Zionism! Why should the communist State subsidise your medical studies when you wish to be a doctor elsewhere?' Indeed, Zionist as he still was, my brother continued to listen, silent and motionless. Annoyed, Dorel dealt the final blow: 'The new education system, my dear friend, promises the principle of equality of opportunity, which is certainly a very good principle, except that the working class, which in our society is the ruling class, is more equal than the others. It follows that in key universities, the entrance exams are held in rooms sorted by categories! The candidates considered politically healthy get easier questions and are marked generously, while the candidates perceived as unhealthy get extremely difficult questions and are marked with maximum severity. Unfortunately, you are now considered to be unhealthy and you suffer as a consequence... Obviously, if you want, you can court good luck and try again.'

My brother did not insist. Discouraged by Dorel's clinical analysis, and also to escape from the house and the gossiping of the courtyard, he accepted the movement's leaders' proposal to go to the farm in Iași. My mother and I feared that, without him, we would feel like children abandoned in the dead of night in the deserted streets of a forbidden city. Even if Leo's angry and dominating nature frequently exasperated us, and his failure had made him even more difficult than before, his strong and assured character had brought an element of confidence and stability into the home since the erosion of my father's authority.

My father, on the other hand, was in no way troubled by Leo's absence. A reduced family circle suited him perfectly. Often, when the three of us ate our meagre dinners in silence, his mocking look seemed to say to us: stop playing this comedy. Leo is not dead. The Earth is no less round without him at the table. He loved Leo, of that there was no doubt, but he was returning the contempt his son had disdainfully shown him. He did not accept his son passing judgment on him. What did Leo know about life, except rubbing his backside on school benches? Had he, at age thirteen, already carted heavy sacks of flour around to feed his family? Would he have risked his honour for them, his life even, as he had done during the war of 1914–18? It was rather to this absent Leo that my father's mocking and defiant look was addressed, to this Leo who, after so many years of costly education, had gone off to learn how to milk cows!

As for me, saddened by this new family disaster, I parted from my parents one August morning to go to the *Shomria*. It was beautiful weather, the air warm and humid. A marvellous tranquillity reigned in the courtyard as I embraced my mother warmly. My father hugged me tightly and placed a big kiss on my forehead and I assured them that I would know how to look after myself when I was far from home. Then, before tears betrayed me, I ran into the street with my bag on my back and a bundle in my hand on my way to the *ken*. It was the meeting-point for going to the Gara de Nord train station, where we would take the fast train for Piatra Neamtz, the town closest to the *Shomria* campsite.

16

Shomria.
Farewell
to My childhood

We had learned from our instructors that the journey to Piatra Neamtz would offer us the chance to admire landscapes of a rare beauty. Except for the long journey with my mother and my brother to visit our family in Dolhesti and Fălticeni, I had scarcely had other opportunities to admire the landscapes of my country. This time, as soon as the train left behind the capital's suburbs and was crossing the green and fertile plain of the countryside, I wondered if rancour towards my anti-Semitic country was not going to get in the way of my [ix] desire to know it and to love it. I had read that Emil Cioran, a young Romanian philosopher and fervent sympathiser of the Iron Guard, described exactly this feeling in his book, *Transfiguration of Romania*: 'The Jews are unique, peerless in the world. Nowhere do they feel at home. They are the only people to feel no bond with the landscape and have a nationalism without geographical expression.' Cioran also thought that 'the Jew is not like us, he is not our fellow man, and, however intimate our relations with him might be, a gulf separates us.'

However, I thought, already more than half a million Jews feel 'at home' under the British mandate in Palestine. Over there, nationalism finds its geographical expression at the foot of Mount Tabor; in the valleys of Jezreel and Beit Shean; on the banks of the Dead Sea and the Sea of Galilee; in Metula and Jerusalem, and among the ruins of Massada. They sow and cultivate the fields, they build factories, they live on the land of a nascent State, that of the first Jewish State to be born!

Leaving behind the great plains of Muntenia, the train passed through Buzau, Focsani and the heroic town of Marasesti, continuing its journey on the heels of the river Siret, which had its source in the distant eastern Carpathians, in the north of Ukrainian Bukovina. Arriving on Romanian soil, this brave river made its way across six hundred kilometres to the south-east of the country before throwing itself, exhausted, into the arms of the Danube, to flow on into the Black Sea. Being neither wide nor deep enough for its praises to be sung, the Siret bathes the banks of a multitude of towns and villages, bringing joy on its way to children, fishermen and especially timber merchants who send their tree trunks floating in its waters as far as the port of Galati.

From my window seat, I contemplated the Siret's peaceful course with a feeling of familiarity; this impression you have in front of a face you have met before without paying attention, but which, at the second look, reveals features as unforeseen as they are fascinating. Indeed, the Siret does not pass far from Dolhesti, the village where Mosh Copel and Auntie Brana lived. My mother, brother and I had got to know its sparkling water from the train that took us to them. But, this time, the train for Piatra Neamtz was taking a different route, and, near the town of Bacau, the view allowed me to follow the river's course more closely. I even thought I heard its murmuring each time the train slowed down to follow the undulations of the terrain. The river's curious tendency to widen here only to narrow there and the magnificence of the landscape had freed me from anxiety about soon being trapped in a tent with unknown boys and at the mercy of their tomfoolery. I was enchanted by the view before my eyes, and, after some time, I had the strange feeling that it was me, and not the train, who was running against the wind, carving out a passage through the fields, hills and valleys. And it was me, my unknown *me*, who sang the praises of the river, the forest, the willows, the poplars, the frogs and the wild ducks. I opened the window, greedily breathing in the scent of lilac, green grass and the flowers of the fields.

Never before had I felt so close to nature, the nature of great airy spaces rich in colour, of the tranquil and picturesque countryside, with its clay houses and churches with bell towers. I had grown up in the big city. My parents did not spend holidays in the country. The capital's parks were my only contact with nature; I liked to walk there, but I had little interest in the names of flowers, plants and trees. I was completely ignorant of nature – of its flora, mysteries and marvels. In the train, I reflected on that with shame.

Interrupting my thoughts, the locomotive whistled three times in succession and picked up speed. We passed Bacau and from then on it was the turn of the river Bistritza to guide us to our final destination: Piatra Neamtz, the 'pearl of Moldavia'. I shut the window and, without expecting it, my mother's face appeared, reflected in the glass like in a dream. She looked neither sad nor joyful, but as though she was about to speak to me. Was she worried about me? Was she talking about me to my father at that instant? I felt a strong desire to embrace her, to thank her for her devotion, her love for me, her youngest son.

When we arrived at Piatra Neamtz, a dozen lorries covered with dusty canvas took us to the camp of the *Shomria*, which was ready to welcome us. A group of instructors and 'adults' had carried out all the preparatory work during a week of hard effort. In addition to a multitude of small tents equipped with camp beds and oil lamps, the campsite included six wide tents for the kitchen, the infirmary and the latrines, as well as water cisterns and tin huts where they had installed showers. From afar, the whole camp seemed to be made up of square and round shapes on a wide plateau covered with pebbles and wild grass, at the foothills of the Ceahlău massif.

That same night, we gathered around a big campfire, the *medourah*. The *madrichim* announced the activities planned for the days to come, dwelling on the excursion to the Bicaz Gorges and the sports competitions that would precede the closing ceremony. All of us, boys and girls, wore the movement's blue shirt with white lace-ups, symbolising equality between us and the bond with Eretz Israel. The reflection of the flames, entwined in fleeting dances, played on our faces, as the moon illuminated the plateau and the mountain slopes in a wan and silvery light, like that which reigned in our kitchen in Bucharest when my mother did the washing-up late at night. The meeting continued for several hours with languorous and nostalgic Hebrew songs and ended with a peasant dance in a circle whose vibrant and frenetic rhythm annihilated the chilly wind coming down from the mountain. We separated from our *madrichim* with the Hebrew greeting *Hazak Veematz* ('strength and courage'), shouted out in unison from a hundred enthusiastic mouths. Then, in little groups, boys and girls, we made our way to our tents, all softly humming a keenly melancholic melody. Appearing more numerous than I had ever seen before, the stars sparkled in the immensity of a cloudless sky. The mountain air, of unadulterated purity, prickled my nostrils unused to such freshness in midsummer. And as the camp fell asleep, armies of crickets, invading the plateau and infiltrating our tents, began to rub their elytra – males to attract the females, and females to offer themselves to the males – producing a musical chirping that no orchestra could ever reproduce. In our camp beds, legs tangled beneath coarse woollen blankets of army green, the sexual calls of the crickets had no effect on our subterranean desires. Fatigue had quickly closed the eyelids of the chaste 'young guards'. Anyway, we were voluntary martyrs to the cause of chastity, having sworn an oath to our Zionist-Socialist movement to 'safeguard sexual purity' until the age when we would be ripe for the servitude of marriage.

Lying on the narrow, hard camp-bed, which in terms of comfort, had nothing in common with the bed I shared at home with my brother, I refused to go to sleep. Arms folded under my head, I reviewed my first day far from my family, and started to fear the eventual failure of my sporting ambitions. Suddenly, without knowing why, nor where the thought had come from, I realised with disappointment that communal life hindered me as much as scouting bored me. Following this troubling realisation, the queen of the night intervened, my resistance wavered and finally I fell asleep, despite the loud snoring of my tent-mates.

The Red Lake and Gorges of Bicaz had always figured among the most frequented tourist sites in Romania. That the organisers of the *Shomria* had chosen them as the highlight of that year's great excursion surprised nobody. The lake was formed in 1837 when an earthquake caused the collapse of a wide stretch of land into the Bicaz river and the subsequent flooding of an entire forest of conifers. It took its colour from the alluviums of iron oxide or, according to other sources, the reddish branches of the pine trees that stood imprisoned in its waters.

We stopped in front of the lake, like so many tourists before us, to contemplate the spectral image of the tree tops piercing the water's surface like petrified heads stubbornly bearing witness to their tragic fate. After a frugal lunch, we left the lake, still dazzled by the view, and took a winding route down towards the Gorges of Bicaz, alongside the forests of fir and beech encircling the lake. High cliffs rose so closely on either side of these famous gorges, carved out by the river Bicaz, that one could hardly distinguish the tiny piece of sky separating them.

I had learned from our distinguished professor of history and geography, Marcu Weintraub, the importance that the mountains framing these Gorges of Bicaz occupied in Romanian mythology. The Ceahlău massif, dubbed the Olympus of Moldavia, was said to have been the place where the Dacian god Zamolxis had his throne. The Dacians were those Indo-European barbarians from the branch of the Thracians of Asia Minor who had mixed with the Roman conquerors to give us the Romanian people. And according to the legend, it was on one of these mountains that Dochia, daughter of Decebal, the famous king of the Dacians, escaping from Emperor Trajan's captivity, was turned to stone by the cold.

The long wars that Decebal and the Dacians had waged against Emperor Trajan – the different episodes of which are engraved on Trajan's column in Rome – embody the tenacity of the Romanian people and their determination to safeguard their identity down the centuries. Decebal and Zamolxis played no small role in arousing the interest of the young history lover that I was, in a period so important to Romania's history.

On the subject of history, one did not forget professor Weintraub's lessons, because often during them, he was playing pocket billiards with his testicles. He also distinguished himself by simplifying facts to make them easier for us to commit to memory. Thus, in a particularly confidential tone, he had explained in the course of his lessons on the history of Antiquity, that the Punic wars (not to be forgotten!) were three in number: the first, the second and the third!

After two or three days, we returned to camp, filthy, exhausted and famished. In the evening, after a good shower and as soon as I had finished my dinner – soup that tasted like washing-up soap, aggravated by a stew that was tough to swallow – I fled to my tent. I needed to be alone and to sleep. Meanwhile, the indefatigable others started to dance around the *medourah*, like Indians in westerns around a sacred fire. The noise of their singing and shouting prevented me from going to sleep and in addition, I had noticed on my legs the appearance of several itchy red spots that I had unconsciously scratched. The following morning, the spots began to be painful. A young medical student, substituting for the nurse who had fallen ill, explained to me in a knowledgeable manner that I had furunculosis and that there was 'a discernible formation of pus'. According to him, the sanitary conditions during our excursion were the main cause, as well as fatigue and my organism's weak resistance to infection. 'As the organism's power to resist diminishes, so the virulence of the germ increases,' he lectured me. But, why was I struck by this misfortune and not the others? 'Well, that's because you are more sensitive to all these factors,' he said, thinking he was reassuring me.

When Moshe saw me coming out of the infirmary with my legs all bandaged-up, the colour drained from his face. He made it clear to me that in the state I was in, I could not take part in the competition and if, through utter folly, I persisted, my chances of success were almost nil. I reminded Moshe of the huge effort we had made together for the honour of my kvoutza and our Bucharest ken, and implored him to help me carry out my commitment to the end. Eventually, he gave in to my arguments and we decided to act discreetly, for the infirmary had warned me to stay away from any activity that could aggravate the infection. At the end of our conversation, the pain was overwhelming and I felt faint and feverish and shivered all over. Moshe noticed and he pressed me with no more questions. Just like toothache, boils cause pain that pierces flesh and bone, sometimes even the heart. I reflected to myself that the core of a boil looked a lot like the crater of a volcano filled with bubbling lava.

The following morning, in the shower hut, I saw myself in the mirror: I had a sad and downcast face, which made me decide to stay in bed all day. I would have been ashamed to show myself to the others, especially the girls, with this frightening face and my mummified legs. Anyway, I had acquired the reputation of someone who was 'socially reclusive', so it was the right moment to take advantage of it.

My madrich and the shaliah came to visit me. Impressed by the bandages and my sickly appearance, they did their best to console me with encouraging words. That evening, in the light of the hurricane-lamp, I tried to sedate myself by reading *The Adventures of Percy Stuart*, that serialized novel published in Germany before the First World War, at a time when the Germans could still glorify the courage, nonchalance and adventurous spirit of an English gentleman. The novel had been successfully translated into Romanian and published in booklet form. I had thrown some of them into my bag at the last minute before leaving home. To entertain myself, when I was a child, I had preferred Percy Stuart to Sherlock Holmes. He wanted at any price to be accepted as a member of the prestigious 'Eccentric Club', made up of elite military officers and influential members of the British administration and of the aristocracy. In order to succeed, Percy had to go on a great number of almost impossible missions. If he failed once, he had to start all over again. Like when I stepped on the foul line and Moshe pitilessly sent me back to repeat the jump.

With nightfall, after reading a few pages, I put the booklets back in my bag and managed to fall asleep before my companions turned in and unleashed another cannonade of snores.

At last, the day of the competition arrived. At sunrise, the first to leave the tent, I felt the full force of all Nature's fragrances. Instantaneously, the green of the wild grass, the red of the poppies, the white and yellow of the jasmine, lily of the valley and daisies together composed a joyful melody traced in my head like coloured notes on a musical score. Breathing in deeply the pure mountain air and the smell of wildflowers and cedar, I stretched my arms skyward where a pale moon, slowly disappearing with the night, looked down on me. I had forgotten my boils momentarily, as one might briefly forget a great misfortune, which, barely forgotten, resurfaces to crush one's heart again. I congratulated myself at that instant on my decision to take part in the competition, despite the bandages and the pain, and on having secured Moshe's support.

A trumpet announced the opening of the athletics' contest. Groups of boys and girls, the latter in shorts, showing bronzed, provocative thighs, made their way slowly to the expanse cleared of stones, where competition tracks had been set out. On a small mound, a sort of rostrum had been built with empty wooden crates turned into seats. A dozen flags – those of Romania (red, yellow, blue) and those of the Zionist movement (blue and white) bearing the Star of David – fluttered in the wind all along the route.

Noah Eitan, the envoy from a kibbutz founded by Jews from Romania, and who presided over the *Shomria*, read out the names of the competitors, unleashing thunderous applause and enthusiastic shouts of encouragement. In the crowd I noticed faces of comrades from my *ken* and *kvoutza*. Standing up, they were chanting my name, like masses stupidly chant the name of their leader during street demonstrations. I wore the sports shorts and shirt that Moshe had found for me. The bandages around my legs made me look more like a footballer than an athlete and I caught the looks of a group of girls staring at me, no doubt mocking my appearance. Too bad. I was going to show them who I was and what I was capable of, despite the bandages.

By the time they announced the quarter and semi-finals of the one hundred and two hundred metre races, the sun had climbed well up into the sky and it was beginning to get very hot. The sun had always been my skin's worst enemy. It was its fault that I had never been able to learn to swim: in summer, at the big municipal pool, while my brother and his

189

friends delighted in the freshness of the water, I, hidden away in a shady corner, watched them, envious and bitter. After each attempt to enjoy a blessing as elementary as a refreshing swim, I fled the pool, betrayed by my body's inability to expose itself to the sun, and I was forced to shut myself up in the house for two or three days. Going to school was out of the question: burnt by the sun, my skin did not tolerate wearing clothes and I counted on my mother to soothe the most affected areas with yoghurt. I spent the time reading and feeling sorry for myself, but soon Nature, showing a more benevolent side, replaced my old skin with another, brand new one. Alas, it turned out to be as white as the previous one before it was roasted. I understood that I would never be able to sunbathe and that, even in this province, I was not like the others. Fortunately, on the day of the competition my legs were protected by the bandages, while the shirt looked after my front and back. Only my face and the nape of my neck sent me distress signals. I was going to suffer. I knew it.

Finally, the moment of the high jump competition arrived. I had long legs, but a short torso, so my build was a little above average. On the other hand, my adversaries, representing the *kens* of Iaşi, Brasov and Focsani, were all very tall – an apparent advantage. Anyway, I hardly gave myself a chance of winning. At the first attempt, I grazed the bar and it fell. I landed roughly on the mat, hurting my elbow. First place went to the boy from the *ken* in Foscani, jumping 1.18 metres. Second place went to the boy from the *ken* in Brasov with 1.14 metres. I got third place with 1.12 metres. Satisfied, Moshe came over to me with a big smile on his face. 'One medal's already not that bad. But I'm expecting more effort from you, more ambition at the long jump,' he told me. 'That's where you'll have your best chance.

At the triple jump, you'll have one as well, but less big.' He put his arm affectionately around my shoulders. 'Take your run-up like a lion,' he went on, 'hit the ground hard, and try to leap high, but not too high, so you can go as far as possible. And watch out! When you land on your backside, be well balanced, stretch your legs and arms out as far as possible in front of you, like you're trying to stop your head hitting a wall. Understand?' I listened to him with gritted teeth as he patted me on the shoulder and quickly walked away.

Remaining alone, waiting my turn, I thought of my father and that in the fox fur affair, he had not deserved to be treated so harshly by us. It was clear that his 'friends' had cheated him – 'Uncle' Sandu as much as the others. I had not forgotten that he had turned up empty-handed at my Bar-mitzvah, apologising and promising that my present would come (but, of course, it never did...) What a disappointment this fake uncle was! I thought of his huge belly and his audacity in flirting so casually with my mother. Suddenly I heard my name called. It was my turn to jump. While I anxiously took my place, something unexpected happened. At first, there were isolated voices, probably from my comrades from the ken, then, gradually, most of the boys and girls began chanting my name: I had become the hero of the Shomria! The brave boy in bandages who refused to give up despite his handicap! I must not disappoint them...

I knew that my most formidable adversary was Avram, the one who had won first place in the high jump. After two attempts, we were the only competitors left, he with 3.85 metres and me with 3.81. At the third attempt, he fell back to 3.80 metres. He was tiring more quickly than me, a weakness that gave me a small chance. The thunderous support of the spectators rose from the stands. Unfortunately, I started my approach too confidently and overstepped the line. My attempt was disqualified. Avram won once again; I got second place, but was no less disappointed for it. I ran to Moshe after, brushing against Avram accidentally, who, the bastard, rewarded me with a malicious smile. Moshe, always patient, always positive, took me aside, away from the track, and said: 'Did you see that? Avram's fragile, he tires quickly, you must take advantage. Before, I didn't give you much of a chance with the triple jump, but if you don't commit another fault, you can win. It's up to you!'

The spectators roared again when they heard my name among the finalists for the triple jump. At the first attempt, the third competitor committed a fault and was disqualified and again I found myself alone against Avram. Lifted on a wave of encouragement from the two 'stands', I obtained a good result: 7.42 metres. But Avram overtook me with 7.44. At the second attempt, I made 7.45 metres while he fell back to 7.43. I summoned all my remaining energy into my third attempt. Suddenly, the shouts of encouragement were cut off as though a heavy door had slammed shut behind me, insulating me completely from the outside world. Launched into my approach, all I could hear was the sound of my breathing and all I could see in front of me was the track with the white line approaching vertiginously at the speed of my strides. The hop was perfect: I hit the take-off board with force and precision, without stepping on the line, and I executed the jump exactly as Moshe had taught me. I landed further than ever before, perfectly balanced, on my backside. The imaginary door separating me from the rest of the universe burst open and I heard the tumult of all the *Shomria* when the result was announced: 7.50 metres!

Dazed and unsteady, I staggered from the landing pit like a drunk. My bandages were dirty, covered in sand and coming undone. From afar, Moshe was waving his arms triumphantly to attract my attention, but victory was not yet assured: vexed by the lack of encouragement from the stands, Avram made his way hesitantly to his starting place for one last attempt. A tense silence fell on the camp. Avram executed a good run-up, did not touch the foul-line, but then lost his balance and his final jump suffered: only 7.39 metres. My spirits soared sky-high: I had won! I had fulfilled my dream of being first!

◇◇◇◇◇

'Back home, back home, back home' were the words spinning in my head to the rhythm of the pistons and connecting rods that propelled the fast train to Bucharest. Home in a few hours. Heavy clouds covered the sky and a few leftover raindrops struggled against the wind to stay on the steamed-up glass. I had made sure that again I had a window seat: the train was taking me back to Bucharest by the same route as the outward journey; the landscapes were the same, except that they flew by in reverse order, giving me the impression of reliving a dream backwards. The train entered Bacau station and pulled up with a great sigh as an army of porters rushed onto the platforms hunting for customers. In my compartment, a graceful young girl, whose name was Sarah, raised her eyes to me with encouragement and I liked what I saw. Though she was not from my *ken*, I intended to get to know her and could then boast to my brother that I too had a girlfriend: his, Erna, was beautiful and blonde, whilst my Sarah was a brunette...

My victory in the triple jump gave me the feeling that I had 'grown up' and left childhood behind me. Leo would surely notice this change immediately. The distance separating us would shrink as my experience of life grew. But why had I not felt I had grown up immediately after my Bar-mitzvah? In the Jewish tradition and according to my Hebrew teacher, who had prepared me for the ritual, a boy is no longer considered a child after his Bar-mitzvah; on reaching his religious majority as 'son of the commandments' of God, he enters the adult world. I remembered the teacher's words, like sweet and pleasant music to my ears, but, in the depths of my being, I did not believe them. I did not like rabbis and, even less, the religious ceremonies held at the temple, that neither my brother nor I frequented. To be old enough to apply God's commandments did not mean much to me. In future, I did not intend to pray wearing the shawl and tefillin, those cumbersome accessories from a bygone age. When the time came for my Bar-mitzvah, I did not really take to heart the preparations nor even the ceremony of this Jewish rite from which, in a certain way, the Christian confirmation draws inspiration. My belief in God, which came to me in hospital when I had scarlet fever, was a personal one. But on the day of the ceremony at the 'Choral Temple' in Bucharest, the ritual of the 'ascent to the Torah' awoke deep emotion in me. As I climbed the thick Oriental carpet-covered steps, my heart began to beat so fast that I had to stop for a moment to catch my breath. The rabbi accompanying me also stopped, turned to me, concerned, and took my arm to lead me to the altar where the liturgy is celebrated and where I was to read from the Torah.

For the first time in my life, I found myself right near the Holy Ark where the legendary scrolls of the Torah containing the five books of Moses are kept with sanctity and, to my surprise, I felt my Jewishness awaken. The blue velvet curtain covering the door to the Holy Ark was artistically embroidered with gold and silver threads in the motifs of the crown of the Torah (*Keter Hatorah*) and the Tablets of Stone. The Ark, pointing towards Jerusalem, was flanked by two gilded columns supporting the lintel above which a triangular decoration in gold leaf led to a Hebrew inscription that was difficult to read. The rabbi took the scroll of the Torah from the Holy Ark and my heart began again to beat wildly as he put it on my shoulders, helping me to bring it in the procession to the reading table.

The reading of the Torah was preceded by the benediction and I believe it was me who pronounced in a shaky voice: 'Blessed be the Lord our God, king of the Universe, who has chosen us among all nations and given us his Torah.' And while hearing my voice, I could not help thinking that I had never really believed that we were the chosen people. Unless God had only made this choice to make us suffer more than all the other peoples on earth... With time, between secularism and religion, I had chosen to remain neutral. It was Moses the revolutionary, rather than Moses the spiritual guide, who had inflamed my imagination! I had got my composition prize at school by treating precisely this theme. But, on the altar of the Holy Ark, religion broke my neutrality to remind me like a revelation: *Do not doubt this God of Moses, do not forget that you believed in HIM, when illness put you face to face with death at the Caritas hospital.* After the blessing, I had to read a passage from the parchment. For one terrifying second, I wondered if I was going to remember what I had learned with my Hebrew teacher during the long apprenticeship period. But I did it, and I did it well. After which came the moment to make my required speech. And there, I encountered a problem. The ascent to the Torah had moved me so much that when I opened my mouth, the tense faces of the men in the great hall and those of the women in the gallery troubled me so much that the words refused to come out.

Sergiu, Nellu, Dica, and Hershcu, all sitting together in the second row with their parents, but especially Pouia, Rozica, Chichi and my female cousins in the gallery, watched me with the sort of detached amusement they might have shown observing an animal cycling in a circus ring. Finally, I managed to begin, but right in the middle of my speech, I twice stumbled on a word and had to pause before remembering the continuation. I could read the anxiety on my mother's face as she was seated directly opposite me in the centre of the gallery. In the front row, my father, Leo, Uncle Max and Uncle Pincu sent me discreet signs of encouragement and I ended my speech firmly, but without joy, convinced that I had disappointed my parents and Leo.

I consoled myself when I got home by opening my presents. From Uncle Max, there was an envelope containing some banknotes; from Bercovici, Rozica's father, a soft woollen pullover from Galeries Lafayette; a beautiful tie from Dica's father and various little gifts from the other guests, but the big surprise was the present I received from Fanny the pharmacist – a magnificent Waterman pen, black with a 14-carat gold nib! I was overwhelmed by happiness. But not for long...

One day, alerted by a loud commotion, I left the courtyard and went into the street where a funeral procession was approaching. I bumped into a boy from a neighbouring courtyard and wanted to show-off with the beautiful pen I had received for my Bar-mitzvah. The procession was then about fifteen metres away. It was not the first time that one had passed down our street: a giant of a man holding up a heavy cross led the procession, followed by a strident brass band, a priest, a hearse carrying the coffin, members of the family of the deceased, and, bringing up the rear, a dense crowd. I took the pen out of my jacket to show it proudly to the boy from the other courtyard just at the moment when the procession stopped to allow the priest, as is the tradition, to throw coins for the needy onto the pavement.

At that precise instant, some lout, swift as an arrow, tore the pen from my hand and disappeared into the crowd, leaving me no chance of catching up with him. I returned home devastated. Tears oppressed me. I adored that pen. What could I say to Leo, to my parents? I won't tell them anything. I'll lie. The day one of them notices, I'll confess that I lost it at school or somewhere else. But how could I explain to myself what had happened? Was it my stupidity, my vanity, or the will of God that had pushed me, so imprudently, to expose my precious Waterman? A bit of all three, no doubt. Between tears, I smiled at the idea that childhood did not have a monopoly on crying, and that on becoming an adult I continued to enjoy this privilege.

◇◇◇◇◇

Moshe, sitting in a row further away in the compartment, sent me one of his tender smiles. I waved to him and felt my cheeks flush. Having ended its stop at Bacau, the train set off again and, slowly, the platform slipped away, and the station and its grand clock in the façade of the central building, along with the bustling crowd of travellers, conductors and porters, vanished into the mist. Peacefully, I put my head against the window and fell asleep, content.

17

My brother Has an Experience I Should Have Learned from

Back from the *Shomria* all proud of myself, as triumphant at the *ken* as at home, I received an unexpected letter from my brother that I hastened to open.

My dear brother,

The farm I am writing to you from, if it can even be called that, is a former goods warehouse, partially damaged during the war when the troops of Marshal Malinovsky occupied Iaşi. It is situated fifty metres from a miserable road used exclusively by lorries, buses, tractors and any other heavy-duty vehicle. I reached it by bus with my friend from the *ken*, Silviu, who you know. As we got off the bus, a convoy of five Russian lorries passed us – ZIMs with the driver's cabin and the doors painted in all the colours of the rainbow. They were transporting hundreds of slant-eyed soldiers brandishing, despite the war being long over, signs bearing the slogan 'NACH BERLIN'! The heroic songs that the Red Army soldiers were hurling at the top of their lungs, the deafening noise of the engines and the piercing sounds of klaxons were just a minor prelude to the adventures that awaited us – the young secondary school pupils who had come from the big city to taste pastoral life in an agricultural commune.

The farm's central building is constructed out of old bricks. Windows and doors are missing, probably stolen before the movement set up the hachshara. Panes of glass cut to size and stuck with putty directly onto the bricks without any wooden frames substitute for windows and sliding panels replace missing doors. Inside, we have created separate dormitories furnished with bunk beds for the girls. Near the dormitories, we have two shower cabins, toilets, a room for the shaliah, a room for Baruch, a big guy aged twenty-five, for the administration office and one room for reading and games. The shaliah comes from a kibbutz in the valley of Beit Shean, near the river Jordan, and his job is to teach us agriculture.

On the left of the big open space in front of the entrance of the building, there is the cowshed, a long concrete structure with two wide doorways and a few broken windows. A corner of the shed, separated from the cows by a half-built low wall, is an area reserved for a horse and its equipment – blinkers, bridle, reins – as well as hay and oats for its feed. Forks, pickaxes, saws, axes, spades, scythes, sickles and rakes, all in various states of rustiness, are kept near the shed in a hut whose rotten flat roof does little to stop the rain from getting in. The hut, lost in the darkness, stinks of mould. I avoid as much as possible venturing there, fearing it is the home of two-headed snakes!

Wheelbarrows and large milk cans are strewn about the area outside, alongside a cistern and a cart with a harness for a horse.

Although the movement preaches equality between men and women, the girls' main tasks are cooking, washing and ironing. Agricultural work is for the boys. Behind the building there is a wide piece of land where we grow lucerne, clover and various vegetables. Another area, protected by a hedge, serves as pasture for the cows, and on a neighbouring plot there is grass that we mow and leave to dry to make hay. Under Baruch's instruction, we have also built a food silo: a mixture of grass, beetroot and alfalfa left to ferment to feed the cows in winter. The agricultural products, mainly vegetables, are collected by an envoy of the movement who, despite being thirty, arrives from the city centre in shorts and adolescents' socks. He honours us with his presence only on these occasions.

The sale of milk in town requires particularly demanding work. Each of us, in turn, must undertake it. We go there in twos: one keeps the cart and the horse, while the other distributes the milk from door to door. Sure enough, the one who has to handle the two heavy milk cans returns to the farm with a broken back and painful loins.

Milking cows by hand, my dear brother, is just one of the dozens of chores linked to cattle-raising which Baruch, the *shaliah*, had to teach us mostly bourgeois Bucharest students. In very little time, we learned that without calving there is no milk, and that the lactation period only begins after nine months gestation, when the cow, by natural coupling with a bull, becomes pregnant, from which results the birth of a little calf that suckles its mother. Then, after a brief theoretical introduction, Baruch initiated us to the daily work, which is anodyne and repetitive and less exhilarating than the birth of a little calf. It involves imprisoning the cows' heads in a special yoke when we feed them; trimming their horns and hooves so they won't wound each another; shortening the hair at the end of their tails so they do not get dirty whisking away flies; cleaning their bedding in the shed, and so on...

Now that you have a better idea of work on the farm in Iaşi, I am going to describe the tough conditions in which we live. The water needed for us and our animals is supplied, via a long pipe, by a timber business, in exchange for our vegetables and milk. Washing is a problem. We have two cabins with showers and basins, one for the girls and one for the boys. But as we do not have any central heating, we shower in cold water; at the onset of winter, the previous *haloutzim* had heated the bedrooms with the help of three stoves, and took their baths in wooden tubs, the girls on Saturday and the boys on Sunday. Hygiene suffered because of this and still does: almost all of us have scabies. As a remedy, we use a sulphur-based ointment, which makes an awful stink, and on top of that we scratch ourselves until we bleed. At the same time, we wage a merciless war against fleas.

At less than a kilometre from the farm, a very dense area of forest crawls with criminals hunted by the police and raises another question mark over our presence in this environment. The authorities have decreed the forest a 'forbidden zone'. Even the police don't dare venture in there. From time to time, they just approach its edge and light it up with projectors to prevent the brigands from settling too near the city. During the war, in a field neighbouring the forest, the Romanian Army had dug hundreds of individual graves for the soldiers defending the road leading to the centre of Iaşi. These graves no longer have a use, but we regularly discover naked corpses, cooked by the sun like meat on a grill. The bodies are so burnt that they no longer even smell. Imagine the horror this sight inspires in us.

The farm is not a rational target for theft: there is no object of value, and the neighbourhood knows this. Our big worry is the girls. They risk attracting undesirable visitors. Baruch has forbidden them from showing their faces in the part of the building that is exposed to the road. As we need means of self-defence in case of danger, the movement has placed at our disposal three German Parabellum semi-automatic revolvers and a hundred 9mm cartridges. But, with the exception of Baruch, none of us has ever used a firearm. During the hours of outdoor work, we never leave the girls alone inside the building. Baruch and his assistant, Sorin, patrol the front yard, both keeping a revolver in their pocket, while a goliath of a *halutz* by the name of Simon inspects the ground behind the building, armed with the third revolver.

Fortunately, under the reading room is a spacious cellar, accessible through a trap door we cover with a mat. As soon as danger is signalled by the *halutzim* on guard duty, the girls go down into the cellar and we mask the trap door and the rug with a big table and chairs. It is the task of Simon and I to hide the clothes the girls leave behind as they flee.

The real danger comes from the occasional visits we receive from the Soviet soldiers. The 'Ivans' (the nickname we have given the Russian soldiers and their slant-eyed brothers in arms) like to stop in front of the farm to sniff out something to eat or steal. As soon as they appear, Baruch and Simon must do two things double quick: firstly, alert the girls to go to the cellar and, then, remove their watches from wrists and hide them between socks and boots, at ankle height. Why? Because bizarrely, as soon as the Ivans see the watches of men, women or children, they sink into the mysticism of medieval magic. The watch ('*cheass*' in Russian) has acquired for them fetishistic powers, incompatible with Marxism-Leninism. To see the soldiers of the Red Army – our saviours, our liberators – cover their arms from wrist to elbow with watches stolen at bayonet point does not augur well for the future of socialism. If you remember, the famous Romanian comic, Tanasse, published a pamphlet on this subject entitled *Davai cheass, davai moshie, harasho tovarashie!* ('Give me your watch and your wife, and we'll be friends for life!'). Thank the Lord, Baruch and Sorin speak Russian sufficiently well to explain to these smartasses that we are only young workers (*maladir rabotnikov*) and that, apart from milk and vegetables, we have nothing to offer them. On each visit, one of the soldiers asks 'innocently' for the time: *Katoriytchas?* It would be enough for Baruch or Sorin to glance involuntarily at their wrists to fall into the trap. But Baruch, as smart as the Bolshevik, replies quickly and politely: '*Ya nie znayou, izvinitie*' ('I'm sorry but I don't know').

I ask myself, dear brother: are we normal taking part, so young, in this unreal experience, or do we belong to a generation so precocious that no one in the movement cares about our age? The ordeals we are subjected to on the farm would pose serious problems even to experienced adults. How to explain the ineffable fraternity that these difficulties have cemented between us? Does it come from the ambition to emulate the heroes we admire in novels and films? Or rather, which seems to me more probable, is it the fear and the shame of each of us at being the first to crack and dishonour himself in his eyes and those of his comrades? But the biggest question I dare ask myself is if, ultimately, the 'raison d'être' of this farm justifies the price we are paying to make it exist? I cannot comprehend how the movement could send young city-dwellers like us to live in such conditions. I bet it is the credulity, naïve or not, of these leaders: they must believe that communal life, the absence of money, and daily confrontation with immense difficulties and dangers are the best ways of preparing the future *halutzim* for the living conditions in a kibbutz in Palestine. But, for my part, I doubt it strongly.

I hope that you have beaten world records at the *Shomria*, Bébé, and that you are bringing back to the *ken* at least a dozen gold medals...

Your brother,
LEO

A wave of warmth washed over me: he was thinking about me. He was not indifferent to what I was doing. The allusion to the dozen gold medals, whether it was humorous or even slightly sarcastic, still showed me that he had understood why I had chosen to take part in the competitions, that my real motivation was the desire to get away from home, and to assert myself as a person. At the same time, his description of life on the farm and the disappointments he felt regarding the movement made me sad. Through brotherly osmosis, his doubts became mine. But the worst happened not long afterwards.

Via a desperate telegram, Leo informed us that his friend Silviu had caught typhoid fever and died in a hospital in Iaşi, age seventeen and a half. He was buried in the old Ashkenazi cemetery of Filantropia in Bucharest. My family was not invited to the ceremony, Silviu's parents believing that their son had gone to the farm under my brother's influence. The rumour that there had been a case of typhoid fever on the farm had quickly spread around the *ken*, sowing panic in the families of three other young Bucharesters who had been sent there for instruction. The idea that Leo could also be infected devastated my father. His son was in danger and it was the fault of those scoundrels who had created this farm in the middle of nowhere. So that was Zionism? Leaving young novices to their own fate, then attributing responsibility to bad luck? He felt he had to go to Iaşi and bring his son home, but he did not dare take the risk of being absent from the factory: if someone denounced him, he would lose his job. That is how the idea of going to Iaşi took hold in my mother's head. Helped by Fanny the pharmacist, she bought a train ticket, prepared a small suitcase while my father was at work and I was at school, and, at dinner, announced her departure the following morning. My father and I were at a loss for words: had we heard correctly? She did not hesitate to confirm her decision, staring at us with implacable firmness. I did not recognise her. I had never seen her so resolute, so intransigent before. My father warned her of the dangers of such a journey for an unaccompanied woman, but she showed no intention of giving up. She wanted to see Leo at any price, reassure herself that he was well, and, if needs be, do all she could for him. Without forgetting the most important thing, to convince him to leave the farm and return home with her, for he had to decide on how he would continue his studies and what direction to take after his failure at the faculty of medicine! I remained silent. Already sufficiently terrified at the idea that some misfortune could befall my brother, I now saw my mother in danger and that paralysed me even more.

Fortunately, in the end, she did come back from Iaşi safe and sound and the journey was a success, even if Leo had refused to abandon his comrades and return to Bucharest with her. Learning that she had found my brother tanned and 'as handsome as a film star' raised my morale. But how had she dared to make this journey all on her own and how had my brother reacted on seeing her arrive at the farm? What kind of vicissitudes had she been subject to during the journey? I immediately replied to my brother's long letter, asking him all sorts of questions. His reply did not take long.

Dear Bernard,

Even in my wildest dreams, I could not have imagined Mother arriving like an angel from heaven into this mad farm. All alone, in shabby trains full of brigands, drunken Russian soldiers, uncouth peasants and gypsies with nasty eyes. They must have wondered what this woman from another world was doing in their midst.

I was just finishing some work in the area behind the building when one of the *haverim* alerted me: Leo, your mother has just arrived from the station and she is waiting for you inside. Can you imagine my surprise and joy at seeing her again? But how had she found her way to the farm? She had had to take the same bus as Silviu and I: that nightmarish vehicle, stuffed with baskets full of eggs, sacks of potatoes, demijohns, animal cages – and, on top of that, smelling of sweat and sauerkraut. For long minutes, we embraced and exchanged tender words stifling our tears. She asked me if I knew how much she loved me, and to what point she had missed me. I looked at her with affection, noticing that she had lost weight. To the rare and delicate beauty of her features, that no one could have contested, were now added fine lines drawn by fatigue. She was there, our mother, right next to me, despite all the difficulties that I could not ignore. Before I joined her inside the building, she had asked a few of the girls about Silviu's death and our living conditions on the farm. We sat down in a quiet corner and from a little bundle she held firmly on her lap, she took out some grilled chicken and that miraculous cake, made with nuts and loukoum, that we are so crazy about. Then she took my hand and in a determined tone, said to me: 'Let them manage here without you, Leo. I have come to take you home. I want you to return with me to Bucharest.' With a broken heart, I replied that it would be an act of betrayal towards my *haverim*, but that other members of the movement were going to arrive in two or three weeks at the latest to replace us and she did not insist. Expecting me to refuse, she took from her blouse a roll of notes held by an elastic band and placed it in my hand. It was her savings, the money she had earned from her sewing. I took it so as not to offend her and because I needed it, and asked her again to forgive me for not being able to return to Bucharest with her. Then, with sadness, I accompanied her to the station in the same shabby bus she had taken to get to the farm. I helped her onto the train and we separated. I glimpsed her face through the window of the carriage from where she was looking at me in tears. Then the train slowly pulled away and her face vanished in a cloud of greyish steam. What a miserable life this fine woman, Jenny, our mother, has had! How has she been able to hold on? As for me, at that moment, seized by despair, sadness and bitterness, I hardly managed to.

That very evening, I shared the nut cake with my *haverim* and *haverot*. However, betraying the spirit of the commune, I hid the money under a stone behind the cowshed. I used it when going to the city to sell milk. I sold the milk quickly then, immediately afterwards, I would run into a patisserie where I swallowed profiteroles, eclairs, mille-feuilles and macaroons, until the point that the sugar overdose made me giddy! On the farm, people began to be amazed by my enthusiasm about going to deliver milk.

My dear brother, this period of *hachshara* in Iaşi represents above all a sad chapter for me. I have just lost a precious friend. We often ate rice pudding from the same bowl. Inevitably, when he caught typhoid fever, I expected this terrible illness to get me as well. Ever since his death I am gnawed by doubts regarding the leaders of the movement in Iaşi and elsewhere: their share of responsibility, their indifference to the difficulties we encounter on the farm. The rumours, true or false, concerning the relative advantages they enjoy – their salaries, their accommodation, as well as their behaviour in their personal life – play a big role. Faith in an ideal suffers severely when one loses confidence in the men that incarnate it. When that happens, both the faith and the ideal raise persistent and justified doubts. These thoughts worry me, for I fear that our nature and our ambitions are not compatible with the demands dictated by an agricultural commune like the kibbutz.

I hope to be back in Bucharest as quickly as possible.

Your brother who loves you,
LEO

18

'Long ago
and far away,
I dreamt a dream
one day'

My dear mother! We both loved cinema, although our tastes were not exactly the same... she remembered Rudolph Valentino with nostalgia, whom she had seen in *Camille* and *The Son of the Sheik*, but her favourite film remained *The Jazz Singer*, with the Jewish actor Al Jolson. As for me, I had been under the spell for some time of American and English films that had been forbidden by the censors in Romania during the war. Two films in particular had captured my imagination: *A Matter of Life or Death* by Michael Powell and Emeric Pressburger and *Cover Girl* by Charles Vidor.

A Matter of Life or Death tells the love story between the pilot of a British bomber that returns in flames from a night mission to Germany and a young American woman, the radio operator who intercepts his message before he crashes. As surgeons operate on him and he struggles with death, he hallucinates that he is on trial in Heaven fighting for the right to return among the living. Apart from the touching love story, what had impressed me in particular was the clever cinematographic idea of using images in colour and images in black and white to represent differently the world below and the world above.

As for *Cover Girl*, its huge success was due to the presence of the ravishing Rita Hayworth and of the song *Long Ago and Far Away*, the film's leitmotiv.

> *Long ago and far away, I dreamt a dream one day,*
> *And now the dream is here beside me.*

The words of the song were translated into Romanian, but as I had eyes only for Rita Hayworth, I paid little attention to the subtitles and, without understanding the words, the melody as she sang it, swept me up in a torrent of undecipherable feelings, towards an intimate dream, that of a young boy who seeks a way towards the future to escape the past and the present.

I had wanted to see *Cover Girl* when one of the main newspapers offered a coupon for a free ticket, valid for matinees only. I knew perfectly well that playing truant to go to the cinema would be considered unforgivable behaviour. How did I, such a good and studious boy, dare be such a rascal? Quite simply because the school board had indirectly encouraged me: confronted with serious financial difficulties, it had decided to send home any pupil whose parents had not paid the tuition fees at the end of the semester.

The day I spent four hours in Rita Hayworth's company at the Trianon cinema my name was on the list of pupils to be sent from class, as my mother had not paid the fees before going to Iaşi. On the morning of my escapade, she had slipped the money into an inside pocket of my satchel for me to pay them, but when a young student teacher with a stammer came to call out the names, the devil – yes, the devil – incited me to do something that only the devil could have thought of. Acting as though I did not have the money, I got up silently, cleared my things off the desk, put them in my satchel and made for the door.

In the street, I met my comrades-in-exile, three of whom cynically boasted about having the money on them, but preferring to enjoy a day off in the open air rather than being bored at the back of the class. Refusing to join common cause with mischievous boys, I walked off alone, taking a roundabout route to reach my destination whilst all along I could feel the burning presence of the coupon for the Trianon cinema in my jacket pocket. The theatre was not too full and, finding a good place quite easily, I settled down in a red velvet seat that was so much more comfortable than my school bench. I remained there bewitched for two consecutive performances until one in the afternoon – sufficient time for my memory to retain the film's most beautiful melodies. In the darkness of my childhood, at the invitation of Rita Hayworth, I had substituted for the real world where fear, hunger and sorrow reigned, a dream world sheltered from earthly misfortunes.

After the film, I reached the canteen just before it was closing. The lady with the potato nose threw two big bones and a paltry quantity of mashed lentils and purée, into my bowl, forgetting the meat. Had she read the crime in my eyes to treat me so harshly? I emptied my bowl in a minute, like a starving dog, and hurried to return home, to avoid raising useless suspicions in my mother's mind. She was chatting with a neighbour at the kitchen door when I got back and after I had greeted the neighbour and kissed my mother, she asked: 'Did you give the money to the teacher?' After a short pause, supposed to indicate annoyance at having to confirm something so flagrantly obvious, I told a barefaced lie: 'Yes, Mother... of course!' I then went straight to the living room, took the money from my satchel, and hid it under the bed and felt all my blood rush to my head as I did so. In the bathroom mirror, I saw my beetroot red reflection and put my head under cold running water to calm myself down. Yes, I thought, I had betrayed my mother's trust abominably: I had swindled her.... And what if I had lost the money? Or what if someone had stolen my satchel at the cinema? May God forgive me, for I had duplicated, at my own level, my father's ignominy.

I sat down at the table with my exercise jotter and mathematics textbook. Leo not being there to help me, I spent hours finding the solution to two algebra problems and one of geometry. Apart from the fact that mathematics was my Achilles heel, I had also to wrestle with my feelings of guilt while the melodies sung by Rita pursued me relentlessly. That evening, when my mother called us for dinner, I took my place next to my father, feeling, thanks to my hunger, less troubled at having collaborated with the devil.

No one in the world cooked better than my mother when she had something to cook... That day, my father had brought a fresh carp back from the market. Sprinkled with ingredients of which only she knew the secret, she cut it into pieces, which she then fried, including the head, in olive oil. While my father sucked on the fish's head, I hummed the film's melodies. And as my mother gossiped about the Breicher couple, who had just announced their intention to split up, I imagined seeing in my plate the beautiful mouth of Rita Hayworth that bewitched men and made the women jealous.

After dinner, my bad conscience started to get to me again. I was obsessed with anxiety that I might forget to put the money back in my satchel as well as by the awful realisation that, in certain circumstances, I could be as despicable as the good-for-nothings at the back of my class. Trying to free myself from this torment, I settled on the bed with my brother's history book to read the chapter on Giuseppe Garibaldi and the national movement in Italy. About ten pages in, the image of Rita Hayworth suddenly appeared to me superimposed on the bearded face of Garibaldi and then I was devastated to discover that the film's melodies had fled my memory without leaving a trace. I went to bed and switched off the light, seeking the consolation that only sleep could provide.

The following morning, my father woke me up gently and, as soon as I opened my eyes, the film's melodies resonated in my head, one after the other – clear, luminous and bright. I had a musical ear!

As soon as I got to school, I handed the money over to the young teacher. He apologised for having sent me home the day before: he had been obliged to comply with instructions, and 'the instructions are... ri-ri-rigid,' he stammered with emotion. The school fee affair was settled.

That afternoon, I went to the ken, after an absence of five days. Opening the door, I found myself face to face with Carol, the shaliah. He had noted my absence and had been worried about me. When I explained to him that I had had difficulties at home and was worried about my brother after Silviu's death, he took me by the shoulders and reassured me that everything was now fine on the farm. The movement had taken the necessary measures, but tragic accidents like Silviu's were always a possibility. I was not to worry about Leo, for two days earlier a leader of the movement returning from the farm had reassured him that Leo was in good shape. I thanked Carol and went over to my brother's wall newspaper to see what state it was in without him, when suddenly hands covered my eyes and I heard a familiar voice say to me in a jokey way: 'Guess who?'

It was Moshe, the sports *madrich*. He embraced me and told me he had wanted to speak to me about something extremely important. The urgency of his tone was intriguing: 'What important thing? What are you talking about, Moshe?'

'Not here, outside,' he whispered.

In the street, we walked away from the *ken* and stopped on a quiet corner. Impatiently, I pressed him: 'So?' He smiled and patted my arm, as he did during training to calm me down. 'Listen. You remember I told you that in Palestine they would need more from you than jumping?'

'Yes, and?'

'Well, you'd better hurry! A list has been opened for emigration to Palestine for boys and girls under sixteen, but it is going to close soon. If you want to sign up, all you need is your parent's written agreement.'

'This is the first I have heard about it, Moshe.'

'Precisely. Do you believe such a thing would be announced with great fanfare in the newspapers or on the radio – to alert the English, maybe? According to rumours, the Party, with the personal support of Ana Pauker, has authorised several thousand Jews to emigrate to Palestine. It's secret. There's talk of two big ships which together will leave a port the name of which is also being kept secret for the time being.'

Disconcerted, I thought of the *Struma* and asked him: 'What kind of ships? Like the *Struma*?'

'Big ships, Bernard. Forget the *Struma*. American ships, solid ones that crossed the Atlantic during the war. Each with more than five thousand emigrants on board! Do you realise? So many emigrants leaving on the same day, from the same port! It would be unprecedented in the history of the Aliyah and the history of Zionism!'

The great adventure, the one I had dreamed of for so long, without knowing what form it would have, began to take root in my imagination as a tangible reality: to cross the sea, fight the English, and work the fields in a kibbutz – all that ahead of my brother for the first time and inviting him to follow me! But what would I do if my parents refused to give me their agreement?

'Neither my mother nor my father will agree to me leaving,' I replied bitterly.

'And your brother?'

'My brother is at Iaşi in the *hachshara*.'

'Do you want me to speak to them?'

'No, I'd prefer to speak to my brother first.'

'The list will soon be closed! And after that, it will be all over. The regime will no longer allow it.'

'I'm going to write to him... I'll send him a letter first thing tomorrow.'

A week later, without warning, my brother returned from Iaşi, handsome as a film star, it was true, but exhausted and alarmingly thin.

19

Between Brothers

After Iaşi and such a long separation, Leo wanted to talk to me about his plans: his future in the movement and the urgent need to take another direction in his studies, to avoid losing another precious year. Taking a walk in Carol Park with me was pleasant and useful relaxation for him. 'It's interesting,' he said, 'I only learned from books of the suffering a soldier endures in war and the strange feeling he has when he returns home unhurt; but that's exactly how I feel after returning from the farm. These days, I enjoy the luxury of getting up later, organising my day as I like, being able to choose to be alone, sleeping in my own bed and eating out of my own plate.' Despite this, I was surprised to learn that my brother missed the daily contact with the cows and with old Hercules, the tired horse who pulled the milk-cart to Iaşi.

We made our way to Carol Park. It was a park that was less chic than Cismigiu, in the eyes of the people of Bucharest, but we preferred it because of its proximity to our home, in the south of the capital, and because its landscape architect, Edouard Redoni, was French, while Cismigiu had been designed by Germans.

On arrival, we avoided the popular sites, and even passed on taking a turn around the lake in a rowboat, a routine that my brother, passionate as he was about this type of nautical exercise, imposed on me nearly every time we went to the park together. This time, our legs guided us along secluded paths, covered in a carpet of rust-coloured leaves and planted with conifers, poplars, elms and various shrubs, finally leading us to a bench where we sat down in the shade. The approach of winter had made the flowers wither, except for the jasmine and daphnes.

Finally, in a hushed, almost inaudible voice, my brother resumed: 'I left the farm on bad terms with the *shaliah* and the leaders.' I dared ask him why and he replied: 'Because they delayed our replacement by a new group of *halutzim*. It was the second time they'd done it and it exasperated me. I wanted to return to Bucharest as quickly as possible to find a university that would accept me, but also because I had serious thoughts of quitting the movement.'

'Under the influence of Dorel Baraban? To join the UTC?'

My questions annoyed him.

'So you don't understand? I'm disappointed. I no longer trust the movement's leaders! That has nothing to do with

217

Dorel Baraban. You know full well that I don't want to join the UTC. Are you just saying that to irritate me? It's about my future. Zionism's an ideal, not a vocation. And my vocation is medicine, not Zionism!'

'That's news. You've never told me that before, or, in any case, not in this way... And what about me?'

'You? What have you got to do with it? You still have four years in front of you to decide what to do with your future.'

It was the moment I had been waiting for. I was not going to miss it. 'I've already decided!' I exclaimed.

Thrown randomly, my little bomb, far from shaking him, amused him. As if I had just told him a joke. He rewarded me with an affectionate smile and a look of endearing gentleness, which was unusual from him. Quite obviously, he had not taken me seriously, neither my tone nor the determination in my voice. But taking care to stifle any nuance of irony in his response, he chose to turn on the charm: 'And what have you decided, little brother?' he asked, placing his hand tenderly on my shoulder.

'I've decided to leave for Palestine!'

This time, I had thrown a real bomb. Leo exploded, raising his arms skyward and seized by a jovial, somewhat inappropriate, light-heartedness: 'Bravo, my boy! And since when have you decided that?' Ignoring his mocking tone, I told him of my meeting with Moshe and the urgent need to obtain our parents' consent, without which I could not register on the emigration list. All of a sudden, his face took on a serious expression. 'But what are you going to do over there? They don't need a featherweight like you in Palestine.'

Used to his malice, I could sense that this was just the aperitif before the arrival of a whole menu of arguments that he was cooking up for me in his head. 'A featherweight who won three medals at the *Shomria*, and despite my boils!' I replied indignantly.

'Bébé! Wake up! Palestine is not the *Shomria*! Emigration is illegal: the English will not agree to open the gates of Palestine to the thousands of emigrants Moshe talked to you about. There's therefore the risk of another tragedy, like that of the *Exodus*. Don't expect to reach the Holy Land, but Cyprus at best! In an English internment camp, behind barbed wire. Without us! Without me! Lost in the crowd! Are you well prepared for that? Certainly less well than the others! You know it. And if the plan to divide Palestine is adopted by the United Nations, the English will quickly pack their bags and, the very next day, it'll be war against the Arabs!'

Bursts of laughter suddenly interrupted us. A young couple in love fled, like doves, as we turned our faces towards them, allowing me a moment to get my wits back before replying in a voice strangled by emotion: 'I want to go to Palestine and I need your help, Leo. Don't be a coward and don't try to scare me with the English and the Arabs!' Leo scratched his head and, when he studied me out of the corner of his eye, I could see that he had chosen not to take what I was saying lightly. 'Explain to me one thing, little brother,' he went on, 'your desire to go to Palestine is such that you don't care about breaking Mother's heart? Because you know well what it's going to be for her to be separated from you! And as for Father and me, it won't be less hard. And then, what makes you want to leave us with such rage and passion?'

He must have known that by mentioning our mother, he was twisting the knife. I loved my mother with all my heart; the idea that I might never see her again swirled in my thoughts

219

like a mad chimera. And yet, I wanted to leave. At any price? Yes, but in truth I did not know what the price would be, for, had I known, I would doubtless not have had the courage to pay it.

'I have a question I've been burning to ask you for a long time, Leo... Tell me: when they buried me in the commercial high school, you did not intervene. Why? Because the same thing had been done to you four years earlier? Can you explain to me what future awaits me here when I have finished these four years of accountancy? And another question: don't you know that next year, our Cultura will no longer exist as a Jewish school? That means I'll be forced to spend my next years in a Christian environment, like in primary school. You'll tell me it's not the same thing, that the class struggle has replaced the Holy Trinity as the State religion. But the fact that the ritual of crossing yourself is no longer practised at school does not make the Romanians any less anti-Semitic than before.'

'I'm listening patiently, but you're coming up with nonsense bigger than you are. I too will be in a Christian environment at university. So what? Am I going to swallow cyanide, like Goering? No! I'll get used to it! "Necessity is the mother of invention." You too will find your vocation like I've found mine. That will depend entirely on you. It matters little that your classmates will be mostly Christian.'

'You want me to get used to anti-Semitism because what counts for you is becoming a doctor. But the Jews are going to have their national State, and I want to find my vocation in the Jewish State, not in Romania.'

He approached me and his face lit up with encouragement and sympathy, 'Bébé, if you don't see yourself as an accountant,

I can see you even less as a farmer. I think that you're born for something else. Everyone who knows you thinks that. I'm not the only one. What vocation will you find in the kibbutz? The commune will devour all that is promising in you. In a commune, it is the shrewdest and the least fragile who cope the best. I learned that all too well on the farm.'

'I want to leave, Leo. I have to leave! It's not simply idealism, or to flee Romania...'

'But, what else are you fleeing from?'

'You really want me to tell you?'

'Yes, of course.'

I stared at him in silence, as I did not yet know what words I would use and I was afraid of what they would be. He felt my apprehension. I think it made him smile unintentionally, a smile that annoyed me, and the words poured out in the mysterious order they had to follow: 'Well. I'll tell you then... I want to flee the past and the present, our home, our courtyard and our street... I want to get away from you... I want to flee Mother's tears, Father's sad appearance, the expression of defeat in his eyes and the way you speak to him, look at him. Do you think I can't see how you observe him when he talks, when he eats, when he gets dressed? Why do you look at him like that? And why do you no longer embrace him? You're the one who poisoned Mother with the idea that he needed his head examined. All that is what I want to run away from. And I also want to flee the future that awaits me if I stay here with you. I want to run away from all that!'

Leo's face darkened. He did not like my speech at all, and softness was not in his nature. 'Is it Moshe who's put all these ideas in your head?' he asked.

'It has nothing to do with Moshe.'

'Oh yes it does! He stuck his nose into our business. He's encouraging you to go off to Palestine alone, but he knows nothing about us and doesn't realise how fragile you are. He doesn't know you like I do.'

'You think you know me!'

'I know you sufficiently well to worry about the consequences of your naïve... if not childish... enthusiasm about wanting to leave. And where does this obsession with Father and me come from? It's true I found it hard to forgive him for ruining us and stealing from Mother. But what happened to us was not theatre. Your outburst is a balloon that you blew up too much and it exploded a long time ago. One day you can tell someone that you don't forgive them, and another day, you forgive them anyway. Someone who promises to never do such and such makes a commitment that he can very rarely keep.'

'You only think of yourself. If forgiveness were so simple, the Jews would not have invented Yom Kippur – or the *Kapparot* ritual! Remember?'

'Ah, the *Kapparot*!' he said, his mood suddenly lifting. 'It's a great pity we no longer do it.'

On the day of Yom Kippur, we would roll around laughing in the kitchen as we watched our parents waive a cock and a hen three times above their heads to transfer our sins onto those poor innocent creatures. Afterwards, it was for Leo and me to take them to the *shohet*, the ritual slaughterer, whose fetid cellar was a few minutes' walk from our house. When he had finished, we took them back home, drained of their blood, where Mother plucked and then cooked them for the great festive dinner that followed the endless day of fasting.

'Yes, it's a great pity,' I confirmed, thereby agreeing to the truce he was subtly proposing. 'But, I'm afraid that ever since we don't practice it, Heaven has stopped forgiving us our sins.'

He gave me an indulgent smile, then got up and continued: 'Are you aware of what you are asking me to do? To convince Father and Mother to give their consent to you leaving for Palestine on your own and wish you, with broken hearts, good luck and a safe journey?'

'Yes,' I replied, getting up to stand face to face with him.

'And if Mother is against, I'm sure Father will be against it as well. So, what to do then, Mister Emigrant?'

'Do all you can to convince them!'

'And if they are still against?'

'You double the blows – I mean, the efforts...'

On the following Saturday, while I accompanied Mother grocery shopping, Leo took the opportunity to approach our father and discuss my desire to go to Palestine.

Father was sitting in the kitchen reading the newspaper Universul and smoking a Carpati, his favourite cigarette. Leo put his hand on his shoulder and said to him softly: 'Taticu'le,[20] I have two delicate questions to ask you. May I sit down?'

Father turned his head to him, visibly surprised. What could it be about? He felt guilty of nothing. The home was quiet. He hadn't quarrelled with Leo or Mother for a long time. Whatever the nature of these delicate questions, to have an intimate conversation with Leo delighted him. It seemed an eternity since they had had a chance to talk like it is good to do between a father and his son. 'Yes, of course. Sit down. What's it about?' he asked. He put the newspaper on the table

20 Romanian term of affection for *tată*, father.

223

and looked at Leo with eyes, which, on certain days, were of an amazingly intense blue.

'Tată,' said Leo, 'you know my friend Dica, the one who has very rich parents?'

'I can't say I know him, but I've often heard you talk about him. I've seen him once, maybe twice. Why?' he asked in surprise.

Leo leaned over to Father and said in a low voice: 'He has caught terrible gonorrhoea. He needs to see a doctor but he doesn't dare turn to his father. Do you think you could recommend him to Doctor Lebensart and tell me how much it will cost?'

Father relaxed in his chair and smiled. 'Since when has he known about this? One day? Two?'

'No, no,' Leo hurriedly replied. 'Not two days. Yesterday, I think. It's yesterday that he felt it. It's not something serious, is it?'

'Serious? No, it's not serious, unless you neglect it.'

He got up and went to make a Turkish coffee. 'Do you want one? he asked. 'No thank you,' said Leo. When Father returned with his cup of coffee, he sat down, took a sip and addressed Leo, taking his time:

'And what is the other delicate question?'

Leo insisted: 'Do you have something against Doctor Lebensart?'

Father took a few more sips, then put down his cup, pushing it a little away. Annoyed and impatient, he added: 'Why the hell do you want to involve me in this business with your mate Dica? Do I not have enough problems without him?'

'Because when you caught it, you went to Doctor Lebensart, didn't you?' Leo challenged drily. He had never seen Father turn so red. In a hoarse voice Father replied: 'Who put that in your head?'

'I've known it for a long time. How I found out is not really important. When Bébé and I went to Fălticeni with Mother, you caught it from a prostitute and you ran to Lebensart to get treated. Hard as he is, and out of respect for Mother, because you did not have the courage to tell her yourself, he contacted her and told her to be careful. She's never forgiven you. Like she's never forgiven you for stealing her furs and jewels!'

Leo could read on Father's face the huge effort he was making to resist the urge to hit him. But Father managed to control himself and found the strength not to give in to the demons who delight in our misfortunes.

'You bandit! What do you want from me?' Father said in a wounded tone.

'Why "bandit"? Because I had the nerve to remind you of your thieving and your lying? Mother has had to put up with it, afraid it could be the end of our family. But have you thought about Bébé? Because the breakdown in our family, because of you, has left deep marks on him. Have you spoken to him about it? No! And you haven't spoken about it to me either!'

'So, you're Bébé's lawyer now?' my father asked sarcastically.

'Yes, I am his lawyer, if you like. When I returned from the farm, he confided in me – in me, not in you! – a thing that you and Mother must know urgently.'

'And what is this "thing"? If it's so urgent, why are you talking to me about Lebensart. Is it Bébé who's caught gonorrhoea?'

'No, Bébé has not caught gonorrhoea. He has caught the will to leave us. He has heard from Moshe, his sports instructor at the ken, that the government has just authorised emigration

225

to Palestine for children under sixteen and he wants to be on that list.'

'And so?' asked Father, astonished but not shocked.

'Well, the list will be closed in ten days' time and he needs your consent, signed by both of you. You must convince Mother to be separated from him, for who knows how long. You asked me what I want from you: you must let him leave, Tată. That's what I want from you.'

Father's face flushed with anger, and his fists hit the table, knocking over the coffee cup.

'You scoundrel! To ask me that, you had to break my heart? I sold the furs and jewellery I had given your mother because I had no other way out. I was ashamed, but in my rage against myself at having got involved in that terrible business with Sandu, I didn't have the courage to tell her openly that it was the only solution we had left to get out of our predicament.'

'Taticu'le...' Leo tried unsuccessfully to interrupt him.

'And as for the prostitutes, you know fine well that they've not stopped me loving your mother more than my own life. It's in a man's nature to do what I did. It's an animal need that every man feels. It'll happen to you as well, you little shit.'

Tears appeared in his blue eyes, making them shine more brightly. If my brother is to be believed, he too felt tears well up, he who thought himself so strong, so emotionally well prepared for the profession of surgeon.

'Forgive me, Tată,' he mumbled.

And Father ignored him.

'I'm not against him leaving if he sees his future elsewhere. At the first opportunity, we'll do the same. It's time for us to have our own country. I will speak to Mother. She'll also understand.'

'Forgive me, Tată,' Leo repeated, placing his hand on Father's. They looked at each other silently, after which Father replied: 'It is what it is.' And Leo had no answer.

On 29 November 1947, the General Assembly of the United Nations approved the plan to partition Palestine and to the creation of a Jewish State and an Arab State, the city of Jerusalem being placed under international jurisdiction. We had a family meeting and in tears, Mother acquiesced. Two weeks later, the movement announced the departure date: 26 December 1947. We spent the final days preparing my bags and consoling my mother. But her sorrow was inconsolable.

20

On the Way to Burgas

The secret location where the two big American ships awaited us was the port of Burgas, situated on a discreet peninsula on Bulgaria's south-east Black Sea coast. Originally, boarding was to have taken place in Constantza, the Romanian port where the ships had finished being prepared for the transportation of thousands of emigrants, but under pressure from Great Britain, the communist government had refused to allow embarkation in Romania. We therefore arrived in Burgas after more than sixteen exhausting hours spent in a Romanian train from Bucharest to the river port of Giurgiu, then on an old ferry across the Danube – at that time, there was no railway bridge between Romania and Bulgaria – and, finally, in a cattle train from the Bulgarian port of Ruse on the Danube, in freezing, stinking trucks carpeted with a thick layer of hay to allow us to at least sit down and try to sleep.

How did I, anxious as I was, get through those endless hours? By alternating between sleep and tortuous thoughts, up until the moment when a lad with thick, red, curly hair made his way through the boys and girls, some of whom were accompanied by their parents, to come and sit down next to me. I thought he had probably done so because the corner where I had had the luck to settle was near a window, even though dirty and barred. He introduced himself as Izi Pfister, I told him my name was Bernard, and we shook hands cordially. I learned that he too had not been accompanied to the station by what was left of his family – an uncle, an aunt and two female cousins, the only family survivors of persecution by the Antonescu regime. His parents had perished in the ghetto of Obodovca, in Transnistria, during the winter of 1942, and he owed his life to a brave peasant couple who had hidden him in their home at the risk of being shot by the gendarmes. He said that he would speak of it another time and I did not insist, but I asked him how he had got to Bucharest, and when he had joined our organisation, as I had never seen him take part in any of the *ken's* activities. He told me that with the help of the Joint and the Jewish Agency, he had been repatriated from a camp for displaced survivors where he had been transferred after the war, to return to Dorohoi, his home town. There, assisted by the local Jewish community, he had been able to trace his uncle, who had moved to Bucharest. One of his two cousins had put him in contact with a friend, Michel Hirschberg, from our *ken*. And it was Michel who had got him on the list, ensuring that, in Palestine, he could join our group.

Meanwhile, sleep had overcome everyone in the wagon except the two of us as the train sped across the wide and fertile plains of Bulgaria's north-east, the plains of the Danube, shrouded in the absolute blackness of a moonless night. Fatigue also began to settle on our lowered eyelids, and I suddenly found myself asking Izi whether he was afraid. He lifted his eyes slowly towards me and in the guttural, mellifluous and slightly husky tones of his regional Romanian, corrupted by Russian and Ukrainian, he replied tersely: 'Afraid of what?' 'Of the English...' I stammered. 'Do you think they'll force their way on board at sea and we'll be obliged to defend ourselves with our bare hands?' With an impassive look, and an even more guttural inflection, he replied: 'If the order is given to defend ourselves, we'll do it without fear. When you've gone through what I went through in Transnistria, you're no longer afraid of anything. But this time, unlike in the camps, we'll be able to choose to fight, and even die if needs be, but as free men!' I ventured with irony that I had not been planning to die so young. 'Don't you worry,' he went on, 'there will be a few thousand of us on each ship. They won't dare massacre us all.' I continued in the same vein: 'That's a huge relief that they won't kill all of us....' but, fearing that my irony might offend, I tried to redeem myself by offering him a fraternal pact. 'No joke. I would like us to be friends, and whatever happens, remain together,' I heard myself say. 'It's a deal,' he replied, cracking a smile. Then, he proposed we try to give sleep a chance. We closed our eyes and he seemed to fall asleep quickly, his back to the side of the carriage, just below the window. But I was sleepless, waiting impatiently for sunrise, wondering at what time the sun rose on the plains of Bulgaria in winter. This Slavic country, traditionally a friend of Russia, had been Germany's ally during the First World War and had joined the Axis in 1941, which seemed a good reason to distrust it. King Boris had not deported Bulgaria's fifty thousand Jews, but eleven thousand from the Thracian and Macedonian provinces lost in the 1914–18 war, were handed over to the Germans and died when the Bulgarian Army took back these territories in 1941. I said to myself that I had never seen a Bulgarian in my life except in Ruse, but that was incorrect, as, long before that, I had been to see a football match between Romania and Bulgaria. As soon as the Bulgarians thought they detected the whiff of defeat, they set about biting the legs of the Romanian players. This very 'unsporting' behaviour raised questions for me about the character of the Bulgarian players, if not of their entire nation...

The train had passed through the towns of Razgrad and Shumen and continued south-eastwards across hills and forests. Izi was in a deep sleep. Because of him, I now saw myself differently: I was no longer the 'hero' I had imagined I was: had I not offered my friendship to this strong and determined boy, who I had liked right from the outset, solely because this journey terrified me? By asking him if the English frightened him, I was signalling, in a roundabout way, that it was they I feared when, in truth, my problem was Cyprus. In the light of my experience during the *Shomria*, and my brother's on the farm in Iaşi, the misery and promiscuity which were rumoured to reign in the internment camps, as well as the idea of finding myself in forced intimacy with strangers, even Jews like me, exacerbated my anxieties. However, I was neither spoiled, nor snobbish, nor pretentious. I had seen the face of hunger and poverty, felt the full humiliation of frequenting a charity canteen five days a week and eating my meals out of a tin bowl. But I had experienced most of my suffering as part of a family, under my mother's eyes. And although her tears had often made me furious, as soon as the smile returned to her lips and

231

I read in her eyes the overwhelming love she had for me, my worries vanished. However, during the *Shomria*, far from my own kin, and especially my mother, only Moshe the sports *madrich* had provided me with some support. I doubt I could have won the ambitious wager of bringing back medals to my Bucharest *ken* without him. It was surely a beautiful outcome, but dearly won. Days before the sports competitions began, I had remained apart from my group and the rest of the participants and, despite my success, I had ended up in the eyes of the *madrichims* as an odd and puzzling boy.

Why did I remain isolated from the others? Did they intimidate me that much? The girls undoubtedly, as I was not sufficiently sure of myself in front of them. But the boys hardly intimidated me. I overestimated myself in relation to them. I fled them because I resented them. I begrudged them their banal, vulgar normality. They were too comfortable together. As a group, they adapted better than me to changing living conditions. Even though I desired change, I was ill at ease when it happened.

From this point of view, the *Shomria* was, in the story of my adolescence, as much a failure as a success, although clearly the failure had had its use. It had taught me to know myself better, without which I would not have sought remedies for my weaknesses. In an unusual, if not hostile, environment, where one has constantly to face up to new challenges, isolating oneself and withdrawing into a shell is a guarantee for failure.

A terrible cold came from the window where I was sitting next to Izi. He was still asleep, his head had slipped towards the corner of the carriage, finding refuge in the angle where the two sides met. I got up to take a look outside. In the breaking Bulgarian dawn, the train sped past villages covered in a thick layer of snow, turned grey by the grimy windowpane. The long silhouettes of bare trees and the obscure contours of peasant houses and deserted stations raced before my eyes and slipped away again as quickly as they had appeared. I left the window to return to my place on the straw next to Izi. I thought of looking for something in my bag to cover him with to protect him from the cold, but I was afraid to wake him.

Images of my parents and of my childhood began to whirl in my mind. Fanny, the pharmacist cousin, had reminded me one day that I had had very few toys as a child, but the one I liked the most was the little wooden boat with its miniature steering wheel that Uncle Max had given me as a birthday present. We both shared a longing to travel, though he had interrupted his great journey to America to return to his family, that he had nevertheless run away from. I made my first journeys in this little boat, where I was both captain and passenger at the same time, imitating the roar of the engines, with deafening 'brrrbrrrbrrrs', before announcing to my imaginary passengers: THE MOTOR BOAT IS LEAVING!

The train was hurrying towards its destination. I tried to sleep, besieged by guilty thoughts that I could not chase from my mind. A great anxiety had filled me immediately after we left the train station, before I had met Izi, as the train took me away, perhaps forever, from Bucharest, from my family and from my roots. My heart had started beating feverishly, waves of heat rose from my chest, drenching my entire body in sweat. I had taken off my heavy pullover and stuck my forehead against the cold windowpane. As my discomfort subsided and I calmed down, I remembered the day when Moshe had informed me that I had a real chance of emigrating to Palestine and I had walked all the way back home with my head in the clouds.

233

Crossing the seas, working the fields in a kibbutz – the great adventure I had dreamed of! I rejoiced at the thought that for the first time I would be ahead of Leo, although he had warned me of my fragility and the danger of taking my dreams for reality, I had not wanted to believe him until the day of departure, the hour when the train left the station. At that precise moment, I paid the price for having broken my mother's heart, that price that I feared so much and of which I had not taken full measure. Cheating myself, I had asked my family that no one see me off at the station. I had told them: 'I don't want to see your tears, your saddened faces, your downcast looks, and I don't want to hear your tearful voices pursuing me throughout the journey. That will drain me of the courage to keep going. Do you not remember Uncle Max, and what happened to his dream of settling in America? I don't want to fail like him.' They said nothing, and so our tears had dampened the floor of the family home instead of disappearing on a bustling platform at the Gara de Nord.

I had been to this station before the war when we had gone to visit Auntie Brana and Aunt Golda and, another time, to leave for the *Shomria*. I had been dazzled by its majestic six columned façade, its long platforms, and especially its great hall, with the beautiful and luminous steel-framed glass roof supported by dozens of iron pillars. But on the night of my departure, this Bucharest cathedral ('cathedrals of modern times' was the name given to the stations built at the end of the 19th century), which had miraculously survived the American bombings in 1944, looked more like a synagogue, although, for a synagogue, it appeared overcrowded and incredibly noisy. Its various halls had been invaded by a hectic mass of people, hurrying toward the platform from which my train was preparing to leave for its secret destination. And, apart from the mechanics, conductors and station personnel, this mass of people was eminently Jewish: believers and atheists, rich and poor – a crowd of all ages and all types, colourful and inclusive, excitedly chatting, with a variety of comical gesticulations, in Romanian, Hungarian and Yiddish. The youngest, in their hundreds, were clinging in clusters to the carriage steps, and I suspected that some of them had even climbed onto the roofs. People shouted, cried, laughed, jostled, hugged, waved handkerchiefs and flags, elbowed their way through. Old people fainted, children stood on tiptoe to see better, and organised groups, belonging to all the various Zionist youth movements, sang patriotic marching songs to their hearts' content, in a language, Hebrew, which they did not even understand.

Through the carriage window, my eyes did not stop searching and hoping. I observed this seething crowd, thinking that its vitality embodied the incomparable cohesion of the Jewish family, the core from which all the eternal energy of Judaism springs. But, behind this thought, I dwelt, disappointed and bitter, as if possessed, on the regret of not seeing my own family in this multitude. I consoled myself with the idea that my mother would not have stood being in this crowd and that my father would not have come without her. He would never have left her all alone in the house in her distress. But where was my brother? He had accompanied me from the house to the *ken*, helping me to carry my little suitcase and my bag with the few things I was taking with me. When we arrived there, he put them down, hugged me and said bluntly: 'You must be strong, little brother.' He had then turned on his heels and didn't even look back once. No doubt he had thought that by embracing me in this way he had done his duty of expressing tenderness without soppy sentimentality. Coming from him, this behaviour had hardly surprised me, as I was used to it. And had I not consented myself to stifling all the usual emotion by asking my parents and him not to see me off on the train? Except that, out of brotherly love, he could have ignored my manly request and come all the same to find me at the last minute and before the train set off, inexorably taking me away from him, I would have insisted that we write regularly so as not to be so brutally torn from each other.

But my brother had not come. Had he gone straight home, or had he chosen to go and see his girlfriend, Erna? In either case, I doubt he had suffered from our parting as much as I had. In his girlfriend's arms, he would no doubt quickly forget his younger brother, 'the idealist'. But in the days, weeks and months to come, in whose arms was I going to find the equivalent of the tenderness and love with which my mother had so fully nourished me? Faced with such a mass of people on the platform and the strange diversity of faces around me in the carriage, I realised how alone I was. I knew no one, and no one knew me. I remembered the image of a woman aged about forty, God knows where she had suddenly appeared from, pushing me from my seat as she held up a small girl, and both had begun to shout and blow kisses from the window. I had reclaimed the right to my seat by pushing her in turn when, staring at me, she said in a heavy Moldavian accent: 'But you're all alone, my boy.... Where's your family?' I had hesitated for an instant, but the need to share my pain was too strong to resist: 'I told my parents not to accompany me to the station...'

'How could you have asked them such a thing? Maybe they have come, but they haven't found you...'

Troubled by the recollection of this encounter, I too finally fell asleep next to Izi. And it is very possible that he was the one who woke me up as the train approached the suburbs of Burgas. It was broad daylight and through the windows could be seen the lakes surrounding the city. Everyone was standing in the carriage. Some members of the Haganah,[21] or of the Palmach[22] – young Sabras, handsome and strong, dressed in dark green uniforms – came to supervise us getting off the train and organise the last stage of this part of the journey: transporting us by lorry from the station to the port and, from there, assisting us in boarding the ships.

21 The Haganah (literally 'defence'): Zionist paramilitary organisation created in 1929 and integrated into Tsahal in 1948.
22 The Palmach: (Hebrew abbreviation for Plugot Mahatz, strike force) was the elite unit of the Haganah before the independence of the State of Israel.

237

21

Crossing the Seas

I had come down from the main deck to regain my place two floors below in the hold. I had gone up in the hope of finding Izi, from whom I had been separated at Burgas in the chaos of boarding, when the men from the Haganah, the Palmach, the Mossad Le'aliyah Bet[23] and various Zionist movements had regrouped us according to our emigration card, with its multiple forgery-proof signatures, which we held in our trembling hands. Even if Izi had been on the deck, as I had hoped, it would have been impossible to find him. A human tide spread from the prow to the stern, around the cargo winches and the masts, between the big exhaust stacks, but also on the lifeboat deck and even on the ladder leading to the bridge. I had no chance of

23 The Mossad Le'aliyah Bet: Hebrew for 'The Institution for Immigration "B"' – secret code for the Jews' clandestine immigration to Mandatory Palestine. Mossad was a branch of the Haganah.

making my way through this deafening anthill of men, women and children, who had come there to escape from the subterranean smells of the hold and breathe the fresh sea air. I was distressed at having been separated from Izi. If destiny were to take us first to Cyprus, the idea of finding myself alone and not having the support of his camaraderie niggled at the back of my mind.

Two ships, the *Pan York* and the *Pan Crescent*, awaited us at [x] Burgas, but due to the circumstances, it turned out that Izi had boarded the *Pan York* and me the *Pan Crescent*. Built in the United States in 1901 for the transportation of bananas, they were bought in 1947 from a fruit company by the Mossad, in the name of an American citizen. In Bucharest, Moshe had assured me that they were not old tubs like the *Struma* or the *Exodus*, but two solid and stable cargo ships, each with a capacity of five thousand tons, and measuring one hundred and ten metres long and nineteen wide: they were the biggest ships in the history of illegal emigration to Palestine! Oh, how I regretted Izi was not with me to share this unique moment.

Before going up onto the main deck, I had tried several times to find him by going through the four decks built in the hold. But how could I be sure I had not missed him amidst all these people packed like sardines on the wooden platforms that served as dormitories? On each floor, more than one thousand eight hundred people were crammed, with only a forty-two centimetres allowance for each person. As much space for the fat as for the thin... In the end, there were seven thousand five hundred of us on each ship, well more than planned. Right up until the last days, the Jewish Agency and Mossad had added new names to the list, with the result that many emigrants had to sleep outside on the decks.

239

My ship, the *Pan Crescent*, was the first to bid Burgas farewell; it lifted anchor at about half past ten on the morning of 27 December 1947. As it left the quayside, a multitude of blue and white flags, bearing the Star of David, had been raised, fluttering in a rather gentle wind for late December. The song *Hatikva* ('The Hope'), destined to become the national anthem of the future Jewish State, had sprung from a crowd burning with pride and hope. A little later, it was the turn of the *Pan York* to leave port, and Izi had no doubt joined the crowd on his ship to take part in this moment of exaltation.

Oh, my beautiful dream of crossing the seas! But other than a lungful of bracing air, being on the deck had provided little benefit: the unyielding mass of people had prevented my eagerly-awaited encounter with the secretive, so called 'Black Sea' – though the 'Hostile Sea' might have been more appropriate given its tempestuous nature, characterised by unpredictable and violent storms. I had been unable to admire the splendour of its immensity, or its harmonious fusion with the blue sky on the horizon. The crisp air had, however, alleviated my distress.

The way to my row, on the second floor, was close to a clinic, which helped me find my place more easily. There were two clinics in the hold, as well as a hospital with eighty beds, an operating theatre, kitchens, toilets, water distribution centres and giant air vents. And yet, the air was terribly stale. A journalist had written that he wondered if the smells of latrines, cooking, sardines and sweat had not penetrated into the passengers' skins as it had the wood and metal of the ships. Nonetheless, one could still breathe and we were all reassured by the knowledge that there were twenty-four doctors and forty-eight nurses on board.

My place was situated between that of a young man aged about twenty, who had the advantage of being at the beginning of the row, and that of a couple in their forties. Beyond this couple, I could see only a mass of blurred faces of men, women, girls and boys huddled together in an opaque light. Some ate, others smoked, argued, slept, played cards, or tried to read old newspapers from an already bygone age. The youngest children – there were more than five hundred of them – stayed with their parents on the first floor, below the main deck. That was fortunate for me, as I would not have been able to stand either their wailing, nor the ridiculous grimaces and the baby babble that parents do to entertain them.

My neighbour had big piercing eyes, fine black hair, a prominent nose and round, well-fed cheeks. In the heat of the confined space, he pulled off his shirt and I caught the smell of his sweat and noticed the strength of his upper body and of his brown muscular arms. As soon as I had settled myself, he shot me furtive looks, as though he wanted to start a conversation. The ship had begun to roll, as the humming of the machines grew louder, and a thin cloud of smoke seeped into the dormitory. The pitching inconvenienced the woman of the couple to my right, who complained of feeling sick. Finally, the young man addressed me: 'Where do you come from, where are you going and why are you alone, my friend? My name is Yakov, what is yours?'

'Bernard,' I promptly replied, ignoring his outstretched hand. 'I come from Bucharest, with the Aliyat Hanoar.[24] My parents and my brother have stayed back there.'

24 Aliyat Hanoar (Youth Immigration): organsation created in 1933 in Germany to allow persecuted young Jews to emigrate to Palestine. Later, as a department for the Jewish Agency, it played an important role in the immigration and assimilation of young Jews in Israel.

'With the Aliyat Hanoar, I see, but to go where?'

'To a kibbutz.'

'To which kibbutz?'

'The one the movement chooses.'

'And what movement do you belong to?'

'The Hasomer Hatzair. And you?'

'Gordonia, my friend... But tell me, why did you join a movement that wants to combine Zionism with Marxism-Leninism, knowing that the two hate each other? Would it not be best to trust in the ideology of Ben Gurion and simply be a Zionist and social democrat? It's Ben Gurion who will give us the State, my friend!'

Why, I asked myself, did he repeat 'my friend' every time he spoke, if not to irritate me?

'Social democracy,' I riposted, 'wants to reform capitalism instead of burying it. Do you think we can put an end to social injustice by asking the exploiting class to offer trifles to the exploited one? Only a socialist revolution will put an end to the exploitation of man by man. And as far as I know, it's thanks to Theodor Herzl and the Zionist movement, the Aliyah and the kibbutzim that we will obtain a Jewish State. This State must be socialist and binational, and that's the reason why I joined the Hashomer Hatzair!'

'Fanaticism aside, what you're saying is not totally stupid, Bernard. The problem is that the binational State that sounds so nice to the ears is pure utopia, my friend. What we need is a Jewish State full stop, and without Ben Gurion, I don't know how we'll have it. I too am for a socialist State. But on condition that it is democratic. The beautiful socialist revolution you're talking about, well you can see what happened in the USSR. The tsar's tyranny has been replaced by the dictatorship of the proletariat, the pivotal concept of Marxism-Leninism. Individual freedoms have been suppressed and all power is in the hands of a single party, and even worse, a single man: Stalin! But anyway, whether you agree with me or not, I have another question to ask you: why did you leave your family so young to go to a kibbutz?'

Surprised by his argument as much as by his question, I quickly came out with something in which childlike enthusiasm served to disguise my confusion: 'Because I'm an idealist... Or a utopian, as you say.... I don't want to be a merchant or an accountant like my parents would like me to be. I want to build my country!'

He looked at me for a long time, and suddenly, without me being able to stop him, he grabbed my frail wrist and said: 'With hands like this, you want to build your country?' Humiliated, I tore my wrist from his grip and, without replying, I turned towards the neighbours on my right. He quickly added: 'Forgive me, my friend, I did not intend to hurt you.' And after a moment, as I had not replied, he asked: 'Do you play chess? I've got a small chessboard with me.'

I took my time and finally answered: 'Yes, I like playing chess.'

And that is how this initial contact, that started rather badly, turned into a close relationship for the rest of the journey.

We spent a few hours that day playing chess and he won every game, generously explaining to me after each defeat where and when I had made my mistakes. Between games, he told me that his kibbutz, Hulda, south of Tel Aviv, belonged to a group of kibbutzim politically affiliated to Mapai, the party of David Ben Gurion. His parents lived in Rehovot, not far from his kibbutz. He had been sent to Romania as an instructor for the youth movement Gordonia, and he was going home. In his kibbutz, he worked as a tractor driver, but dreamed of teaching mathematics to the children, as he had been born with a gift for this science whose object and methods had always seemed to me difficult to define. When he confessed his ambition to me, I chuckled to myself: good luck to the children of kibbutz Hulda!

On the morning of Sunday 28 December, my second day at sea, it was announced that we were approaching the mouth of the Bosphorus. Yakov, who had taken me under his protective wing after wounding my pride by making fun of my fragile arms, took me up onto the deck as a sign of friendship. We stopped right next to the bridge to savour the view. The Asian coast of the north of Turkey could be made out through a veil of light mist – fishing villages, orchards with leafless trees and, in the background, snow-covered mountains. Suddenly, Yakov surprised me by recalling the *Struma*: 'One of those villages,' he mumbled, 'must be Sile, whose fishermen saved the life of David Stoliar, the sole survivor of the explosion that sank the *Struma*. Do you know the story?'

'Yes,' I said bitterly.

To dispel my bitterness, he asked: 'Do you know? Our captain is Ike Aronovitch, the hero of the *Exodus*. I've met him several times. I've contacts with a few members of the Palmach and the crew,' he proudly added, and taking me by the arm, he led me to a small upper deck near the bridge. From there we could observe, thanks to the binoculars he kept on him, the mouth of the strait separating the Asian part of Turkey from its European shore. Ships were going in and coming out continually, like giant, tireless ants. I felt my heart leap. The great adventure I was living through helped dull my homesickness and in the absence of Izi, I had only Yakov with whom to share my deep emotion.

'How old are you, Yakov?' I asked.

'Twenty-five and a few crumbs,' he replied, smiling candidly.

'I think you're incredibly smart, Yakov! You know lots of things... What should I expect when dealing with the Turks in the Bosphorus?'

'We'll soon go through the health check,' he replied. 'On the way from Palestine, the check was done at the entrance to the straits of Dardanelles. I was on a big tourist ship, and everything went quickly. With us, it will be different, my friend. It's not so simple to ensure good health conditions on an old cargo ship with more than seven thousand emigrants in the hold! If the Turks get it into their heads to find health problems with us, they're going to find them, that's for sure... Except that, fortunately, in Turkey, baksheesh is king. With a few gold coins, pens, lighters and watches, everything can be sorted.'

'I hate the Turks, Yakov. You too?'

'Let's see if they let us pass without a problem, my boy, then I'll tell you if I hate them or not!'

He had suddenly replaced 'my friend' with 'my boy'. That suited me better. I was beginning to have a lot of sympathy for him. His good humour made me relax and I liked his big black eyes shining with intelligence and vivacity. It was a great pity that he suffered from a strange nervous tic: every now and then, he would wriggle his nose and sniff twice.

'Look,' he suddenly said. 'We no longer need binoculars. We're right near to the Bosphorus.'

I looked, and we were not the only ones to scrutinise the coast. The main deck had filled up with a swarming and excited crowd. Hundreds of men, women and children. Right next to the steps leading to the bridge, a voice in the crowd asked a Mossad member what the ship's maximum speed was. 'It doesn't go above twelve knots,' he replied. 'How can you explain then that we've taken twenty-four hours to get to the Bosphorus, instead of seven or eight?' the voice insisted. 'That's a good question to ask the higher authorities, but they can't be reached for the moment,' the man retorted, and the crowd burst out laughing. The voice persisted: 'Would it be to confuse the British by hiding our intentions with irrational manoeuvres?' Evasively and curtly, the man from Mossad replied: 'It's quite a plausible hypothesis, that's all I can say.' He smiled, satisfied, and the crowd relaxed. I turned to Yakov and asked him how much time it had taken to go from the mouth of the Bosphorus to Constantza on his way from Palestine. He said: 'It's not the same thing, the distance neither, for Constantza is further away than Burgas. I don't remember exactly how much time it took us. Surely not as much as twenty-four hours.'

It was clear that he knew more than he wanted to say. His reply, just like that offered to the crowd by the man from Mossad, had seemed to me too vague, if not dishonest. My incredulity did not disturb him. As the weather was mild and the sea was calm, he changed subject and in a didactic tone, which reminded me of my peculiar teacher Weintraub, informed me that the Black Sea stays calm for one hundred and twenty days per year and that we were lucky this was the case today.

Also changing subject, I took the risk of asking him why, with all his contacts, he had not tried to get a better place instead of sleeping on the 'sardine platform' like us. 'Oh no!' he said indignantly. 'I could have, but that wouldn't have been

246

me... I wanted to share this experience in the same conditions as everyone else.'

At midday, the ship slowed down and manoeuvred to allow a Turkish pilot to come on board. A little later, with the tug in front, our ship crossed the mouth of the Bosphorus, followed by the *Pan York*.

The sky was cloudy, but it was not raining. Up above, where Yakov and I were standing, a north wind lashed our faces and made the boat pitch as it confronted powerful marine currents. The sight took my breath away. The deep blue waters of the strait snaked along the European coast of Turkey to the right and the Asian one to the left, although the gap between the two was so narrow that here and there they seemed to meet.

We passed between two lighthouses erected on the rocky soil of two fishing villages situated on opposite sides of the strait. Yakov knew their names: Anadolu Feneri and Rumeli Feneri. The first, he told me, had been built in the 18th century by the Turks at fifty metres above sea level. The other was the work of the French, not long before the Crimean War. The view was spectacular, but I was cold and hungry. I told Yakov I wanted to go back 'home' and we separated.

We did not eat badly on the ship. Many of our meals came from America: tons of vegetables, meat, flour, rice, and enough tins for a fortnight! What's more, we received generous rations of biscuits, salted or sweet, and a whole variety of jams. And not to forget the chocolate, the delicious chocolate, which was also American! As it melted in my mouth, I thought of the pilots of the flying fortresses shot down during the war in the Romanian sky. Still wearing their airmen's jackets, made of leather with a fur collar, they ate chocolate while smiling to us from the windows of the buildings the authorities had hastily requisitioned to house them. Whilst the American pilots were treated with great regard in Bucharest, I had witnessed Soviet prisoners trudging through the snow, barefoot and chained together like slaves...

I had my hot meal, potato soup and meat, then returned to my place in the dormitory. I looked at my watch: one o'clock in the afternoon. With a full belly, fatigue numbed me. I closed my eyes, while my body stretched out, borrowing some of the space Yakov had freed up by his absence.

An hour later, Yakov came to take me back on deck. While climbing the stairs to regain the fresh air, he confided to me that he had important news concerning the next part of our journey.

'Our ships, my skinny friend, will not go directly to Palestine. We will not repeat the tragedy of the Exodus. The Yishuv has agreed a compromise with the British authorities!' he announced triumphantly.

'Tell me! Tell me!' I shouted in excitement.

22

New Year with His Majesty's Fleet

Suddenly, whistles and brief siren calls disturbed our conversation; three Turkish inspectors boarded, two wearing red fezzes, the third holding an officer's cap under his arm. A sailor from our crew accompanied them and they quickly made their way to the bridge. Yakov let out a great sigh and told me: 'From now on, our fate is in the hands of those fezzes and that cap.' I encouraged him to continue with his interrupted story. He replied that the result of the health inspection could completely change the equation, for if it turned out to be negative, we would be forced to return to Burgas: This was a possibility that I refused to accept. I told him I was too young to be inclined to pessimism: my dream of going to Palestine was finally being fulfilled and there was no question of me returning to Burgas! My destiny was to go forwards, not backwards! He looked at me in amazement and was seized by that nervous tic with his nose. Visibly, on the list of factors likely to set it off, hearing me come out with such nonsense was right at the top. As soon as the tic passed, he kindly patted me on the shoulder and said that he was not inclined towards pessimism either, but he doubted our temperament would have any effect on the Turks' decision. 'What they decide to do will depend on their temperament, not ours,' he concluded. Then he returned to his story at the moment when the Turks had interrupted it.

According to his 'secret source', a member of the Haganah who he had met in Palestine during a meeting of his movement, the British were panicking. The cargo of our two ships represented a quarter of the immigrants to arrive in Palestine since the end of the war. They had to act quickly to stop these ships, but they could not and did not want to repeat the grave errors made with the storming of the Exodus: to open fire again on concentration camp survivors and risk killing women and children in a confrontation with thousands of emigrants. As a last recourse, they had prompted the intervention of the Americans, managing to convince them that most of the emigrants were members of the communist party and that their settlement in Palestine would be a Trojan horse for replacing the United States with the USSR as the dominant power in the Middle East. Although the information was totally erroneous, George Marshall, the Secretary of State for the United States, warned the leaders of the Yishuv and the Jewish Agency that the ships' departure could compromise his government's support for the creation of a Jewish State in Palestine. Thus, under the pressure of the American warning and especially under the influence of Ben Gurion, but also of Moshe Shertok, the Yishuv representative at the United Nations, a decision was taken to postpone the ships' departure scheduled for 14 December 1947. This set off direct conflict between Ben Gurion and Mossad, for Mossad was firmly in favour of the ships setting sail on the planned date. Ben Gurion accused Shaul Meirov, the Mossad chief, of ignoring the fact that such a provocation of the United States risked compromising the creation of the State. Pausing here, Yakov laughed loudly and said: 'You must understand that to rebel against the political branch of the Yishuv is not in Shaul Meirov's nature! And moreover, Moshe Shertok, who is Ben Gurion's right-hand man, is his brother-in-law! Believe me, I would not want to be in his place!'

I had absorbed this fascinating story as if each word was a precious sip from an exquisite drink, but I could not resist the temptation to ask Yakov what he now thought of his idol, Ben Gurion. Serenely, he retorted: 'The same as before, my boy! It's quite normal that the men from Mossad, who have made superhuman efforts to enable fifteen thousand Jews to leave Romania, do not agree to give up just at the moment when their plan is about to become reality. What's more, they had responsibility for the fate of thousands of emigrants waiting in Constantza or Burgas like you, my friend, and even worse, like those who had to sell all their possessions and who have definitively lost their homes. But we mustn't ignore Ben Gurion's point of view either. He is carrying on his shoulders the responsibility for something much more important than the consequences of a temporary interruption to emigration: the creation of the Jewish State. And then, when at the end of their mandate the English withdraw from Palestine, a war with the Arabs is inevitable. It's not my personal theory: all the Yishuv knows it and is preparing for it. It was therefore not the moment, from Ben Gurion and Moshe Shertok's point of view, to upset America, whose support for us is as vital to us today as it will be tomorrow.'

As Yakov paused, I intervened to torture him with another fine question: 'You tell me that Ben Gurion and Moshe Shertok forced the leaders of Mossad to prevent the ships from leaving. So how is it we're here in the Bosphorus and not sitting on our bundles in Burgas?'

The triumphant inflexion in my voice amused him.

'You've got some nerve, my little Bernard!' he said affectionately. 'In fact, all that's very complicated... Here's what I've learned: the decision to freeze the ships' departure astounded Moshe Averbuch, the Mossad envoy to Romania, and his colleagues in Europe. They all belong to an elite – mainly of kibbutzniks– young men used to winning through action on the ground. They are distrustful of politicians and diplomats who believe in the art of negotiation and compromise. Averbuch alerted Shaul Meirov to the risk that the Romanian and Bulgarian communist regimes might decide to close the borders, thus condemning thousands of emigrants to confront the freezing winter sitting on their luggage. He had apparently received an ultimatum from his 'contact' in Romania, demanding that the ships leave Constantza within a week, otherwise, emigration to Palestine would be forbidden.'

'And who's this "contact"? Do you have an idea?' I asked.

'He's the head of the secret services and deputy Prime Minister. His name is of no importance to you,' he said in a mischievous tone.

I quipped back with an ounce of irony: 'I am familiar with the names of the leaders of the communist party in Romania; the contact could only be Emil Bodnaras, the Romanian minister solely responsible for the army, religions and the Securitate.'

Yakov swallowed my pill while groaning between his teeth: 'Bravo... Shall we continue?'

'Of course,' I replied with a smile.

'Well then,' he resumed, 'having received no reply to his telegram concerning the Romanian ultimatum, Averbuch informed Meirov that he had ordered the ships to leave Constantza on 21 December at the latest and to board the emigrants at Burgas. He felt that Shaul Meirov had lost control of the situation, that he was reduced to being just the powerless witness of a collision between two fundamentally opposed generations: on the one side, the men of Mossad – ambitious, intrepid and committed to their mission, which is noble but partial in nature – and, on the other, the leaders of the Yishuv: politicians in the prime of life, responsible for the bigger picture, in other words, the nascent State.'

'That points again to Ben Gurion,' I remarked, scratching my head.

'Yes, my dear Bernard, because for him, the departure of the two ships is less important than the State!'

Suddenly, the *Pan Crescent* sounded its siren twice, to which the *Pan York* responded from afar.

'It's taking them some time to decide if we conform to the health rules,' Yakov said with a sombre face. 'That could be as much a good sign as a very bad one.'

'I think it's a good sign!'

'May God hear you! But... I don't believe in God'. And he added, mockingly: 'Besides, it seems to me that you don't frequent synagogues either, zealous adept of Marxism-Leninism that you are.'

'There you're mistaken. I don't go to the synagogue, but I'm a believer... Don't laugh. I do it my own way.... It's an intimate, mystical feeling that I have had since I was little. I know what you're thinking... Marxism doesn't like mysticism... It's an obvious contradiction, that's true. The same perhaps as courage and fear, those twins who quarrel then finally make up in all of us.'

He gave me an affectionate look mixed with something I could not decipher. It was at that moment that the Turkish controllers, escorted by half a dozen men from Mossad, reappeared on deck, filled with exuberance. The precious gifts, the feast and the alcohol had made them ecstatic. Our men did not seem less happy, for the *Pans* had clearly passed their exam, being decreed, no doubt thanks to the baksheesh, as conforming perfectly to health regulations.

As soon as the Turks were back on their boat and had disappeared from view, the *Pan Crescent* started up its engines and, followed by the *Pan York*, gradually regained its cruising speed. Holding his binoculars, Yakov explained to me that we were approaching the exit to the Bosphorus and the entrance to a wide and spectacular fork, with the Golden Horn to our right, and the Sea of Marmara in front of us. Shortly afterwards, although it was beginning to get dark, we could make out the impressive silhouette of the famous Blue Mosque with its six minarets, as well as the monumental basilica of Saint-Sophia, built by the Emperor Justinian. Neither of them made my heart race. My interest in the architectural pearls the Turks had accumulated in the course of their glorious history was as low as it could be. I reminded Yakov that he had to finish the story about the man from Mossad. That interested me much more than the churches and mosques of Istanbul. He told me he was tired and famished, and preferred to continue later. According to him, it was better to return to our platform, get a bite to eat, play two or three games of chess – he assured me that, in principle, I always had a chance of winning one – then go to sleep and rest before the great unknown of the following day. I agreed to follow him and we made our way back down into the hold.

After the meal, we played chess: he won three games without my firing a single dangerous shot at him. My constant losing depressed me. The fact is that, theoretically, I was not playing the middlegame that badly. Yakov would surprise me with unusual openings, which obliged me, still at the development stage of the game, to place my pieces on the wrong squares. Thus, he mercilessly captured a pawn or two right from the start. Against a better player, and he was one, this disadvantage condemned me to lose. I detested him when he won in this way and when he tried to console me, I hated him. We turned in late and I hoped that sleep would bring me some solace.

I was dozing peacefully in my forty-centimetre space when I heard Yakov get up. Half opening my eyes, I glimpsed his silhouette disappearing behind the clinic, in the direction of the stairs. Where was he going? Everyone has secrets. He had his and I had mine. What was his that night: a romantic encounter with a young nurse, or with one of those Bulgarian girls I had noticed on the main deck, the day we left Burgas? There, I gave him no chance, for those girls, about ten of them, were part of a group that included twenty boys and two *madrichim* belonging to the same movement as me, the Hashomer Hatzair. I had jealously observed this group: it was close-knit, inseparable and they kept themselves apart. How had these Bulgarians managed not to be dispersed, to remain together joyful and sure of themselves, while I was all alone, confused and full of self-doubt, entirely dependent on Yakov in the absence of my *kvutza* and my *madrichim*? One of the girls was called Thea and she played the accordion marvellously. She looked about sixteen or seventeen. I could not take my eyes off her when I saw her. She had a slender build and short, black, smooth hair that reminded me of Pouia, big brown eyes, prettily arched eyebrows, and a radiant smile that revealed gleaming white teeth.

And as for me, what secret was I hiding? Did I leave Romania for Palestine through idealism, through rejection of anti-Semitism, or to run away from the conflicts in my family? Neither of these propositions satisfied me. Was it not more reasonable to think that the drive to go to Palestine came simply from the appeal of a great romantic adventure, from the desire to escape everyday life? I could not wait to cross the seas on a ship, asking myself if I didn't grasp the opportunity when it presented itself, when would I? As for my fervour at joining a kibbutz, did it not mask the attraction of the unknown, of the unforeseen in any new thing? But since the *Shomria* I knew that I was not made for communal life, so why choose this path? Moreover, how could I explain my enthusiasm for Marxism-Leninism?

Around me, on the platform, everyone had gone to sleep. The couple next to me breathed heavily under a woollen blanket pulled up to their noses. The noise of the engines could be heard only faintly. The Sea of Marmara was particularly calm that night, and the ship moved smoothly.

A thousand thoughts collided in my head. Where did my revolutionary spirit come from? From the time when we did not have enough money to eat? From the period when my father did not have enough to pay for the electricity and when we were afraid of spending the nights in the faint light of gas lamps? From the humiliating situation where my brother and I were forced to find sustenance in a canteen with other poor schoolboys, and eat out of mess tins rather than plates? Certainly, a bit of all of that, but the driving force had surely been the anti-Semitism gripping Romania and the Shoah in Europe.

I remembered what Michel Hirschberg, the intellectual of our movement in Bucharest, said during one of his lectures to the ken: capitalism had not eradicated anti-Semitism, even in the most developed countries of western Europe, be they constitutional monarchies or republican democracies. It was only in the socialist countries that anti-Semitism and any other form of racial discrimination were outlawed. That did not mean, Michel had stressed, that hatred of the Jew, motivated by age-old prejudices, religious or of other nature, disappeared as soon as socialism was established. That justified my fears for the future, when Cultura would cease to exist as a Jewish high school and, later, when at the university I would find myself in an environment subject to the anti-Semitic reminiscences of the old regime. It was one of the arguments I had used to convince Leo to support my decision to leave for Palestine. As Michel had demonstrated well, a Christian-born Romanian, even if he became socialist and atheist by conviction, would always remain marked by the prejudices he had been steeped in since childhood, the first one being the accusation that the Jews were responsible for Christ's crucifixion. In the regimes of Popular Democracies installed by Stalin, Romania being one of them, socialism had rapidly and radically changed the condition of the Jews. Not only had they won equal rights, they had reached the highest echelons of the hierarchy of the communist party and the government. However, it could not be said that socialism offered a real solution to the Jewish problem.

I questioned Michel Hirschberg on this subject and raised Soviet anti-Semitism and Stalin's decision, in 1929, to create a Jewish autonomous province in Birobidzhan, an arid region on the eastern edge of Siberia, six thousand kilometres from Moscow. I added that by offering the Jews of the USSR a national territory, Stalin contradicted his own theory that the Jews were not a nation. Michel had replied that Stalin was offering them a territory where they could express themselves in a common language, Yiddish, not as a Jewish nation, but as a 'Soviet nationality'. Birobidzhan was to be the alternative to Zionism, defined by Stalin as 'bourgeois nationalism' and by Trotsky as a 'reactionary utopia'. In a hurry to put an end to our dialogue, Michel had concluded that at the time when he was speaking, the Jewish autonomous district resembled a grotesque and sad caricature of a plan that was ambitious but suspect and futile from the start. Birobidzhan could not be the alternative to Zionism. However, I put one last question to him: the General Assembly of the United Nations in New York had adopted the decision to establish a Jewish national homeland in Palestine, and the USSR had been the first to vote in its favour. What had happened? It was Stalin who decided everything. Why had he changed position? Michel had then replied that Lenin and Stalin were not always in agreement on the national question. Stalin made no distinction between the nationalism of the oppressors and that of the oppressed. Lenin, on the other hand, recognised the right to self-determination of the dominated nation in relation to the dominating nation. For him, the right of nations to govern themselves was in line with the principles of proletarian internationalism. For

Stalin, these principles had above all to be compatible with the interests of the Soviet Union. 'At the current time,' Michel went on, 'the USSR's interest in the Middle East is to weaken Anglo-American imperialism and to increase Soviet influence and presence'. That explained Stalin's pragmatic volte-face in supporting the creation of two independent States in Palestine. However, his rejection of Zionism remained. We would, Michel promised me, talk about it another time, thereby putting an end to the meeting.

Next to me, the middle-aged man snored rhythmically. His head had slipped onto his wife's shoulder. As she opened her eyes, ours met. I smiled at her, she smiled back and then, gently pushed her husband's head away, which stopped his snoring. It was time for me to try and fall asleep as well. In the morning, Yakov would tell me the rest of his story, and I would know at last what compromise our leaders had reached with the English!

◇◇◇◇◇

Early in the morning of the third day of our journey, Yakov and I took up our usual places below the bridge. The sky was lightly overcast, the air pleasantly fresh, and the Sea of Marmara, at times turquoise, at times a deep blue-green, was completely calm like the park lakes in Bucharest on windless days. We had long since left behind the big island of Marmara, famous, Yakov had explained to me, for the marble quarries from which its name came and that of the sea surrounding it. Devoid of vegetation, the island seemed to me poor, sad and unwelcoming.

'We'll soon be at the mouth of the Dardanelles,' Yakov went on. 'We'll have the peninsula of Gallipoli to our right, on the European coast of Turkey. And if the visibility improves, from there we'll be able to make out the snow-covered summit of Mount Olympus, in Greece.' Instinctively, I lifted my head and looked into the distance, but could see nothing resembling Olympus.

'Tell me the rest of what the man from Mossad said to you,' I asked impatiently. 'I know the story of Gallipoli well: it's there that thousands of men were killed for nothing. And then Mount Olympus and its Greek gods, that's mythology, and I'm not on good terms with mythology.'

That amused Yakov. Thanks to a sudden tumult coming from the deck, we understood that we had just left the Sea of Marmara, and were now indeed making our way through the strait of Dardanelles. From our position, we could see with the naked eye, the outline of the mountainous coast of the Gallipoli peninsula to our right and to our left, the coast of the province stretching from the eastern side, Canakkale, according to Yakov. He always seemed to find a new pretext to avoid finishing the story of the conflict of opinions between Mossad and the leaders of the Yishuv. I pressed him again and he responded impatiently: 'I've got pins and needles. Why don't we walk a little on deck?' Though a little put out, Yakov did return to the subject he seemed to want to dodge: 'There is not much more to tell. The main thing is that we're here, on the point of leaving Turkey through the strait of Dardanelles, and not in Romania or Bulgaria, where the politicians would have wanted us to stay, waiting for God knows what and for God knows how long.'

I insisted: 'Yes, but still... if we're here, it's no doubt because there has been a compromise between Mossad and the political leaders!'

The starboard side of the bow was not too crowded. After a few steps, Yakov stopped and turned to me: 'Well then, here is the rest of the story in a few words. We were talking yesterday about Averbuch and his order to the ships to leave Constantza... That was done, and the *Pans* arrived in Burgas a few days before our departure. At Geneva airport, Moshe Shertok met Shaul Meirov and the man responsible for the illegal Aliyah at Mossad's Paris bureau, and announced the good news to them: the British had agreed to take command of the *Pans* in the Aegean Sea and then lead them safely as far as Famagusta. That means there is an agreement based on Jesuitical cunning: we won't be going to Cyprus voluntarily, but if we are forced to, we won't say no... That's the essence of the compromise. The problem is that the conditions of this agreement have not been put down on paper or signed by the two parties.'

'So who'll guarantee that once we are in the Aegean Sea that the British will respect the agreement?' I asked.

'No one, as far as I know. Yossi Harel has not received precise instructions from the Yishuv in the case that the British decide, despite the verbal agreement, to use force to come on board. In this case, will we meet force with force, or give in and accept the inevitable? I know that Ike and the young members of the three branches present on our ship will oppose any compromise with the British. They want to fight and are ready to accept the loss of life. On the other hand, Gad Hilb, the captain of the *Pan York*, thinks that resisting the British would only lead to a useless massacre, for, in any case, the emigrants should only stay in Cyprus for a short period before being authorised to proceed to Palestine. Everything will be decided when we're on the open sea. Will the orders from both sides get through clearly and on time? That's the big question. We'll know more soon, once I get rid of you, I'll go fishing for the latest news.' Laughing, he added quickly in a mocking tone: 'You are now party to a great State secret, my dear Bernard. Don't say a word to anyone!'

'That's a promise, captain,' I said, and we shook hands. And at that moment, I do not know if it was his strange laughter, the sparkle in his eyes, but suddenly the question that I had buried since the previous night sprang to my lips: 'Tell me, Yakov, your kibbutz sent you as a *shaliah* to Romania, so why are you not returning on a tourist ship like the way you came? You're not an emigrant. What are you going to do in Cyprus with us?'

His laughter had not yet stopped when he replied: 'I was expecting this question, Bernard. You're an intelligent boy, but it's taken you longer than I thought. It doesn't matter. Your question comes at the right time. Tonight, we'll leave each other. I will sleep elsewhere. As for the rest, you'll understand later. Once in Palestine, I'd like you to write to me. My address is not difficult to remember, just four words: Yakov Tzafir, kibbutz Hulda. Please don't ask me any more questions.'

I had imagined the possibility that Yakov was linked to Mossad, the Haganah or the Palmach, but the prospect of the sudden separation stunned me. I understood that what I lightly called 'the meeting with the English' was not the kind of adventure you see in films, but a confrontation that could have tragic consequences for all of us.

'When are you leaving?' I mumbled.

'I told you, Bernard, tonight... Do you like cinema?' I nodded silently and he smiled before adding in a hushed voice: 'I will disappear into the night like an image which slowly fades to black in the films. In English, this technique is called a *fade out*. And I will reappear from the black somewhere else. That's called a *fade in*. Don't be sad, Bernard.'

Sad? It was worse than that. But he too, despite the effort he was making to appear poised and sure of himself, could not hide the upset I read in his eyes. In an emotional voice, he added: 'I had told you not to ask me any more questions, but you have the right to one more.'

'I now know where you go when we're not together and why you often disappear at night. You are a member of Mossad or the Haganah, no? So why have you spent so much time with me, revealing things that you haven't shared with anyone else amongst the passengers?'

'You're the new generation of idealists, Bernard. I needed to talk to you about this moment of history, which is on the very point of happening, in circumstances that you'll never forget. I'm confident. I know I've not wasted my time.' I felt very proud and blushed. 'I want to tell you, sincerely, that I feel very lucky to have met you,' he confided with emotion and hugged me briefly. 'Don't worry. This time we won't fight with the British. We'll reach Cyprus without shedding blood.' And on these last words we parted company.

Evening was approaching and finding myself alone again and still feeling very emotional, I joined a large group of men and women surrounding a young Palmachnik who was acting as a tourist guide. He explained that we were close to Cape Helles, at the end of the south-western peninsula of Gallipoli, on the European shore – an expanse of rocky land, with its white lighthouse, overlooking the entrance to the Dardanelles. On the Asian side, what we saw in the distance were the lowlands of Kumkale. Between 1915 and 1916, these Turkish lands bore witness to the bloody battles of the Gallipoli campaign. I left the group to contemplate the dark and silent cliffs and said to myself that soon we would be welcomed by the waves of the Aegean Sea, but I no longer wanted to stay on deck. I went down into the hold. Before going to get my dinner, curiosity pushed me to go and see if Yakov had taken his things. The couple who were my neighbours said hello, curiously happy to see me. The man informed me that my friend, 'the young halutz', had found himself a better place to sleep and then, in unison, they asked if it was not possible, now, to take advantage of the place left vacant... I moved my things twenty centimetres and they were visibly glad. Then I rushed to the place where food was being distributed.

◇◇◇◇◇

On the morning of our fourth day at sea, I woke up to shouts of: 'The English, the English!' Six British warships greeted our arrival in the Aegean Sea, outside Turkish waters, ships whose types and names we would learn much later.[25] On deck, some early-risers were admiring our formidable escort: a destroyer ahead of the *Pan York*, one in front of us, while the two battleships and the frigates joined the party on both sides.

25 Two battleships, the *HMS Mauritius* and the *HMS Phoebe*; two destroyers, the *HMS Chequers* and the *Chivalrous*; and two frigates, the *Cardigan Bay* and the *Whitesand Bay*.

264

A sign from heaven or just by pure coincidence, the weather suddenly turned stormy; great waves were lashing the decks when the destroyer in front of the *Pan York* abruptly changed direction, moving westwards. It seemed that the commander of the British ship had communicated to our ships that he was obliged to divert the convoy away from the storm. A dialogue had thus opened for the first time between the *Pans* and the British.

The bad weather and the inhospitable Aegean Sea, with its high dark waves, incited no one to go up on deck. Its numerous islands held little interest for me, and I was bored without Yakov. With his absence, I no longer had insight into what was going on behind the scenes. Infrequent announcements on the loudspeakers and rumours that constantly circulated from one floor to another became my only sources of information. When evening fell, a rumour took hold, that Yossi Harel had received a telegram from Ben Gurion ordering him to obey the British if they asked him to redirect the ships to Cyprus.

The following day, our fifth at sea, in dazzling sunlight and gracefully cutting through calmer waves, HMS *Mauritius* took the lead of the convoy. In the crowd, rumours spread that Yossi Harel had confirmed to the English admiral that he had received instructions from the Jewish Agency to follow the fleet to Cyprus, under his orders. The admiral's order coming soon after, the *Pans* complied and changed course, in the direction of the port of Famagusta.

Everything now seemed to progress in a satisfactory manner. The reassuring rumours calmed the masses on deck, made them confident and even, occasionally, joyful. But, in fact, the British had suddenly claimed that the agreement included the right to search our luggage and question crewmembers. Most of the sailors were anti-Francoist Spaniards and the British wanted to repatriate them, but Yossi Harel was not the man to give them what they wanted and he set out his own conditions to the Admiral: that the crew would be guaranteed to keep its authority over the emigrants and over day to day administration; that there would be no searching of individuals; that the emigrants would keep their luggage and that no member of the crew would be arrested or forced to return to his country against his will. The Admiral accepted all the conditions except the treatment reserved for the crew. Yossi Harel could not allow his men to be incarcerated and the brave anti-Francoist sailors be handed over to Spain, where they would no doubt be sentenced to death by Franco's courts. He replied immediately: 'In this case, I will head for Haifa!' The consequences of a total breakdown in dialogue being as unpredictable for the Admiral as for his country, he took the surprising decision to give his word to allow the foreign sailors and members of the Jewish crew to mix with the emigrants and leave the ships without their identities being checked. Yossi Harel knew the weight an Admiral carried in the social and military hierarchy of the United Kingdom, so he replied unequivocally that he accepted his word.

In the afternoon, the two British battleships, HMS *Mauritius* and HMS *Phoebe*, approached us and, in a deep silence disturbed only by some sharp whistles and shrill orders, the British lowered boats with the crews designated to board us. In proper fashion, command of the *Pan York* was handed over to a captain of HMS *Mauritius* and that of the *Pan Crescent* to a captain from HMS *Phoebe*. For Ike Aharonovitch, the captain both of my ship and also of the Exodus, having the British on board wasn't acceptable. But in the end, he was forced to submit to

266

orders coming from both Yossy Harel, the commander of the *Pans*, and from those of the Yishuv. He deeply disliked Yossy Harel, whom he used to refer to sarcastically by his previous name: 'Hamburger'. The Sabras hated the British. They would have liked to resist them and felt betrayed by the politicians. I hated the British as much as they did; their presence on board troubled me deeply. But they had come on board unarmed and without military caps, and had quickly made their way to the bridge, ignoring our hostile looks. In truth, they definitely did not look like the wolves in green uniforms that we came across in the streets of Bucharest at the time of Antonescu. Nevertheless, they were our enemies, as I was yet to feel in the camps in Cyprus.

During the night of 31 December, leaning on the portside railings with hundreds of other emigrants – a hostile block of silence – I saw the elated sailors of a British frigate preparing to celebrate at midnight the New Year, 1948! Lit up by hundreds of light bulbs, the frigate cut through the waves, while on the deck sailors danced and shouted with joy. When the twelve strokes of midnight were carried on the BBC's airwaves, followed by whistles and triumphant sirens, a multitude of signal flares burst into the sky and drifted down slowly, covering the sea in a carpet of stars. *God Save the King* then filled our ears, solemnly asserting the omnipotence of the British Empire in front of a cargo of fifteen thousand Jews on their way to detention.

On 1 January 1948, at seven thirty in the morning, we arrived in Famagusta, at the end of the long journey of five days and five nights. I did not see Yakov again. I imagined he had melted into the darkness in the crowd of emigrants engulfed by the *fade out*, that cinematographic notion I had learned from him. I hoped that the *fade in* which normally follows the *fade out* would at least bring back the lost face of Izi. And, indeed, it did.

23

The Winter Camp in Cyprus and Arrival in Palestine

After all the emotions on my journey across the seas, our ships' arrival in Famagusta and the landing procedure took place in a remarkably uneventful way. It seemed almost routine, dealing with ordinary visitors and not detainees sentenced to indefinite imprisonment. The *Pan York*, benefitting from the privilege of being the command ship, was quickly moored alongside the central quay, perhaps as a sign of respect, and this facilitated its passengers' disembarkation. My ship, on the other hand, had to lay anchor quite far out, where we were transferred onto small boats to bring us ashore, a more than uncomfortable inconvenience for the old, the women and the children. Despite that, the atmosphere was good: after such a long sea journey, people rejoiced at soon being able to put a foot on dry land, and the British soldiers who had come on board to help with the transfer behaved in a correct and friendly manner.

We were told that they belonged to an artillery unit of the 6th airborne division, but like the soldiers who had come aboard the previous day, they were not armed.

Izi was among the last passengers to disembark from the *Pan York* and I was one of the first to reach land from the *Pan Crescent*. But we did not find each other on the quayside or in the long convoy of army lorries that took us to the internment camp. Izi was in the lorry at the head of the convoy, while I was in the last with a few boys from my *kvutza*, whom I had finally met up with on disembarkation.

The convoy of lorries left the coast at Famagusta and crossed a low limestone plain that dazzled in the sunlight. It was midday, the hour when the star of heat and light keeps terrestrials in its sight and pursues them relentlessly. It was warm for January and we lacked air as we huddled under the thick dark green tarpaulins that covered the lorries. The only opening was at the rear of the lorry, obliging us to kneel in rows to get some air and in order to see something of the landscape. Luckily, we were the last in the convoy and our view was unobstructed by other vehicles.

The road leading across the plain separated a vineyard with bare vines from a wide olive tree orchard. With long rakes, men and women were gathering the olives left on the trees, while young girls emptied their baskets into small carts. I reflected that they would do this same work all their lives; they did not fear the unexpected, unlike us. Before the sun sets, they would return to their peaceful homes and the evening routine of a shared family meal. Bold little birds would perch on their windowsills to chirp, or come to peck at crumbs on their doorsteps.

The passing convoy interrupted the pruning of the vines. A few men ran towards us with their left fists raised in the communist salute, shouting 'Markos, Markos!' at the top of their lungs. A boy asked shyly who this Markos was, and I explained: 'Markos Vafiades was the hero of the Greek guerrilla war against Germany. Under the name of "General Markos", he is now the commander of the communist guerrilla forces in the civil war against the royalist government and the nationalist army'.

Another boy, Gabi, who was small and aggressive, asked me, circumspectly, if I knew how this civil war had started. I replied that one learned these things from newspapers. Had he not read that the Greek royalists of the Populist Party had won the general elections in 1946, held without the left's participation, and that, in the following plebiscite, the majority had voted in favour of the monarchy, allowing the return of King George II to Athens? The new royalist government had wanted to dissolve the communist party, which was unacceptable for the heroes of the anti-Nazi resistance, and that had unleashed the civil war.

'The royalists obey the orders of Anglo-American imperialism,' asserted Gabi.

'Yes, that's true,' I conceded. 'The royalists have the full support of the British and the Americans, while Markos has won that of Bulgaria, Albania and especially Tito's Yugoslavia. At the beginning, I hoped that the guerrillas would have the upper hand, but now the balance can change at any moment with the massive intervention of the English and the Americans.'

Gabi insisted: 'You've forgotten that the USSR, in solidarity, supports General Markos!'

'No, I haven't forgotten, but it's more complicated: the USSR and the West are dividing up spheres of influence. Stalin has exchanged Greece for Bulgaria, Romania and Hungary.'

'And what's the closed-fist salute of the vineyard workers?' intervened the timid voice of a boy kneeling near me.

This time it was Gabi who replied: 'Cyprus is a British colony! The communist salute shows that the population here is in solidarity with Markos's fight in Greece and with the communist party of Cyprus, which is struggling for the island's independence against British colonialism!'

By chance, our convoy had just overtaken an old lorry transporting some dust-covered workers who made the same salute accompanied by the same shouts of 'Markos, Markos!' This time, we echoed back loudly the name of the popular general, but our shouts quickly turned into giggles, no doubt to diffuse the tension that seized us at the idea that the 'tourist journey' was approaching its end. As soon as our laughter had died down, we fell into silence. The row of heads at the back of the lorry broke up, each boy returning to his place on the wooden benches. Only the roar of the engines and the screeching of tires on the sharp turns could be heard. We remained pensive for a long time, staring at the floor, until the moment when Gabi suddenly stood up and said: 'Haverim, let's sing to warm our hearts!' And we sang with joy and at the top of our lungs Shirat Hanoar – the Song of Youth – that celebrates the rediscovering of the land on which to build the reborn nation. We often sang it at the ken, after having learned the meaning of the Hebrew words from our madrichim. In the meantime, our convoy passed some carts, an old tractor, blackened stone houses of a medieval-looking village, fields covered with sparse vegetation, cows and sheep, peasants in traditional dress, and also a very beautiful church that reminded me of the one of Dobroteassa in Bucharest. We left behind the last images of a world where men still lived in freedom, for the convoy slowed down at a crossing, took a rutted and stony side road, and finally stopped. It was the prison CAMP! I can remember the noise. Paratroopers in red berets and moustachioed policemen with ruddy cheeks barked orders in their language to make us get down from the lorries. Around me I could see only barbed wire, fences, barriers and a few sinister hangars. One of the policemen seized me by the shoulder and I shouted furiously at him in Romanian:

'Ia mîna de pe mine, englez murdar.' ('Take your hands off me, you dirty Englishman!')

Disconcerted, he stepped back, and, at that moment, I could read in his eyes that he was ashamed. He knew perfectly well that we were not miserable crooks like those we had seen in films from his country, that we did not smell of bad beer and that our hands had never shed blood. If we were there, it was because his government wanted to prevent us from building a home on our biblical land. He knew the tribe we belonged to. He had certainly seen the heaps of bones, hair and spectacles, and he had no doubt come across with horror the human wrecks, a yellow star on their scrawny chests, as they emerged from the shadows to beg for a piece of bread, when his unit had entered the gates of the death camps.

On turning my back to him, I noticed, in the distance, Izi, my friend I thought I had lost. He had seen me shout at the policeman, and was running over to bring me his support. 'Come,' he shouted. 'Let's stay together and never leave each other again!'

Gradually, the noise abated and the English managed to calm us down and gather us together. We were about a hundred boys and girls lined up in three rows like soldiers at morning parade, except that, instead of rifles and bayonets, we presented bags, rucksacks, torn parcels and cardboard cases, carried in our hands, or placed on the ground next to our filthy boots. Heads covered with caps, bonnets and berets, necks protected by brightly coloured scarves, and bodies dressed in overcoats, sheepskin coats and big roll-necked pullovers – you could say we looked like the soldiers of a ragtag army, or, according to a Romanian expression, an 'army in slippers'.

Surrounded by paratroopers and exhibited in this ridiculous posture before a fat and moustached sergeant major, we were called up by the dozen and pushed inside a wide Nissen hut to be searched and sorted like lentils.

When our turn came, Izi, me, and ten other boys found ourselves opposite a dozen English soldiers seated behind a wide table. Each of us stared into the eyes of one of them. Standing behind the table, some red berets armed with Tommy Guns paced nervously like stallions.

'Get the muck out of your bags!' shouted the sergeant major.

Concentrated as I was on the Englishmen sitting at the table and on the red-bereted thoroughbreds behind them, I had not noticed the presence, to my left, of the fat sergeant major near the first boy in the row, a brave little orphan by the name of Sami. Not understanding a word of what the Englishman was shouting, we turned towards him and froze. The sergeant major, a brute who was perceptive enough to sense that there was 'a language issue', furiously grabbed Sami's bag and tipped out its contents onto the table, indicating that we all do the same. We put our things on the table, exactly as the sergeant major had, but calmly. The twelve Englishmen began to search them carefully, as the men from the Haganah had warned us on the ship that they would do, looking for firearms and

274

subversive books written by renowned troublemakers like Marx, Engels, Lenin and Stalin. I had a few of these books in my bag, Gabi and two other boys did as well, and all were torn up and thrown into bins by the paratroopers, as we looked on furious. The British monarchy was saved!

'Get your rags back in your bloody bags!' the sergeant major hurled.

We still did not understand a single word of what the Englishman was spitting out and he was obliged yet again to use poor Sami, forcing him to put his things back in his bag. Silent and defiant, we imitated Sami. The soldiers in charge of the search stood up and left the hut. But the sergeant major stayed where he was, and I expected another nasty surprise when I saw the paratroopers advance towards us holding buckets. We hardly had the time to wonder what was going through their heads before the buckets filled with DDT were emptied over us. Knowing nothing about this disgusting powder, we panicked. Blinded, we tried to rid ourselves of it by sneezing, spitting, coughing and frenziedly shaking our limbs.

'Come on!' screamed the sergeant major. 'It's only DDT. It's good for your health!'

In response to their hilarity, we looked straight in the paratroopers' eyes with blind hatred. It was explained to us later in the camp that DDT had been widely used during the war to protect the American Army from infectious diseases transmitted by insects. We had therefore undergone a necessary procedure given the severe shortage of water on the island, particularly in the camps, but why in such a humiliating fashion?

When we left the hut, armed sentries opened a tall barbed wire gate and, like with a herd of cattle, they funnelled us through a narrow corridor reserved for patrols and lined with electric fences. At the end of the corridor, shaken and disoriented, we found ourselves abandoned in the middle of a large deserted space, called Winter Camp 69, where the canvas flaps of about thirty empty tents snapped in the wind and a few discoloured huts lined up sadly before our eyes like old tombs in a desolate cemetery. Vegetation was non-existent: there were neither trees nor the slightest shade to protect us from the sun. We had been well informed: the climate on the island was semi-arid, days were hot even in winter, and temperatures only fell drastically at night and during February. However, there were signs of recent rain, for here and there puddles and mud lingered.

Suddenly, out of one of the huts, an incongruous and bizarre vision appeared: an adult dressed all in khaki – short trousers, shirt and Trotskyist cap– to announce in Romanian that nearly all we needed to make ourselves at home in the camp was at our disposal right next to the tents. 'There's enough material for everyone. Off you go, but no panic!' he shouted. On hearing the words 'no panic', the herd ran as fast as it could. I hesitated, but Izi pushed me: 'Don't trust what he says! Run!' And I ran, panicked like the others. It is a dog-eat-dog world, and one only thinks of oneself in such situations. Everyone hopes that by getting there first he will have more than the other, better than the other. Out of breath, the herd stopped in front of a pyramid of mugs, bowls, spoons, and knives and forks all covered in axle grease. Alongside was a stack of long narrow planks for assembling our beds, and three hills of mattresses, blankets, pillows and towels. What was the point in getting there first? Same greasy cutlery, same pillows, same mattresses, same blankets, same wooden planks for everyone! But would there really be enough? Did we not risk finding ourselves without a bed, with neither bowl nor fork or even without a mattress? Yes, there was a genuine risk, it truly is a dog-eat-dog world. And it was a free for all! You fought for a knife, for a cup, for a pillow. I wanted to remain above the fray, to flee the jostling, but Izi dragged me in. He knew the rules of the game, those that ensure survival and to which he owed his own life, for he had returned alive from the nightmare of Transnistria.

The adult in khaki intervened. He re-established order, telling us not to worry: there was everything for everyone. He then advised us to assemble our beds and quickly make our homes in the tents, eight *haverim* in each, before the kitchen opened a few hours later. He also promised that they would soon be distributing oil or kerosene lamps. With patience, everything would be sorted out. He introduced himself as Elie, and added that he had been one of the leaders of the Hashomer Hatzair movement in Cluj, in Transylvania, which explained his thick Hungarian accent. Soon he left us, never to be seen again.

Only four adults – we did not know if they belonged to our movement or not – looked after us every day in the camp: two young women, one thin and the other fat, who prepared our meals in the kitchen hut and who spoke only Hebrew, and a male and a female nurse, aged about thirty, who we noticed were only present in an emergency. The main meal consisted of a small handful of kasha[26] and an orange, which we devoured in a few minutes, making us even more famished. In the mornings and evenings, we received some old black bread, two hundred and fifty grams per day, and a mug of tea. As for the nurses, they did not live with us in the camp, arriving in a mobile infirmary. Where they came from, I never knew, but they were the

26 Porridge made from buckwheat.

ones who shaved the heads and treated the wounds of several girls infested by lice.

We had learned that there were twelve camps in Cyprus: five called 'summer camps', near Famagusta, and seven others called 'winter camps' in the south-east of the island. Life was much easier in the summer camps along the coast, as it allowed the deportees to bathe in the sea even in winter. On the other hand, my camp 69 and the neighbouring winter camps were situated a few kilometres from the coast and at one hundred metres above sea level, near the village of Xylotymbou. From our camp, we had no sight of the sea. We very rarely saw water in general, except when it rained.

The administrative need to pass from one camp to another obliged the British to build bridges over the roads reserved for patrols and supply vehicles. One of these bridges linked my camp 69 to camp 66. But this bridge was not immediately open for our use. It was only after a certain time that we could cross it. And when we did, Izi and I found by chance, David, whom we had known at the *ken*, and who had arrived in Cyprus with his mother and younger brother after a long odyssey during the war. When the USSR annexed Bessarabia, David's father had been deported to Siberia, accused of a financial crime he did not commit. As soon as the Romanian Army retook Bessarabia, David's mother, fearing their fate would be the same as that of the Jews of Iași, had fled with her two children, taking refuge in towns behind the defence lines of the retreating Red Army. In Tbilisi, Georgia, they had learned of the father's death in a Stalinist gulag and, after the war, they had been repatriated from the USSR to Romania, where they settled in Bucharest. The mother, Riva, once invited us into their tent and served us tea and some pieces of chocolate. On this occasion, David

278

revealed to us the cruel irony of the camps in Cyprus: they had been built on the model of the Nazi concentration camps by more than a thousand German prisoners that the British had brought over from Egypt! Another curious thing, the name of Xylotymbou, 'wooden tomb', had been given, he told us, to the village when a dealer in antiquities discovered a tomb there that had beautiful wood engravings that portrayed Aphrodite and Artemis. And then, bursting out laughing, David added: 'What outrageous irreverence on the part of the English towards the cradle of Aphrodite, goddess of beauty and desire, to build, on land that doesn't even belong to them, vile prison camps!'

Crossing the bridge to camp 66 was my passage from hell to heaven, as there we could, thanks to Izi's money, suppress our hunger by eating large quantities of carobs that could be bought cheaply in kiosks that had opened for trade.

I wondered why our camp, compared with the others, had been designed to resemble hell. Why was it that no *madrich* from the movement had accompanied and remained with us in camp 69? Why were we left to our own devices to struggle against hunger, thirst and all sorts of illnesses aggravated by malnutrition, boredom and despair?

Of course, every camp had its problems. Each individual suffered in his or her own way. In David's camp, the deportees did not endure hunger in the same way as we did in camp 69. For David, the worst suffering was not hunger, but the lack of books. In his camp, no one was infected by scabies and none of the girls experienced the humiliation of having her head shaved. There, the deportees even benefitted from a certain social life: representatives of Zionist organisations took care of boys and girls who had come without parents. Nothing like

279

that existed in camp 69, the accursed camp, the camp neglected by the adults.

I had spent all my childhood in the shadow of adults or, at least, near my brother and his friends who were all a few years older than I was. The boys of my age did not interest me. Before I met Izi, I had never had a friend of the same age. I had survived the *Shomria* thanks to Moshe, my sports *madrich*. On the ship, I had Yakov as friend and protector, while in the courtyard Pouia was my only friend. The adult world was indispensable for stimulating my eagerness to learn, while enabling me to constantly take up challenges. I had replaced it in the camp with my ties to Izi, Gabi and Tina, a girl we had met standing in the queue at the kitchen hut. Without books, deprived of any physical or cultural activity, we passed the time, often to forget hunger, talking about the films we had liked in the past, or by exploring what our memories, our ambitions and our aspirations had, or didn't have, in common.

One day, when we were sitting outside the tent on surplus planks, we were surprised to hear the rich and beautiful sound, with its deep harmonies, of an accordion and young voices singing a sad Russian melody. We crossed the wasteland behind the tents and the music guided us to the metal fence and barbed wire separating our camp from camp 70. Usually, there was nothing interesting to see at the edge of this neighbouring camp as most of the activity took place in the centre near the family tents and huts. An idea suddenly struck me, and with great strides, I was quickly ahead of Izi and Tina. As soon as I was near the fence, I discovered that the singers were, as I had hoped, the group of Bulgarians I had admired on the deck of the *Pan Crescent*. When they caught up with me, I excitedly told Izi and Tina that the accordionist was Thea, the beautiful girl with black hair like Pouia's. 'Have you fallen in love with her?' Izi teased. 'Not yet,' I replied. 'But I would like to. That would cure my boredom.'

'Love must not serve practical purposes. Otherwise, it ceases to be love and becomes no better than a pair of shoes,' Tina scolded me.

'Maybe you're thinking of spiritual love,' Izi suggested. And quickly added: 'Have you already been in love?'

'No,' replied Tina. 'And you?'

Izi smiled and, giving her a provocative look, added: 'Me neither. But I'm not far from it.'

Tina blushed. To get her out of her embarrassment, I pressed Izi: 'Who are you not far from falling in love with: the fat one who serves us kasha through the big kitchen window?' He quickly turned towards me and answered: 'Yes, it's her, clearly not the kasha!'

We all laughed, after which Izi started to look at Tina insistently again.

The Bulgarians, sitting on the ground in a circle, stopped singing as soon as they saw us. We praised them with thunderous 'bravos' and 'encores'. Thea stood up, put the accordion back in its box, and came over to join the members of the group who had approached the fence. I could see her more closely: her silky skin, her smiling eyes, her fine build, her beautiful fragile hands waving in a friendly gesture.

What a stunning difference there was between them and us! They wore blue shirts with white laces, traditional in our youth movement, and their faces radiated confidence and the pleasure of being together. They, for one, had no doubt they could overcome all the present difficulties before launching into the great adventure of communal life on the kibbutz. The camp had not changed them. Their poise, their elegance, their joy, their fine manners impressed me as much as the first time on the deck of the ship. But what impression could we have made on them, we, the Romanians, so poorly dressed, so emaciated, so discouraged and wretched, even in our own eyes? We greeted them with a vigorous *Hazak Veematz*, the divine commandment taken from the first chapter of the Book of Joshua: 'Be strong and courageous, for you are the one who will put this people in possession of the country that I swore to their forefathers to give them.' Paradoxically, in order to hide the biblical origins of this greeting, the movement had combined it with the scout salute. It consisted of raising the right hand, with only the index, middle and ring fingers facing out; the thumb had to cover the little finger to remind us symbolically that the 'big' had to protect the 'small'. We therefore added this sign to the greeting, and the Bulgarians did the same with even more fervent enthusiasm than us. That practically put an end to the encounter, for we did not understand Bulgarian and the Bulgarians understood Romanian even less. Thea tried to test our knowledge of Hebrew. Izi spluttered a vague reply, but it was in Yiddish, and the Jews of Bulgaria, who are of Sephardic origin know about as much Yiddish, the international language of the Ashkenazis, as we know Ladino, which is theirs.

Not long after this bitter-sweet encounter, a serious eruption of boils covered my body: first the legs, then the thighs, the buttocks, the back, the arms and the nape of my neck. Penicillin not being widely used at the time, boils were treated with hot compresses, hydrogen-peroxide antiseptic plasters or mustard poultices. But my situation was getting worse. In the absence of a doctor and given the camp's poor sanitary conditions, the nurses hesitated to lance the boils. Although my face was spared, they were beginning to get seriously worried. I often heard them mention the word 'anthrax', the meaning of which I learned later: the formation of a cluster of boils that could lead to dangerous swelling.

I was dirty, I could not take a shower, my bed linen was infected and laundry was rare at the camp. To avoid the worst, the nurses covered me in bandages. Yet again, I was the captive of bandages. I was reliving the traumatic experience at the *Shomria*, but this time my condition was infinitely more pathetic and degrading! I was ashamed to leave the tent. I spent most of my time on the bed, my face buried in a hard and dirty pillow. Neither Izi nor Tina were able to raise my spirits, nothing could console me. I did not want to see or be seen by anyone. I wanted to be invisible. The bandage-covered face of Jack Griffin, the hero of *The Invisible Man*, that film which had so impressed me when I saw it after the war, had come back to me. Claude Rains, the actor playing Jack, was famous for the unique, unforgettable timbre of his voice. In the film, his eyes were hidden behind big dark glasses. When he took them off, unwound the bandages and took off his clothes, his body disappeared completely, becoming invisible...

At night, the pain made me shiver. Who could I ask for help? Ah! If only I could have become invisible like Jack Griffin! To cross the bridge and walk at will from one camp to the other, rid of my bandages, invisible, freed from all complexes, drawing advantage from my suffering! Then there was the hunger that could be forgotten briefly during sleep, but during sleepless nights, I tossed and turned, my whole being consumed by it. I longed for the big comfortable bed I had shared so long with my brother. I thought a lot about Leo. He had written to me that he had finally been accepted as a student in the new faculty of

283

Zootechnic that had just opened its doors and was part of the University of Bucharest. You could say that in a certain way his dream had been fulfilled, except that substituting animal husbandry for medicine seemed to me a poor compromise, albeit the only one compatible with the subjects that interested him the most, anatomy and physiology, unfortunately, not of men, but of animals...

And I thought sadly about my parents. I had sent them two postcards and a letter. Had they received them? No reply had come... They had only reluctantly accepted my departure and Leo had only silenced his doubts to please me. I had forced him to help me with distorted and dishonest arguments. He felt guilty towards me. But guilty of what, exactly?

I philosophised during my sleepless nights. At the ken, during his lessons on Marxism, Michel Hirschberg had summed up the notion of 'philosophising' in six words: 'Search for the reason in things'. I had remembered his analysis of Karl Marx's work, The Poverty of Philosophy, written in response to Proudhon's study, The System of Economic Contradictions, or The Philosophy of Poverty, because I had liked the inversion of words: Philosophy of poverty, or poverty of my philosophy, for, to tell the truth, I was an intruder in this elitist discipline. The syllabus of a commercial high school was hardly designed to give birth to a new generation of philosophers. I had learned from Michel that the basis of Marxist philosophy, dialectical and historical materialism, gave pre-eminence to matter over mind. As Michel had emphasised, all the concepts of the mind emerge in the brain, which is matter. The old theme of my inability to adapt to a new environment and the irritations of communal life came back to me. Did this inability come from my body, matter, or from my mind?

It was in this way that the days and nights passed in winter camp 69. In February, we had to put up with several days of icy, slow and monotonous rain. Water soaked the canvas of the tents and the humidity penetrated the marrow of our bones. Often the rain leaked into the tents, forcing us to abandon our beds, half naked, to save our things left on the ground. On one of those nights, during a storm when the wind was very strong and the tent I shared with Izi and six other *haverim* threatened to collapse, we had to go out in the rain, shivering like puppies, to drive the pegs more securely into the ground and spread the canvas, while reinforcing the guy ropes. Gabi, the tempestuous boy I often argued with about ideological subjects, but who became a friend, was the first to roll up his sleeves when physical strength and courage were needed. He was from Bacau, a small town in the north of Romania, while the five others were from Bucharest, all former pupils of the Ciocanul vocational school whose canteen my brother and I had frequented. For schoolboys like Izi, Gabi and I, 'vocational' was a dirty word. It brought to mind trades where hands were more useful than brains, while for me, the pupil of a commercial high school, the word 'commerce' was no less dirty... Anyway, it was their hands, and not their minds, we needed to re-erect our tent.

The 'gang of five' as we called them from the heights of our elitism, had devised – for they were no fools – a clever strategy to punish us for our pretentiousness. At night, after bedtime, they began to tell dirty jokes and engage in shameless farting competitions. Even more perniciously, two of these boys had the idea, when we were asleep, of lighting matches against the soles of our feet, which always protruded from the blanket, making us jump up like baby deer frightened by lightning. This kind of joke was unacceptable for elite high school boys like us. And as neither Izi, Gabi nor I lacked fighting spirit, the two jokers, at their third attempt, received a good ration of well-placed kicks and punches. Blood ran from the nose of one of them, and peace was signed. The three other members of the group distanced themselves from their comrades, recognising that they had gone too far. It was an imperfect, provisional peace, about which I hardly had any illusions. You do not change boys from a vocational high school overnight.

On rainy evenings, we stayed closed in the tent to have our meal. I was disgusted by the stench created by the incongruous combination of the smell of orange peel the 'gang of five' threw inconsiderately on the floor and the odours of farts, dirty socks and kerosene lamps. These nights in our damp, freezing and stinking tent were particularly difficult for me to bear.

Towards the middle of March, the rainy season stopped. Spring had even reached us in camp 69. I thought of the beautiful spring times in Romania, of the grass and the flowers awakening from their winter sleep. There was nothing particularly spring-like in camp 69, and I did not expect that to change, as the approaching hot and dry weather would make the land even more arid, the air even more dry, life more monotonous, boredom more demoralising and my boils more painful.

One day, a doctor arrived and lanced the boils on my buttocks, the most uncomfortable ones, and treated those that had freshly appeared on my neck and legs. The nurses replaced my soiled bandages and I felt better. Little by little, the days lengthened and I was less famished, since I had begun to eat orange peel, imitating my comrades from the Ciocanul. They, and other hungry boys, had added to their daily menu some Odol, a mint-flavoured toothpaste, which was apparently very tasty if you were to believe them. 'Using Odol guarantees you good

286

teeth, good digestion and increased longevity,' our pharmacist in Bucharest used to say, lampooning the advertisements. But, to eat it? No, thank you. I was not yet ready!

The rains having stopped, our Bulgarian comrades met each evening after dinner on the waste ground along the edge of their camp. Sitting around a fire, they debated various subjects with their *madrichim* in their language and continued the evening by singing Russian and Hebrew melodies, accompanied by Thea on accordion. Izi, Tina, Gabi and I were no longer the only ones to admire them. When the songs began, the tents of our camp emptied and everyone ran to the barbed wire fence to attend the Bulgarians' performance. Moving away from Izi and Tina, I mixed into the crowd to try and get as close as possible to have a better view of beautiful Thea. Occasionally, the group let her play a solo, according to her inspiration. We watched her in amazement, bewitched by her virtuosity. When she ended and we applauded her wildly, she approached the fence to thank us, triumphant and happy. She was aware of the joy her music brought us. Once, I even thought she had noticed me; as her eyes had settled on me. It was when dusk was enveloping the camp with its pale light, giving my bandages a phosphorescent glow. 'Hey,' she must had said to herself, 'a young boy who looks like a mummy! What is he suffering from? Why is he covered in bandages?' I would have replied: 'Why? Because by inflicting boils on me, God has singled me out from the others and this makes me suffer. I feel ugly, dirty, humiliated. I'm ashamed that you see me wretched as I am in these bandages, for I've liked you from the first time I saw you, while what you see of me is not the real me, it's what the Creator has made of me in Cyprus.' That's what I would have wanted to tell her, but it was not possible. So, when I felt her looking at me, I

287

panicked and, abandoning my place by the fence, ran back to my tent. It was empty. I threw myself on the bed and decided to end my infatuation with Thea. Never to return to see her at the fence, to flee to the other end of the camp, as far away as possible, every time the Bulgarians gathered, so as to no longer hear their songs and her virtuoso accordion solos. I had to leave Cyprus! Leave this camp, this island! But where would I find hope? What awaited me in Palestine? First of all, I had to get rid of my boils. And then... and then, it was the unknown yet again. Life was just beginning for me. I had to lift my head high, regain confidence, the will to go forward, to surmount obstacles. Above all, I had to forget this humiliation!

That day, I had wiped Cyprus from my reality. I had put this experience behind me and was helped when soon after, within the quota system imposed by the British authorities for the emigration of children to Palestine, we left camp 69 in late March 1948.

In Famagusta, a *shaliah* from the Hashomer Hatzair organised a first meeting of the forty boys and girls who would form the group I would belong to. Together, we decided that its name would be *Lehava* ('the Flame'). On board our ship taking us to Palestine, the men from the Jewish Agency and the representatives of the Zionist movements had efficiently anticipated all the bureaucratic formalities. The *shaliah* informed us that the name of the kibbutz expecting us was Tel-Amal ('The Hill of Labour'), in the Beit Shean valley. Apart from Izi, Tina, Gabi and the 'gang of five', I knew almost nobody, for they came from all corners of Romania.

The journey took longer than expected: on 7 April 1948, we had to be landed, for security reasons, at Tel-Aviv instead of Haifa. As the port of Tel-Aviv was reserved exclusively for small

288

watercraft, our ship had to drop anchor out at sea and we were then quickly transferred to rowing boats and motor launches to be brought ashore. The few timid efforts to celebrate our arrival in Eretz Israel with shouts of enthusiasm and patriotic songs withered when our ears were struck by the sounds of explosions and machine gun fire from afar. At the frontier with Jaffa, the Arab town right next to Tel-Aviv, only a few kilometres south of the port, there was sporadic fighting between Palestinian militants and irregular units of the Irgun[27] and the Lehi.[28] In the run-up to 19 May 1948, the date when the British Mandate in Palestine expired, the Yishuv, in accordance with the partition plan voted for by the United Nations, was to take control of the territories allocated to the State of Israel. Here and there they were being enlarged as part of the policy to protect the Jewish population living in enclaves considered too close to Arab neighbourhoods and towns.

Tense and silent, we were landed on the quay and were led to buses without having to undergo tedious formalities. In front of the door of one of these buses, a female nurse and a man by the name of Yoel, both of them of Romanian origin, warmly welcomed us and distributed oranges and sandwiches.

27 Irgun: clandestine terrorist organisation in British Mandate Palestine, created in 1931 from a split in the Haganah. Its complete name: 'National Military Organisation', in Hebrew, 'Irgun Zvai Leoumi'. The Irgun was ideologically close to the revisionist party of Zeev (Vladimir) Jabotinsky whose political platform envisaged the construction of a Jewish State on both banks of the river Jordan. In 1943, command of the Irgun was given to Menachem Begin, future Prime Minister of Israel from 1977 to 1983.

28 Lehi: Hebrew acronym for *Lohamei Herut Israel* ('fighters for the freedom of Israel') a terrorist armed group, an offshoot of the Irgun created in September 1940, also known as the 'Stern Gang', according to the name of its founder, Avraham Stern. Lehi was on the nationalist and fascist extreme right of Jabotinsky's revisionist party.

Once we had sat down, Yoel gave us some information about the route we were to take: From Tel-Aviv to Kfar Saba, a small town less than twenty kilometres away, we would pass through only Jewish territory, and at Kfar Saba we would be welcomed by the man who would be our *madrich* at the kibbutz Tel-Amal. 'He only speaks Hebrew, Polish and English,' Yoel told us. 'His name is Zvi Lurie, a very intelligent and cultivated man. He will accompany you to the kibbutz. But from Kfar Saba, we will make the rest of the journey in an armoured bus, for the historic road connecting the valley of Jezreel with the valley of Beit Shean, where your kibbutz is situated, passes through Wadi Ara, a valley populated by the Arabs. The road is often exposed to gunfire from their villages. Among them, Hum al-Fahm is the biggest, and as it is built on the mountainside it has dangerous control of the road. Your group is going to replace the Czech group who, since they have been called up, are leaving the kibbutz to join the Palmach. War is expected any day now. The war for our independence.'

Sitting together, still inseparable, Izi and I looked at each other and smiled with our hearts beating: The war for our independence! The Jewish people were finally returning to their biblical land. We were witnesses to the birth of the Jewish State! Could our adventure begin in a more dramatic and exhilarating way than that?

A young man in a khaki uniform leapt agilely onto the bus, exchanged a few quick words in Hebrew with Yoel, made himself comfortable behind the steering wheel and the caravan set off for the kibbutz. Our bus was second in the convoy of ten identical vehicles, bearing on the top of their windscreens the letters of EGGED, the name of the Yishuv's public transport company. The hangars of the port, the road, the cafes and the little restaurants, the pretty two and three-storey houses with their overhanging balconies had been designed and built by Jews. The men and women we could see through the windows were Jews like us. We were no longer unwelcome and frowned upon by strangers in countries that wanted nothing to do with us. We were at home, on the land of Eretz Israel.

The roar of the engines swallowed up the noise of the explosions and machine gun fire. The moment had come for our joy, contained up until then, to finally escape in shouts, laughter and songs charged with the most ardent patriotism.

After a very long journey across the seas, I had arrived in the land of my dreams. I had left my family, my neighbourhood, my city and the land of my birth, the backbone of my childhood, and now found myself projected into the future, on the point of becoming a man. The fight to live my life was going to begin.

Notes

[i] (p. 65) | On 20 February 1866, in Bucharest, the parliament of the Romanian principalities of Moldovia and Wallachia, weary of fratricidal quarrels between their rival princes, had decided to seal the union achieved in 1859 by choosing as their first king a prince from a foreign dynasty. With the secret consent of Napoleon III and Bismarck, who had both welcomed the union with open arms, the choice was made of the German prince Karl of Hohenzollern. Austria had opposed the unification of the Romanians in order to maintain its stranglehold on Transylvania. So as not to be recognised by the Austrian police, the young prince, aged twenty-seven, had taken the night train, in second class, disguised and in possession of fake identity papers. In Bucharest, he changed his name to the more Romanian-sounding Carol, and, under his leadership, as a sovereign prince, Romania proclaimed its independence in May 1877. A month later, Romania allied itself with Russia in the war against the Ottoman Empire, whose yoke had weighed heavily upon its principalities. The Turks were defeated, the Treaty of Berlin recognised Romania's independence, and on 23 May 1881, the sovereign prince was proclaimed King Carol I.

[ii] (p. 71) | The great Russian writer, Isaac Babel, had served during the First World War in the Russian Army stationed in Romania. Sent back to Odessa in 1918, he joined the Bolsheviks and was attached to the Red Cavalry under the name of Lyutov, the name he gave to the hero of his short story collection *Red Cavalry*. Here is how Babel describes in 'Berestechko' the execution of an old Jew by the Cossacks:

'Just beneath my windows some Cossacks were trying to shoot an old Jew with a silvery beard for espionage. But the old man was squealing and struggling. So Kudrya from the machine-gun section took his head, and stuck it under his arm. The Jew calmed down and opened his legs. With his right hand, Kudrya took out his dagger and carefully, without splashing himself, cut the old man's throat. Then he struck a closed shutter. If this interests anyone, he said, he's free to clear it up...'

[iii] (p. 78) | Bela Kun, born Bela Kohn, on 20 February 1886, of a Jewish father and a Calvinist mother. Taken prisoner during the First World War on the Russian front, he made contact with Bolshevik activists and attracted the attention of Lenin. After the failure of the Hungarian revolution, he took refuge in Vienna. Arrested by the Austrian authorities, he was expelled to Russia in an exchange of prisoners of war between the two countries. He became a member of the communist party of the USSR and chief of the revolutionary committee in Crimea, where his name is linked with the massacre of thousands of White Russians and members of ethnic minorities. Later appointed to an important post in the Komintern, he was accused of Trotskyism and died in the thirties in a Stalinist gulag.

In 1956, the destalinization that followed the 20th Congress of the Soviet communist party led to the rehabilitation of his name. After the failure of the Hungarian revolution of 1919, communism had to wait a quarter of a century to be imposed simultaneously in Hungary and Romania, along the Stalinist model – despotic, corrupt and criminal.

[iv] (p. 102) | The territorial ambitions of Marshal Antonescu were going to cost Romania an exorbitant price: hundreds of thousands of soldiers killed and wounded on the battlefields; the natural resources of the country pillaged and plundered by the USSR as war reparations; and the replacement of the monarchy by a 'people's democracy', a perverse form of socialism concocted by the USSR and imposed in all the countries that the Yalta agreement had abandoned to its zone of influence. Condemned to death, Marshal Ion Antonescu, his Foreign Minister Mihai Antonescu (no relation) and several of his close collaborators were executed in June 1946 in Jilava prison.

[v] (p. 115) | When on 16 December 1941 the ship *Struma* arrived in the Turkish port of Buyukdere, north of the Bosphorus, out of fear of being forced to allow her passengers onto its territory as refugees, and also under pressure from Harold MacMichael, the British High Commissioner for Palestine, Turkey put the boat in quarantine. Only eight passengers in possession of British visas for Palestine and a woman about to give birth had the permission to land. Given the deplorable living conditions on board, on 10 January 1942, the captain Garabetenko sent a desperate letter to the Turkish authorities and the British embassy. On 13 February, after a wait of sixty-three days, Moshe Shertok, of the Jewish Agency, obtained from the British the granting of twenty-eight travel documents for the children aged between eleven and sixteen. But the Turkish authorities refused to lift the quarantine. On 23 February 1942, they ordered the ship to set sail. The engines being beyond repair, the Turkish navy then tugged the *Struma* into the Black Sea, far from the Bosphorus, leaving it adrift. The following day, the boat was torpedoed by the Soviet submarine SC213.

In his defence, Harold McMichael declared: 'The fate of these people has been tragic, but it nevertheless remains a fact that we are dealing with citizens from a country at war with Great Britain and coming from a territory under enemy control.' And in the House of Lords, Walter Guinness (Lord Moyne), who would be assassinated in 1944 by the 'Lehi', stated that 'Palestine is too small and already overpopulated to welcome the three million Jews that the Zionists want to bring over' and that 'anthropologists believe that there is no pure Jewish race'.

[vi] (p. 123) | *The Jew Süss* had been created with the sole monstrous aim of instrumentalising the murder of Jews on a global scale. The film's director, Veit Harlan, was a protégé of the regime. Under pressure from Goebbels, or at his own initiative, we will never know, Harlan altered the novel by Lion Feuchtwanger published in 1925 and, by grossly distorting the facts, created a hideous and repulsive Jew Süss.

At his trial in Hamburg in 1949, Veit Harlan assigned to Goebbels responsibility for the film's poisonous anti-Semitism. According to him, if he had refused, he would have risked being judged and punished as a deserter, for under the orders of Goebbels, working on this film was the equivalent to being at the front. For the judge Walter Tyrolf (a former Nazi lawyer) proving that Harlan had committed a crime against humanity turned out to be too difficult a task. He declared Harlan innocent. During the war, this same judge had sentenced Ukrainian women to beheading for stealing scarves!

The acquittal allowed Harlan to make nine other films in West Germany, until his death in 1967. In September 1940, *The Jew Süss* received the Golden Lion at the Mostra in Venice. Michelangelo Antonioni, a young film critic at the time, found that the film was a

successful combination of art and propaganda: 'Let us not hesitate to say that here we are dealing with propaganda. Bravo! Because the film is powerful, incisive, effective... As for the acting, the appreciation is the same: Ferdinand Marian, the Jew, is simply excellent. He draws the figure of Süss with subtle finesse' (Antonioni Dossier in the review *Positif*).

Under the film's influence, millions of viewers in Germany and the world were persuaded that the Jewish race had to be eradicated from the Earth. A particular effort was made by the Nazis for the film to be seen by all members of the SS and concentration camp guards in order to stimulate their sadism.

[vii] (p. 130) | *Haskalah*, ('education, instruction' in Hebrew), from the verb *lehaskil* ('enlighten through education'), a Jewish intellectual movement born in the mid-18th century in Germany under the influence of the German *Aufklärung* (Enlightenment). The retrograde life in the ghettos and small towns (*shtetls*) inspired the movement's founder, the philosopher Moses Mendelssohn (1729–1786), to envisage the emancipation and integration of the Jews in a more and more modern and liberal European society. As a solution, he advocated that they free themselves from subjection to religious tradition through secular education, by opening the windows of knowledge to the fresh air of general knowledge and science.

Thanks to Mendelssohn, there opened, for the first time, a Jewish school where classes included geography, mathematics and the study of the German and French languages.

[viii] (p. 161) | The Hashomer Hatzair movement was born in 1922 in Poland, from where it spread into neighbouring countries, Romania included, as well as Palestine. From the beginning, it had been under the ideological influence of the Hapoel Hatzair ('Young Worker') party formed in 1905. Its leader, Aaron David Gordon, was inspired by the philosophy of the Russian populist socialism of Tolstoy, and, above all, Poaley Sion ('Workers of Zion'), a socialist Zionist party founded in 1906 in imperial Russia.

[ix] (p. 180) | Emil Cioran was a philosopher and writer in Romanian and, from 1949, in French. With the publication of his first book written directly in French, *Précis de decomposition (Treatise on Decay)*. Born on 8 April 1911 in Rasinari (Austria-Hungary), Rășinari in Romanian, and died on 20 June 1955 in Paris. In 1936, he published the essay *Transfiguration of Romania*, where he developed theories influenced by the nationalist theses of the Iron Guard.

[x] (p. 239) | *Boats or State, the story of the great emigrant boats* Pan York *and* Pan Crescent, Israel 1981. In this book, we learn that, during the war, the Germans had lain mines along the Bulgarian coast to prevent Soviet ships from approaching it. Because of these mines, nearly three years after the war, maritime traffic to the Bosphorus via the south of Bulgaria was still not allowed. Thus, the *Pan Crescent* and the *Pan York* had to make for the north by taking a narrow corridor, demined by the Soviets, which extended to the coast of Romania. From the Romanian coast, at the end of the secured corridor, the *Pans* could reach the high seas without fear, heading southwards to reach the Turkish strait while avoiding the shores of Bulgaria. However, only the Soviets knew this corridor well. It was for this reason that Mossad had chosen as navigator a Russian pilot and ardent communist, who knew the route like the back of his hand. But boarding had taken too long and the *Pans* were forced to cross the most dangerous part of the passage in the middle of the night. By keeping this dangerous episode secret, Yossi Harel, the commander of the *Pans*, had prevented panic from seizing the thousands of emigrants confined to the holds. The long nocturnal detour extended the journey to the Bosphorus by fourteen hours, almost as long as the train journey from Bucharest to Burgas.

DOV HOENIG was born in 1932 in Romania. He is best known as an American film editor, and was nominated at the 66th Academy Awards in the category of Best Film Editing for *The Fugitive*. In addition, Hoenig was recognized for his editing on films such as *Thief*, *The Last of the Mohicans*, *Manhunter*, *Heat*, *The Crow*, *Overboard*, *A Perfect Murder*, *Under Siege* and *Collateral Damage*. He is a member of the American Academy of Motion Picture Arts and Sciences, the Motion Picture Editors Guild and American Cinema Editors. His career as a writer began at the age of 86 with his debut novel, *Rue du Triomphe*. First published in French, it was chosen as one of the 10 best first novels by the jury of the Prix Stanislas and has also subsequently been published in translation in Israel and Romania.

GAVIN BOWD is Reader in French at St Andrews University and has published widely on French, Romanian and Scottish culture and history. He is also a poet, novelist and literary translator, notably of Michel Houellebecq.